THE BOY NEXT DOOR

SIÂN O'GORMAN

B

Boldwood

First published in Great Britain in 2025 by Boldwood Books Ltd.

Copyright © Siân O'Gorman, 2025

Cover Design by Head Design Ltd.

Cover Images: Getty Images and Shutterstock

A CIP catalogue record for this book is available from the British Library.

Paperback ISBN 978-1-83617-825-5

Large Print ISBN 978-1-83617-826-2

Hardback ISBN 978-1-83617-824-8

Trade Paperback ISBN 978-1-80635-278-4

Ebook ISBN 978-1-83617-827-9

Kindle ISBN 978-1-83617-828-6

Audio CD ISBN 978-1-83617-819-4

MP3 CD ISBN 978-1-83617-820-0

Digital audio download ISBN 978-1-83617-823-1

This book is printed on certified sustainable paper. Boldwood Books is dedicated to putting sustainability at the heart of our business. For more information please visit https://www.boldwoodbooks.com/about-us/sustainability/

Boldwood Books Ltd, 23 Bowerdean Street, London, SW6 3TN

www.boldwoodbooks.com

1

If someone had told Claudia that the person she'd been looking for all along was right under her nose, she wouldn't have believed them. And he was the one who knew their connection way before she knew what was going on.

At the time, all she knew was that she'd had enough of men and would be perfectly happy never to see another one. This had seemed the most sensible response to when she'd finally emerged after a year or so of getting over her unceremonial dumping by Dom.

As deputy features editor on Ireland's biggest-selling women's magazine, *Irish Woman*, with an office right in Dublin's city centre, Claudia's job had been the one thing that kept her sane while stewing over the break-up.

She now knew she'd wasted three long years with the eejit and her only regret was not ending it before he had. But worse was the fact it had been his flat they'd lived in, so she'd had to move out. Now, a year later, she barely thought about Dom but it rankled that she'd allowed herself to feel *anything* for him. Claudia was a mere thirty-two and only just hitting her *prime*, as her best friend Grace repeatedly reminded her. But they both knew it was a tricky age to find yourself single. You could either commit fully to the apps or go hunting in the wild, old-school, and beg every person you even vaguely knew to introduce you to the eligible and intelligent men of their acquaintance – or as time ticked on, the ineligible and intelligible.

There was, however, a third option. Go solo. And that was the route that Claudia chose. Enjoy being single, revel in her independence, her joyfully, *manless* existence. However, she had no idea that her life was about to suddenly involve a plethora, a veritable bounty, an *embarrassment* of men; the good, the amusing, the fascinating and even one who was downright evil.

The ending with Dom had been brisk, blunt and

bruising. Worse, when Dom had sat her down 'for a serious chat', the thought crossed her mind that he might be about to propose. But instead of passionate professions of undying devotion, he calmly explained he didn't see much of a future for them, and so Claudia moved out that night, tearfully stuffing her old backpack with some clothes and wobbling off on her bike, wearing two coats because there was no other way of carrying them. By the time she arrived at her sister Fiona's, she had a puncture and had to walk the last mile along the Liffey, her front basket containing her make-up bag, laptop and a single shoe.

After a couple of weeks of sleeping in her old bed in her mother's house, she heard of an available room from a friend of a friend of a colleague which was close enough to work, a doable rent, and she jumped at it, sight unseen. It turned out to be in a large flat on the third floor of a crumbling Georgian building just off Dublin's Baggot Street and owned by the parents of Leesha O'Reilly-Hayes, who had given up her job in a solicitor's office and reinvented herself as a social media influencer. Leesha always looked fabulous, her long golden hair falling over her shoulders, her fake-tanned limbs, face lavishly made-up, teeth white as a glacier mint. But however glamorous Leesha was, behind the scenes she lived in a state of chaos, unable to tidy the smallest thing away and scattering her belongings so liberally around the flat it was almost an art form.

Who knew there were so many very obvious *upsides* to heartbreak? The amount of articles which sprung from her was almost dizzying. Over the last year, she had penned the 'top ten things *not* to do when heartbroken', 'how to fix your heart when someone has broken it', 'how to be alone (when you don't want to be)', 'five things to remember about yourself when a relationship has ended', 'who are you, now you're alone?' And on and on. It had been a therapy, a way of writing herself out of that wound-licking, gruelling experience.

It was Wednesday evening, the first day of September, and in the low-lit surrounds of Luigi's pizza restaurant, Claudia and Grace caught up with each other's lives.

'The problem with Dom,' said Grace, 'was that he had no discernible personality. You deserved so much better. I find a personality to be a basic requisite. Even a bad one is better than none at all.' Grace was the office manager in the Celia Desmond Gallery, back in their home village of Sandycove, just a half an hour's commute from the city centre.

But Claudia was not thinking of Dom, she was thinking of Tom, who had perhaps a little *too* much personality. He and Grace had only met six months earlier but he was already living in her house and busy reshaping her world into one eminently more comfortable for him. Previously an insurance broker, he'd retrained as a psychotherapist and had nailed his framed diploma on Grace's living room wall, a special light trained upon it. Grace fully worshipped at the shrine of Tom so she didn't see that this was perhaps a narcissistic move too far, and over the months she'd changed from independent, know-her-own-mind woman to a slave to Tom's whims and whines.

'Going man-free makes complete sense,' Claudia explained, refilling their glasses with the restaurant's second-cheapest bottle of red wine. 'I can crack on with work, write my articles and save up for my own flat.'

'It does sound *much* easier,' Grace conceded. 'If I didn't have Tom, I'm sure I would be quite happy in my own manless universe. But isn't it ironic that just as you are *manless*, I've found my soulmate.' She paused. 'Except he's so much better and cleverer than me.'

'That's not remotely true...'

'But it is!' Grace's eyes were shining with love and happiness. 'I love that he's so clever. I just soak up all the intelligent things he says. And when he was in the gallery earlier today, chatting away, full of beans, pretending to help, saying the paintings were wonky. It was so funny.' She smiled happily. 'You are coming to the next opening, aren't you? Celia says she hasn't seen you for ages. Tom says Celia is far too indulged and if *he* was married to her, she wouldn't get up to half the things she gets up to.' Grace laughed. 'I think he means how she flirts with other men but her husband Michael never seems to mind. She's just so beautiful and charming she gets away with it.' Grace shrugged. 'You're lucky too. Your hair falls properly in actual waves, your eyes are a proper colour, like brown. Whereas mine are a strange hybrid, like a cat's, said Tom. But he hates cats, so I don't know what he meant by that. And you always look nice, as though you didn't leave the house by accident.'

Claudia laughed, picking up the menu, suddenly starving. 'I am sure Tom meant that as a compliment. Now, shall we order food?'

'*Actual* food? Do breadsticks and wine not count? Tell that to Jesus.' Grace picked up the menu. 'Pasta,' she said, immediately. 'Any kind...'

Claudia read the menu. 'Ravioli with sage butter...?'

'Done.' Grace picked up another breadstick. 'Tom says that pasta is a sedative and that eating too much of it dulls the brain...'

'Is that a fact?' Claudia waved to the waiter, reminding herself that if Grace loved him then she too would have to at least like him. And anyway, Grace had just reminded her of another benefit of being single, you could eat whatever you liked.

2

The following morning, Claudia was working away at her desk on the second floor of Hackett House, the home of Foxy Publishing. Every month, four magazines were produced in the building – *Irish Woman, Irish Man, Irish Music and Irish Knitting*, all wildly different to each other and the staff rarely mixing.

Hackett House was situated right in the heart of Georgian Dublin, which was criss-crossed terraces and squared of beautiful five-storey red-bricked, ivy-fronted mansions, famous for their brightly painted doors.

Stepping through the doors of Hackett House every morning still gave Claudia a frisson as she wondered what the day would bring. She loved her team, who all worked hard on *Irish Woman*, punctuating their day with chat about anything and everything, from meals eaten to holidays taken and updates on family dogs. Home-made cakes were brought in, chocolates handed around and biscuits hoovered up. From the front desk, receptionist Bernadette greeted everyone, some with more enthusiasm than others. Claudia had seen her giving Blake Moriarty, the new editor-in-chief of all four publications, the side-eye, when he'd asked her to order him a taxi. 'Is your arm not working?' Claudia had overheard her saying. 'Too busy scratching yourself? Go outside and wave them about and hail one yeself.'

Blake didn't run the company, however. The owner of Foxy Publishing was the titular Foxy, a man who had a head of fading red hair and perhaps, at a younger age, had a burnished barnet. Now in his mid-sixties, he had started *Irish Man* decades earlier and had grown the business to include all four titles. Claudia wasn't even sure he knew her name, but he always seemed ebullient and cheerful, calling out pleasantries or greetings as he moved quickly through reception.

The only person who slightly ruined the atmosphere was *Irish Woman*'s features editor,

Amanda Buckley, a tiny woman who threw tremendous rages and even occasionally staplers or Sellotape dispensers, but they'd just heard that Amanda was being considered as the new editor of their fellow magazine, *Irish Man*, on the floor above.

No one else had arrived yet in the office and Claudia was powering through a new article, provisionally titled 'One Is Fun – the deliciously empowering life force of being single'.

Their desks were piled high with books and plants, papers, printouts and proofs. There was an old dictionary and thesaurus, which looked like refugees from the last millennium, or maybe the one before that. Cardigans hung over the backs of chairs, spare shoes were lined up underneath desks, the accumulation of twenty years of magazine production, the sedimentary layers of labour, of previous employees and issues, amassing in this slightly cluttered but exceptionally well-ordered office. If you needed anything at all, someone would know exactly which shelf or which pile it was on.

Claudia was soon in the zone, typing away, filling her screen with her thoughts on all the truly wonderful ways life opened up when you were unencumbered. She expounded on how trapped some women felt in relationships, how they put up with second best because they were sold a narrative that to be single was to be sad. She filled another page with famous quotes about the joys of being alone and a listicle about the pleasures of single life. But just as she was about to write another sidebar on famous single women living their best lives, Amanda entered and angrily threw her handbag (this season Chloé) onto her desk. They were all in clear and present danger of being on the receiving end of one of Amanda's infamous strops.

Sensing the need for careful handling, Claudia used her most soothing voice. 'Everything all right?'

Amanda had now slumped into her chair. 'I'm feeling horribly, extremely and completely... *stressed.*' Amanda's eye began twitching. 'You see, they were meant to be finalising my promotion today. Blake says... you know Blake Moriarty, our editor-in-chief... he's the only man I've met who can carry off a padded gilet. Anyway... I'm digressing and I always digress when I'm upset...' The eye was now twitching alarmingly. 'He's just told me I haven't got the job. He says it's out of his control.'

'Who made the decision?'

'Bloody Foxy! As if he has *any* say in the matter!'

'He does *own* the company...' Claudia immediately regretted her intervention.

Amanda's top lip turned inwards as though it was stuck to her teeth. 'He might *technically* own the company,' she growled, 'but why is he involving himself with the hiring and firing? Blake says Foxy is past it. Quite doddery these days. According to Blake, the executive board expects him to retire soon and sell his remaining shares or they will force him out due to incompetence. He doesn't even have a majority. Gave shares away foolishly when he was younger. Anyway, we can't have a doddery CEO, can we?'

'I doubt he's senile...' began Claudia, but Amanda's eyes started to boggle again and she quickly shut up.

'Blake's in charge,' Amanda snapped. 'There's a board meeting arranged in a couple of weeks, which is basically a takeover. Foxy can't expect to hold on to a business if he's not *compos mentis*, can he? It's selfish, if you ask me. And I think they are going to get rid of *Irish Knitting* and *Irish Music*. I mean, who actually *knits* these days?'

'Lots of people...'

But Amanda wasn't really listening any longer, so Claudia gave up, and because she'd skipped breakfast and her writing flow was ruined, she escaped to go and buy herself a coffee and a bun from the café across the road.

Just as she was about to leave through the main door onto the street, the sky was suddenly obscured. A large man with dyed blue-black hair was barrelling through the door forcing her to stand to one side. He had a disproportionately small face and was mainly pinstriped dark grey three-piece suit with the waistcoat buttoned over his large stomach and miniature polished shoes poking out from the end of his trousers.

Claudia *knew* him. A shiver rippled through her as she stared, trying to place him. The memory crystallised and it came back to her. It was the week of her father's funeral, when she was fifteen years old. He'd knocked on their door explaining he was her father's old friend and financial advisor. This man's name – how could she forget? – was Brian O'Brien. It transpired her father, Philip, was liable for a huge debt after an investment went wrong and Brian arrived to collect his money.

And now, all these years later, he was scuttling towards the lift like a cockroach as Claudia watched, heart pounding, wondering what on earth *he* was doing in Hackett House.

Shaken, she left the building, her mind full of Brian O'Brien and that night when he'd arrived at their house, like a portent of doom. The three of them – her mother Patsy, her older sister Fiona and herself – were already in a state of shock after a series of terrible tremors, beginning with the awful call from the hospital telling them about the heart attack and, when they'd rushed to his bedside, he'd looked so pale and small, surrounded by tubes and wires, so unlike their handsome and smiley father. He had managed to put an arm around his two daughters, his voice not like his usual one. 'I'm surer than sure that I love my two girls,' he'd said, which was what he always said, but no one was prepared for him to *never* come home.

A cold dampness settled deeply within their whole family, the house never the same again. They tried to keep each other going and their neighbours rallied, standing with them as the hearse collected the body for that final journey to the crematorium. Their next-door neighbour Mrs Hogan had her arm around Patsy, almost holding her up for the whole day, and her son, Johnny, took it upon himself to carry in extra chairs and shift the sofa to accommodate all the visitors. Mrs Hogan had appeared with plates of ham sandwiches and fruitcakes, her best china, a lace tablecloth, and made enough tea for the stream of hand-shakers and well-wishers and was the last to leave, she and Johnny washing and drying and putting the house back together again.

But then, a day or so later, there was that knock on the front door that somehow made everything worse. Claudia had answered, expecting another neighbour with an Irish stew and a loaf of brown bread, but instead it was a man, looming over her, a sour smell off his breath. She had found herself almost frozen in his shadow and unable to smile, even the fake one she'd been using lately when people asked how she was.

'You must be Fiona...'

'Claudia.'

'Brian O'Brien...' His smile was oleaginous, his hair dyed Elvis-black, and he still had hold of her hand, like the wolf in 'Little Red Riding Hood'. 'I commiserate you on his passing...' He smiled again, little toothy daggers. 'Your mother is in, is she?'

'I'll just get her.' Relieved to be free of his sweaty hand, Claudia ran along the hall and into the kitchen where Patsy and Fiona were washing up.

'Who is it?' Patsy tried to smile, as though everything hadn't been turned upside down.

'It's a friend of Dad's,' Claudia said. 'He wants to speak to you.'

Patsy quickly wiped her hands on a tea towel and left the room.

'I'm so bored of visitors,' Fiona fumed angrily. 'It's constant. I can't bear it. And we have to be so *nice*. We're not allowed to cry or anything because that just makes everyone awkward.'

'No one has said we're not *allowed* to cry.' Claudia tried to remain reasonable. If she was calm and sensible, then she might be able to cope with the chaos which had tornadoed her world. The tears would start and then stop and then start again, as though the cold dampness was seeping through her as well.

They could hear Patsy and the man going into Philip's study. The girls looked at each other.

'Who was he again?' Fiona asked.

'Brian O'Brien...'

Fiona began to laugh, which was good because it was the opposite to crying, a kind of shield against soggy tears. 'Who calls their child *Brian* when your surname is *O'Brien*?'

Under any other circumstances, Claudia too would be laughing, but this last week, she had wondered if she might ever laugh again.

Meanwhile, Fiona was giving it a good go but gave up. Tossing a tea towel towards Claudia, she said, 'You can dry and *don't* try to get out of it like you normally do.'

Claudia began to wipe. 'He looked horrible. Like Cruella de Vil.'

'She was a woman.'

'Yes but...' It was hard to explain.

'Just forget him.'

But that had proved impossible because it turned out that Brian O'Brien was the reason Philip had left them no money. Their father had invested in a company owned by this Brian and, when it failed, Philip's estate was liable. They didn't ever really understand it, but they knew there was no money. Pennies were pinched, they scrimped, they saved and Patsy took on longer shifts on reception at the doctor's surgery. It had been a tough and worrying time, but somehow they'd survived.

The biggest lesson Claudia had learned was that somehow when your world ends, even after being broken up into a million pieces, you managed to stick yourself together again, imperfectly; scarred, chipped... but alive. It was a lesson she'd taken with her through life.

She had hoped she would never see Brian O'Brien ever again but here he was, hale and hearty

at Hackett House, and Claudia couldn't help feeling
it was a bad omen.

3

At least for Claudia's sister, Fiona, the course of true love was rattling along smoothly as she and long-term boyfriend John-Paul Kearney had finally decided to get married. There hadn't been a proposal or anything like that – Fiona hated frills and fuss – but more of a gradual acceptance that after being together so long they might as well.

'We get on,' Fiona explained to Patsy and Claudia when she casually dropped into conversation over a Sunday roast and Viennetta that there was to be a wedding. 'And neither of us is getting any younger.' Fiona and John-Paul were both ancient at the age of thirty-three. 'And anyway, John-Paul is just so *nice*.'

He really was, a fact they'd all agreed upon since they'd first met him years earlier. He and Fiona now lived in a small terrace close to Dublin's old port, just under a railway bridge and next to a shop which never closed. The location caused much consternation for John-Paul's parents, especially his mother, Josephine, who couldn't bear to think of her only child living in such an insalubrious location and had declared she would never visit. Fiona hoped Josephine would keep this vow and so far she had. Josephine, who had a penchant for gold lamé and drawn-on eyebrows, had never approved of Fiona, perhaps because she didn't come from a family who frequented golf clubs or holidayed in the glitzier parts of Marbella.

Despite his unbearable parents, Josephine and Robert, somehow John-Paul had avoided their worst traits and was lovely to his future mother-in-law, solicitous to Claudia and seemingly couldn't ever do enough for Fiona. It was Thursday evening and the Kearneys had invited their 'circle' to celebrate John's father's term as golf-club chairman and also, as an add-on, John-Paul and Fiona's engagement.

Claudia and Patsy stood on the doorstep of the Kearneys' mock-Tudor, double-fronted house clutching bottles of wine and posh chocolates.

'Remember, don't stare at Josephine's eyebrows,' said Claudia, trying to make her mother laugh. But Patsy was determined not to be drawn. Unlike the eyebrows.

'You look lovely,' said Patsy, changing the subject. 'Your hair is beautiful.'

'I'm still letting it grow,' said Claudia. She had had it cut short in a bob for the three years she'd been with Dom, and as a result of being too consumed with her heartbreak, she hadn't kept up with her regular trims, and now her blonde hair was longer than her shoulders.

'It suits you. And the dress brings out the green of your eyes.'

'Thanks, Mum.' She was lucky, she knew, to have the kind of mother who thought everything she did and wore was perfect. Grace's mother was the opposite and couldn't help herself critiquing Grace's every move – from a dress which was too tight, hair which was either too long or too curly and wearing too much make-up or too little.

Josephine answered the door dressed in a shimmering kaftan.

'Patsy... and...' She looked at Claudia for a moment as though trying to remember her name. They went through this charade every time.

'Claudia.'

'Indeed, indeed...' Josephine ushered them in, air-kissing Patsy and then Claudia. 'Well, isn't this nice?' She spoke in a tone of voice that suggested it was anything but.

'It's so lovely of you to host a party for Fiona and John-Paul,' said Patsy, handing over the gifts. 'And beautiful kaftan, Josephine. You look like a goddess.'

'Don't I just?' Josephine was evidently delighted someone had noticed. 'Isn't it div*ine*? Joan Collins has the same one.'

Placing their gifts on the hall console, she led them through to the large living room, filled with men in red trousers and women in floral separates. Josephine swept through, across the nauseatingly swirly burgundy and cream carpet which matched the curtains and past the heavy mahogany furniture which looked as though it belonged in a Bunratty Castle medieval banquet experience. Fiona and John-Paul were on the other side of the room, talking to – or rather being talked *at* by – a large man with a larger moustache. His words floated over the general hubbub. 'And so I said to him, you can't park there, it's members only! He had no choice but to move his filthy plumber's van round the back.'

Fiona waved. 'I'll be over in a bit,' she mouthed.

Josephine came to a halt, beside the unlit, faux-logged fire. 'I'll park you two beside the mantel-piece,' she announced. 'When women are on their own without a man at their side, they can feel a little at sea. Here you won't be so *visibly* alone. Food is on the table, and drinks... you can help yourself, can't you?' Before they were able to answer, Josephine and her kaftan flapped away to greet other far more important guests.

Claudia nabbed two glasses of fizz from a nearby table, along with a selection of canapés on a small plate. 'Next time, we should bring a cardboard cut-out of a man. We could pretend to talk to it,' she said. 'In fact, the conversation might be more animated than most conversations people have with their Tinder dates.' She began to tell Patsy about some of the things her colleagues, Jess and Terri, had divulged about their adventures in online dating. 'It's another reason why I love my manless pact. These sausage things are nice, aren't they?'

'And the salmon pinwheel things are delicious,' began Patsy. 'Now, tell me more about this manless pact. Is this some kind of cult?'

'Well...' Claudia was just about to expound on

her new theory when a man in socks, sandals, green knitted jumper and large glasses materialised beside them, beaming.

'Patsy! What an *extremely* pleasant surprise!'

But Patsy seemed to be making slightly strange movements, along with muffled squeaking sounds, her eyes were watering and she had begun to wave her arms. Instead of panicking, the man, with impressive and decisive speed, suddenly and swiftly hit her sharply, like an assassin, between her shoulder blades.

Patsy swallowed. 'Thank you, Alan. For a moment, I thought I wasn't going to make it...' She began to laugh, perhaps from relief at being back from the brink. 'Imagine, death by salmon pinwheel.'

The man was smiling too. 'Glad to be of assistance. Good to know I haven't lost my touch.'

Patsy turned to Claudia. 'This is Alan Dunne, one of the doctors in the surgery.'

He held out a brown and hairy hand. 'Very good to meet you, Claudia. I've been hearing about you and your sister for a very long time. And now finally face meets reputation.'

Shaking his hand felt like shaking that of a squirrel, or at least what Claudia imagined it would feel like, small, furry and delicate.

'Do I talk about the girls *that* much?' asked Patsy, smiling back at him.

'The right amount, I would say.' Releasing Claudia, Alan turned back to Patsy. 'Although, I don't think you can talk about your children enough. I certainly go on about my Paul. And he's nearly forty.'

Patsy smiled at him. 'What brings you to the party? Do you know Robert and Josephine?'

'I was invited just today, when Robert was in the surgery,' said Alan. 'I hummed and hawed but at the last minute talked myself into it. My Paul is always saying work should not be a substitute for a social life. And he's right, of course. But I enjoy my work... and my colleagues...' His eye lingered a little on Patsy. 'I didn't know that *their* John-Paul was engaged to *your* Fiona. I'd never put two and two together.'

'Oh, what have we here?' It was Josephine again, slowing down to a stop. 'A little gathering of the Sea Road Surgery?' She smiled another of her terrifying grimaces. 'We have a doctor, a doctor's *receptionist* and...' She turned to Claudia. 'What is it you do again? A pamphlet thing, isn't it? You are so lucky to be *working*. Girls these days need to be independent because so few of them have a nice man in their life. All I hear on the radio is about dwindling egg reserves and all sorts of unmentionables and the perils of too-tight underwear.' Her laugh sounded as though she'd been shot in the back. 'Being a medical person, you'd know all about it, doctor. Women think they have it all and then, oh dear... eggs dwindled to nothing.' She sighed. 'I wish young women would realise that you *can't* have it all. Men do not want to be at home minding the baby, let me tell you, whatever those feminists say. Am I right, doctor?'

'Well...' He coughed a little. 'I don't know if... I can't say if... well...' He looked helplessly at Patsy, but Josephine suddenly yelled surprisingly uncouthly at Fiona, across the room, as though shouting for emergency assistance.

'Come and keep your family company! They know no one here, they are quite fishes out of water...'

'They know me,' said Alan, pleasantly.

Fiona and John-Paul hastily came over and Fiona hugged Patsy and then Claudia. 'I have my happy face on,' she said, just loud enough for Claudia to hear. 'Do I look ecstatically grateful for this lovely gathering?'

Claudia whispered back, 'I think your happy face might need a little fine-tuning.'

The two sisters were very different, in their appearances – Fiona was dark-haired and taller than Claudia and her eyes were brown – but also in their personalities. Fiona was methodical, unromantic and corporate and could never have spent a life writing for a living, conjuring articles from her brain. But they'd grown up sharing a bedroom and there was nothing which bonded you more with someone than conversations after dark, from your bed, where you talked about life, the universe and if Jason Fitzpatrick was going to ask you to his leavers' Debs.

Beside them, introductions between John-Paul and Alan were going on. 'Dr Alan Dunne from Church Street surgery,' Josephine was saying. 'General practitioner, isn't that right, Dr Dunne?'

'We call ourselves doc of all trades.' Alan beamed at John-Paul. 'Bit of everything…'

'Expert in choking,' said Patsy, making Alan laugh.

'That's right! I rise to the occasion.' He turned to Fiona. 'And you must be Patsy's eldest.'

Fiona took his hand. 'Fiona.'

'Alan.' He smiled at her. 'Very good to meet you all. I have been longing to put the faces to the names for many years. I am so sorry for your loss…'

Fiona looked confused. 'Our dad?'

'Well, yes... but...' He looked a little awkward for a moment. 'I was actually thinking of your dog. Petal, wasn't it? Didn't she pass away recently? She was also on your mother's list of favourite topics. She sounded like a lovely dog.'

Petal had been one of the ways they had managed to glue themselves back together again and had only died six months earlier after a life of service to the three of them.

Josephine, bored of the conversation, was looking around for a neat exit when her eyes alighted on Cameron Duffy, John-Paul's best friend from school, who had just arrived and was making his way towards them. Tall and handsome, with a wave of brown hair, he was wearing a loose smart navy sweatshirt and navy chinos and a huge smile. He slapped John-Paul on the back. 'How's it going...?'

'Ah, Cameron!' Josephine was delighted. 'I was asking John-Paul where you were. We cannot – I said, we simply *cannot* – have a gathering without him.'

'Lovely to see you again, Cameron,' said Patsy.

'And you two.' Cameron smiled at Claudia and Patsy. 'I just can't believe these two are finally getting married. Never thought they would.' He gave John-Paul another light arm punch.

'Neither did we,' laughed John-Paul. 'I mean, it's not important to us. Bureaucracy gave us the push. Tax and all that. And we just thought we may as well.'

'The last of the great romantics,' teased Cameron. 'Honestly, you'll be writing love poems next.'

John-Paul laughed again. 'Sorry if we can't oblige, Cameron. Anyway, Fiona would hate me to write a poem.'

Fiona didn't seem to be listening to any of this and had taken out her phone to check something. But she looked up. 'Depends on the poem,' she said. 'I wouldn't object to a *good* one...' She gazed back at John-Paul who laughed.

'But I would only be able to write bad ones, so it's probably better if I don't attempt one,' he said. 'I'm not the most romantic person. I like to be practical, don't I, Fi?'

'Hmmm?' She was barely listening again, and was back looking at her phone.

Obviously bored, Josephine interrupted, claiming Cameron by slipping her arm through his. 'Cameron, have you tried the salmon mousse? You really must. It's div*ine*. Even if I say it myself. *Not* that I made it myself...' She gave another of those shot-in-the-back laughs. 'You know me, I wasn't made to wear an apron... Come along, Cameron.'

As she led him towards the food table, Claudia glanced over at Fiona, but Fiona was looking away, a glazed look on her face, as though she had zero interest in what was happening here in this room and wished she was anywhere else.

4

GRACE

Remember opening of new exhibition this evening! It's the John Hogan exhibition. Remember I told you? He's from Sandycove... just met him for the first time today. He's amazing. Just doing the press invites now and I'll put your name on the door. You're going to love it. See you later?

It was Friday morning and Terri cleared her throat. 'Ahem, ladies,' she said to Claudia and Audrey, who were sitting at their desks in the *Irish Woman* office.

'Big news... you know Amanda's definitely now *not* leaving?'

'Not leaving?' Audrey looked a little shaken. 'As in *never* leaving or just not leaving *today*?'

'Foxy is choosing his new editor of *Irish Man* to-day,' Terri said. 'Paulie and Marko in the post room heard it from Bernadette on reception and *she* heard it from Foxy himself.' Terri readjusted her framed George Clooney photograph on her desk. It was her lucky emblem, the only time she had turned it away was the weekend after his Venice wedding. 'It was just nice to think he was single,' she had explained at the time. 'It was a comfort.'

'Foxy obviously didn't want Amanda,' said Audrey. 'He's got better sense...'

'But Amanda said he was doddery,' said Claudia.

Terri let out a kind of horse noise. 'Doddery? Foxy? Hardly. He's as sharp as ever, even though he's looking a little tired and probably should lay off the red wine but his wife left him last year and we all need our little comforts.' She gazed briefly at her photograph of George, who smiled comfortingly back at her. 'She went off to Spain to do yoga on the beach or something, so it's understandable if he's looking a little careworn, as well as the stress of a potential hostile takeover.'

'I know at least four other women who've done the same,' mused Audrey. 'Left the rat race and opened up retreats. It's the new midlife crisis of the disaffected woman.' She turned to Claudia. 'You should write about it.'

Claudia was just about to answer when Amanda walked back in.

'Gossiping again, ladies?' She shot a particularly venomous look at Terri. 'Talking about me?'

They all blushed a little, immediately chastised but also nervous that Amanda might start shouting.

'You've heard about the job, then?' Amanda said. 'Foxy *has* chosen someone else. The old fool. Honestly, he should be locked up in an old folks' home...'

'You're thinking of prison,' said Jess. 'That's where they lock people up.'

'Or perhaps you were talking metaphorically?' suggested Audrey. 'But your metaphor was all wrong...' Audrey always took her editing very seriously, especially grammar, punctuation and misplaced metaphors.

'Oh, do shut up,' growled Amanda. 'Blake has only just heard. He's *furious*.'

'But it's not Blake's decision...' began Audrey, but she was silenced by another of Amanda's looks.

'Well, whoever does get chosen,' said Amanda,

'they will soon find out it's a poisoned chalice. Blake was saying that the *Irish Man* team are all dreadful. Talentless, moody, unmotivated. They tried to revolt against Blake a month ago, which led to the editor leaving. Blake says they are like the Vinegar Hill mob, shaking their pitchforks and dancing at the crossroads.'

'Again...' began Terri, but quickly thought better of correcting Amanda.

A smile flickered on Amanda's lips. 'Anyway, it's only temporary. Foxy will be gone soon and there'll be a new team in charge. And then, Blake says—'

She was interrupted by Claudia's desk phone ringing.

'Claudia, it's Cian from Foxy's office. I wonder if you have time for a meeting?' It wasn't an invitation. It was definitely an order. 'But not here in Hackett House. Do you know Ernie's café on Merrion Lane...?'

'Are you sure you have the right person?' Claudia was aware that everyone was listening in. Amanda even had her head on one side, eyes squinting with the effort of trying to hear both sides of the conversation.

'Yes, yes, quite sure.' Cian was brisk. 'Foxy has a

busy morning ahead. As soon as possible? He's there now. Thank you, Claudia.' He ended the call.

'Who was that?' Amanda had a glint in her eye, sensing something was up. 'Was that *Cian*? Did he say Foxy wanted to meet *you*?' She looked incredulous for a moment, but then that smile again. 'He must be sacking you! What have you done? Stealing stationery? Embezzling expenses? Tax fraud? I knew it! It's always the quiet ones. Well, you all get found out in the end...' She nodded, satisfied with her theory.

Terri, Audrey and Jess looked on, concerned, as Claudia gathered her things and left the office with a breezy, 'See you all soon.'

However, her nerves were beginning to jangle as she stepped out into the world. And even though it was a lovely day in early September, the sky was blue and there was a warmth in the air, she didn't notice any of it, focused as she was on why Foxy wanted to meet her. *Was* she going to be sacked? *Had* she done anything wrong?

Baggot Street was, as always, full of traffic, kamikaze couriers and crowds on the pavements. Outside the golden-fronted pub, Doheny and Nesbitt's, barrels of Guinness were being launched from the back of a truck and rolled through a trapdoor in the street. Large sacks of flour were being hauled into Luigi's restaurant, while besuited office workers waited for coffee at Shot! Claudia turned left onto Merrion Street towards the Merrion Hotel, which was her favourite in the city, one of those old-fashioned, glorious places where there was always a turf fire, or an afternoon tea to be had, or a drink in the lovely bar. Beside the hotel was a small lane, which she'd never been down before, but ahead she could see a striped awning and a blackboard sign.

Speciale!!! Today ONLY!!!! Linguine alle vongole!!! And the finest tiramisu this side of Roma!!! Ernie's Mama's recipe!!!

Audrey would hate those multiple exclamation marks, thought Claudia. Why did Foxy want to meet in this strange little café? Inside, it was like stepping into the backstreets of Rome or Palermo with clattery chairs, pastel Formica tables, Italian opera filling the air, vintage posters of Italian resorts hung on the walls. At the back was a counter with a large coffee machine and a wooden platter piled high with ciabatta sandwiches.

Foxy was at a corner table, beside the window, looking at her curiously, taking her in. She did the same. He was a big man, with a broad chest, radiating the kind of ebullient charm that happy and successful men often did, and today he was wearing a navy blazer over a pink-striped, open-necked linen shirt. His face was lined, his white hair curled around his ears, and his eyes, under his bushy brows, were bright and intelligent. But she felt immediately that his usual swaggering confidence was missing. He looked somehow, although Claudia thought she must be mistaken, almost *nervous*.

5

Foxy stood up in a rush, as though only just recovering his manners, holding out his large hand. 'It's such late notice... You found Ernie's all right? Obviously you did, because you're here...' He smiled. 'This is where I come when I don't want to bump into anyone. My not-so secret office.' He gestured to the chair beside her. 'Please take a seat. I want to... well, there was something I wanted to talk to you about.'

'Of course...' Claudia hesitated.

'Call me Foxy. Most people do. Well, apart from my family. My mother forbade it.' He gave a laugh. 'She didn't like me being called Foxy, but it started in boarding school, when I turned up with my red hair. Coffee?'

Claudia gave a nod, unable to quite find her voice, as Foxy called over to the back of the café.

'Two cappuccino, Ernie, please.' He turned back to Claudia. 'You live in town?'

'That's right...'

'And you like it?'

She nodded and then, due to nerves, found herself rambling almost incoherently. 'It's handy being so close to everything and I was lucky to find a place because I had to move out of my old flat because it belonged to my ex-boyfriend... and he decided that he no longer wanted a relationship with me...' She tried to laugh, embarrassed that her awkwardness and desperation to fill the silence had led her to talk about her failed romance.

Foxy looked aghast. Probably at the quality of her small talk. 'Why did he end it?'

'He said there was no future in us. He didn't love me enough, I suppose.'

'He didn't deserve you,' Foxy said, nodding at her as though it was obvious and the case was closed. 'Fool.'

She hoped he was referring to Dom.

'Anyway,' he went on, 'you're having fun at *Irish Woman*?'

Claudia smiled, feeling her nervousness dissipate. Foxy seemed kind, considerate, caring. And not *remotely* doddery. 'It's my dream job. I feel so lucky to work there. I wake up every day wondering what the day is going to be like.' She sounded like an overly earnest lunatic. 'It's so exciting.'

And he was grinning back at her, this time a proper sun-splitting smile, as though he too had relaxed, his nervousness – if that's what it was – also gone. 'Magnificent... truly. *We* used to... *I* used to go to a school and had a teacher. The only good teacher there. The rest were sadists and godawful excuses for human beings. But this one teacher was inspiring. And he always used to say, "Boys, you're all privileged *young* men, and you will grow up to be privileged older men. Success is many things, it's making money, deals, whatever. It's the first-class seat or the big car... but the only success that really matters is if you make other people happy."' Foxy smiled again at Claudia. 'I'd forgotten that over the years. Too busy chasing all the other kinds of success. Joy stopped being a priority.'

A small man wrapped in a huge white apron, with a face that reminded Claudia of one of the penguins at Dublin Zoo, came over with their coffees. He had a long, faded scar which snaked from his scalp, behind his left ear and down to his neck.

'Ernie, this is Claudia. Claudia, one of my best friends in the world, Ernesto di Lucia.'

Ernie clasped her hand, beaming. 'I'm so happy you're here... you are very welcome.'

'How's the property business?' asked Foxy. 'Any profits to be made these days?'

Ernie shrugged. 'The market is what I call *inattesa*... it's holding out, not sure where it will go.'

'Ernie has a pretty impressive property portfolio,' explained Foxy to Claudia. 'But the café is his real love. Isn't that right, Ernesto? He opened it a couple of years ago now. An antidote to his property empire.'

Ernie nodded. 'You have to do something for love and something for money. This is my love. Foxy, what do you do for love and what do you do for money?'

'I thought they were the same thing,' Foxy said. 'Well, they used to be, for me. Now, I don't know... all my love is gone.' He turned back to Claudia. 'See how it is with Italians? They have Irish men talking about love as though it's a normal topic of conversation. Ernie, we should be talking about rugby and how Ireland is going to trounce Italy in the Six Nations.'

Ernie laughed and pinched Foxy's cheek. 'When Italy beat Ireland, that will be a good day. There will be a lot of love then.' He and Foxy laughed suddenly together. 'I'll leave you two to your very important meeting,' he said, before following a couple who'd just arrived.

Foxy turned to Claudia. 'Now, I'd like to tell you a little story. I started *Irish Man* more than forty years ago. Still a student then, editing the college magazine, the usual route. Anyway, I wanted to make some money. There were women's magazines, obviously, but I had this idea that Irish men would like something just for them. And I was right. Immediate success, advertising off the scale, sales unbelievable. We had something really good.' He paused, almost dreamily. 'Our very first office was on the top floor of Hackett House. A bit shabbier back then, no nice bathrooms, the lift was about to break and the windows were so dirty the only view was a grey haze. In the office next door was this Italian man who was getting into property...' He nodded towards Ernie. 'And in the other office was a lad who was just starting up his own betting business. Toby Rabbitte? You've heard of him?'

'Of course.'

'And Arnold Kennedy, the... whatever he is now. Rugby pundit and communications consultant.' Foxy slid his coffee on the table towards him. 'Sugar, Claudia? No? My wife, Alison, is always on at me to give up sugar. Well, she was.' He flicked a tube, ripped it open and shot the contents into his cup. 'Soon to be *ex*-wife, I suppose. Should have prioritised joy, really. She was the one person who liked me for who I was, but she left a year ago. Moved to Alicante and now teaches yoga on the beach. Now, *that* sounds joyful, doesn't it? If I was *her* best friend, which I like to think I still am, I would have told her to go, to leave her old, boring workaholic husband behind and live her life. She'd spent too long waiting for me to come home or trying to keep me healthy so we'd have a retirement together... Heart problems run in the family, so she was right to worry.' He paused and looked straight at Claudia. 'You, Claudia, are my last chance... I'm going to offer you the job as editor of *Irish Man*.'

Claudia nearly laughed. He may not have been doddery but he *was* deranged and straight-up *mad*.

'You can write,' he went on. 'I like your style. You are a fresh, young voice. And I need someone just like that. And, more than anything, I need someone I can trust to be on my side. You may think I'm getting paranoid in my old age, but I know I need to take back control of the basics of the business and first thing I need to do is choose my own editors.'

Speechless, Claudia concentrated on stirring her coffee, trying to work out how she could say no and retreat from mad Foxy without hurting his feelings.

'The board are trying to put someone as editor, someone *they* can control. I've been firefighting and sometimes I feel like giving up, I really do. But I sacrificed so much for the business and I can't give up on it. I *can't* let it go. This is truly an existential crisis.' He sat back in his chair. 'Look, I know this all sounds whacky, but things are complicated. I need to start gathering support. Cian, my PA, and Bernadette on reception are literally the only two people who wouldn't screw me over. And...' He looked at her. 'I'm hoping you too.'

Claudia felt out of her depth. She was going to refuse, obviously, but hated having to say no to anyone about anything. She didn't want to be editor of *Irish Man*. For one thing, she knew next to nothing about men – an essential prerequisite, she imagined.

Foxy sensed her hesitation. 'Look, what about for a short time? Three months? See it as a kind of sabbatical and then, if you want, you can go back to *Irish Woman.'*

'But I don't know anything about men. Nothing. I grew up with just a mother and a sister. All my friends are women. I'm not even interested in men. They are a complete mystery to me. I don't know how they work.'

Foxy laughed, thankfully. 'Perhaps you haven't met the right ones? We're not so mysterious.' He looked at her kindly, as though he understood some- how. 'Take your time to think it over. But not *that* much time. The weekend? What about telling me on Monday morning? I need you to do this. I really do.'

'How do you know you can trust me?'

Foxy grinned at her, raising one of those bushy brows. 'I just know.'

6

Back in the office, Claudia avoided the searching glances from her colleagues and pretended not to notice the daggers from Amanda and typed away at her 'house buying' piece and began a draft of 'yoga as an alternative midlife crisis' article. She hoped Foxy's wife was having the fun and joy she deserved. She was also thinking of the strange meeting she'd just had. The more she mulled it over, the more she felt protective about Foxy. He wasn't doddery, she was sure of it, but perhaps a little off the wall. She would, she knew, officially refuse him first thing on Monday.

After work, she took the train out of town to

Sandycove, a small villagey-suburb along the coast of Dublin, where she'd grown up, and where her mother lived and where her best friend Grace worked in the Celia Desmond Gallery.

Soon, she was rattling along the coast with all the other commuters, staring out the window at the sparkling sea glinting like sequins in the late-summer sunshine and the birds wading in the iridescent sand flats which stretched the length of Dublin Bay.

Sandycove looked beautiful with the late-summer hanging baskets and the brightly painted shops as the Friday post-work crowd lingered on the suntrap seats outside the Island pub.

Claudia looked across at the Celia Desmond Gallery where 'JOHNNY HOGAN – sketches of home' was emblazoned across the large plate-glass window. *Johnny* Hogan? It couldn't be *the* Johnny Hogan, their old neighbour, who'd always looked out for her and Fiona. He was three years older than Claudia and had gone off to art college in London just before his lovely mother sold their house and moved to Galway. Could it be *that* Johnny Hogan?

If it was, one memory stood out. The summer after their dad had died, their lawn had turned brown, weedy and overgrown. Fiona and Claudia had stared out of the kitchen window at the dismal sight. 'We've a wasteland, not a garden,' Fiona had said mournfully. 'We should try to make it nice like Dad did.'

They struggled to pull the old, heavy petrol mower out from the shed, half wiping away the cobwebs and dust and trying not to shriek too much. Then they spent an hour pulling at the string to start it, eliciting only a whirr and a rumble, poised to shriek again as soon as the engine roared terrifyingly into life. Claudia thought they were going to have to cut the grass with a rusty pair of hedge clippers.

'Need any help?' It was Johnny Hogan, his face appearing over the wall.

'We're giving up,' Fiona said. 'It doesn't matter.'

Claudia shook her head. 'No, it *does* matter. We *do* need help.'

'Why don't I bring over *ours*?' In a few moments, Johnny was knocking on their back gate, having lugged over the Hogans' mower, and the three worked on the garden all afternoon, Johnny mowing straightish lines up and down, Claudia and Fiona clipping the edges, trying to regain that lovely finish their dad used to achieve. They even weeded the dandelions in the flower beds and chopped at the fuchsia hedge. Finally, when they stood and admired their effort, somehow it didn't quite live up to the vision Claudia had had in her head.

Fiona stood there, sweaty, twigs in her hair, her knees stained from kneeling on the freshly mown grass. 'It still looks like a wasteland.'

'It almost looks worse,' Claudia said.

Even Johnny looked uncertain. 'It'll grow. It's just a bit bald in places. I think I went too low on the mower.'

Claudia began laughing. 'I *love* the bald bits and the brown grass and the hedge that looks like it's been attacked...' It was the first time in a year that she realised that she could still laugh.

Johnny began laughing as well. 'It's like a bad haircut.' He pointed to his head. 'Like mine. I look like someone has taken the hedge clippers to it...'

'It's worse than the fuchsia hedge.' Claudia now had tears rolling down her face and she fell to her knees, and she wasn't sure if she was hysterical from grief or the relief that she could still find humour in the world. Perhaps both.

'You two are weird,' Fiona said. 'If Mum asks, tell her we don't know who destroyed the garden.'

When Patsy did arrive home, she didn't think the garden was ruined at all. In fact, she kissed the top of their heads. 'Thank you,' she said gently, 'for making it look so lovely.'

And then Johnny mowed their lawn every week, for the rest of the summer, his dog Scamp lying waiting for him. And he did it every week until he left home for good. Claudia couldn't remember if they'd ever properly thanked him and perhaps it was just something they got used to and took for granted. It was people like him who got you through those times, she thought now. At the time, you accept help almost without thinking, but it's the people who give without expecting anything back that help you along, get you to the next stage, help you survive.

Just as she was about to cross the road to the gallery, she saw Grace's boyfriend, Tom, checking his appearance in a shop window and popping a mint in his mouth. He obviously liked what he saw, because he gave a little smile and a head toss, before disappearing inside. Claudia followed him, taking a glass of wine on her way in and squeezing through the tightly packed crowd. This was definitely the busiest opening she'd ever been to at the gallery, causing the necessity of having to duck under armpits and slowly edge her way to the back of the room, where there was a bit of breathing space. She stood close to two huge beautiful canvasses of dreamy-creamy colours, overlapping to create a gorgeous effect, and stared at them for a moment, thinking how utterly beautiful and calming they were.

'Thank God. A friendly face...' Grace had squeezed through the crowd and thrown her arms around Claudia. 'I can't talk to another journalist or buyer or agent. I just need someone normal...'

Claudia laughed. 'That's debatable...'

'Tom's too busy schmoozing to talk to me,' went on Grace. 'Says he learns so much from observing people. He and Celia are sparring about something or other. Anyway, so, what do you think? Isn't Johnny amazing? We still can't believe that he would exhibit in such a small gallery. But he's from Sandycove and he says he wants to be here. Ah, here's Johnny now!' Grace turned to face a tall man with dark brown hair pushed back off his face, high cheekbones. 'Well, I told you we'd get a turnout,' Grace was saying. 'Every journalist in Dublin is here...'

It *was* Johnny Hogan. And he was smiling straight at Claudia.

'Claudia Kelly! It's so good to see you!' He threw his arms around her, hugging her. 'How long has it been? How old were we when we last saw each other? It must have been fifteen years ago?'

He had the same soft brown eyes and the same

smile that Claudia remembered on the teenage version of Johnny. He was even wearing a battered black leather jacket which looked just like the one he used to wear when he would come home from school carrying his art folder. 'I think it was when you went off to art college.'

Grace interrupted them, 'You didn't tell me you knew Johnny...'

'You said *John* Hogan...'

'Autocorrect,' said Grace, turning to Johnny. 'I should have asked you where in Sandycove you'd grown up... but it's so great you're exhibiting at home...'

He smiled at her. 'My mother is delighted I'm back on Irish soil.' His eyes lingered on Claudia, warmly. 'So how are you? What's the craic?'

'None at all. You?'

'Ah, you know...' They were still smiling at each other.

'I was just remembering how you used to mow our lawn...'

He smiled at her. 'I became obsessed with that lawn. I remember trying to cut it perfectly. I read books on how to achieve the perfect lawn. I bought seaweed fertiliser for it and everything...'

'Did you? I had no idea.'

'I can be too obsessive,' admitted Johnny. 'I did the same to my mam's lawn. Both of our mothers were very happy with their grass...'

'Such talents you have,' said Grace. 'I could have put all this in the press release if I'd known.' She had finish her glass of wine, placing it on the table behind them. 'I have to bring Johnny to meet the journalists. Oscar de la Bournville from *Irish Man* is desperate to talk to him. *Major* fan apparently.'

Claudia recognised Oscar's face from seeing him rushing through reception at Hackett House, always wearing something stylish and striking, his hair never the same colour, sometimes he had eyebrows, sometimes not. Today, his jacket was slung over his shoulders, cape-like, and he teetered in snakeskin boots which looked tight and uncomfortable.

'Duty calls,' said Johnny, apologetically. 'I'll come back and chat again.'

Claudia helped herself to another glass of wine from a passing waiter, and again paused in front of the beautiful paintings, admiring their swirling wash of colours which brought you almost inside the canvas.

'Oh God,' said a voice. 'Don't tell me you're worshipping at the shrine of Johnny Hogan as well?'

Laughing, she turned to see Michael Desmond,

Celia's barrister husband, standing beside her. 'Hello, Michael.'

He kissed her on the cheek and grinned at her. 'You'll have to explain it all to me and tell me how I am to make sense of them? Do you *understand* any of it? I just don't get the mysterious art world myself. All this nonsense about light and shade, or if it is a bird or a plane or just a splodge? That's about death, they say. And of course I don't *dare* suggest it's just a black square. I like to be able to recognise a tree. Or a face. Or a dog. My darling Celia calls me a philistine but as she's the genius in our house, all I can do is agree. The gallery is her true love, I am surplus to requirements.' Michael always performed this little charade of family strife, safe in the knowledge that he and Celia were unshakeable.

They chatted together for a while before Johnny edged back through the crowd and rejoined them.

'Oh, the star of the night! *L'homme du soir!*' Michael beamed at him. 'I was just saying to Claudia how simply marvellous your paintings are. Exquisite! The myriad ways you use colour to express the human experience is breathtaking. Your swirling brushstrokes suggest the whirl of life or perhaps the infinitesimal quality of the intangible. Am I right?'

Johnny was laughing. 'They are whatever you want them to be.'

'Whoever is brandishing the chequebook, is that right?' suggested Michael, archly.

Johnny smiled. 'I learned long ago that once a painting is finished, or as near to finished as possible, once I let it go into the world, whatever someone sees in it, then that is right. Once it's out there, it belongs to them. One man at the New York exhibition was convinced he could see the face of his long-dead dog in one of my paintings.'

'Your paintings are like those Rorschach tests,' said Michael, 'where people see the faces of murderers or ink spots, that kind of thing, whatever their subconscious sees.'

'Hopefully not murderers.' Johnny winked at Claudia.

'I think,' said Claudia, 'it says more about Michael than it does about your paintings.'

'Alas, I think you might be right, dear Claudia,' mused Michael. 'By the way, Claudia, we're having a little supper party for Johnny at ours, I'm cheffing, Celia hosting. Grace and her... her whatever he is...'

'Tom.'

'...her *Tom* will be there as well. Would you join us? I'll text you the details. You *have* to come because we can't be odd numbers, oh no. It's bad numerically and harmonically, according to Celia. You'll come? Oh, marvellous! Now, let me go and recharge our glasses. I have a supply of some decent plonk hidden away. I can't be drinking *launch* wine, oh no. My taste buds would never forgive me. Back in a mo.'

7

'So how did charming the journalists go?' Claudia asked Johnny. 'Did any of them see murderers or dead dogs in your paintings?'

'They didn't say *that* exactly but I just tried not to be too weird or say anything controversial. I think I managed to answer a particularly fiendish question about my motivation, whatever that is, and tried to sound relatively sane.' He changed the subject, as though not wanting to talk about himself any longer. 'How's your mother and Fiona? Both well?'

'They are doing brilliantly. Mum still working at the surgery. Fiona's a management consultant... about to get married...'

'Ah, to someone nice?'

'The nicest... and your mother? How is she?'

'Couldn't be better. Lives in Galway now, out in Barna, stares at the Atlantic for hours at a time, swims in it, paints it. Wears a Dryrobe permanently, you know those swimming coat things? Does painting classes and says she's trying to beat me at my game. But I think she might be the real talent in the family. My sister is married, three children. Also lives in Barna. She has her own café and Mam makes the scones for it. They're both happy out, you know?'

Claudia nodded, remembering Mrs Hogan and how she was one of those people who just made everything all right. Claudia remembered on the day of her father's funeral when her mother stood in the hall, as though she was a statue, frozen in time, and Mrs Hogan spoke so gently, her hand around her elbow, like she was talking to a frightened horse. 'There, now,' she had said. 'One step in front of the other. There now...'

The gallery was emptying out a little, the noise in the room lessening, there was space to spread out a little and to hear each other.

'What about your work?' asked Johnny. 'What do you do?'

'I'm on *Irish Woman* magazine...'

'Really?' He looked interested. 'A journalist!'

She nodded. 'It's not exactly war reporting...'

'No... but still important...'

'Well...' For some reason Claudia found herself wanting to tell Johnny about her meeting with Foxy. 'I was offered *another* job today. For the same company... a three-month trial, really, on *Irish Man*. As editor.'

Johnny was looking impressed. 'I always used to buy *Irish Man*,' he said. 'It was so funny... and it was always so clever and interesting.' He smiled back at Claudia. 'And now you're the editor. But I'm not surprised. You always had a way with words. I remember you won a poetry competition in the *Sandycove Newsletter*, remember?'

Claudia nodded, astonished. 'That was years ago...'

'Yes, but my mother had the poem stuck to the fridge for ages and ages. I'd be eating my cereal every morning and reading your poem. *The blue of the sea meets the grey of the sky, mingling and shimmering, mirroring...*' He smiled at her. 'Am I right? Something like that...?'

She felt herself blush. 'Yes, something like that.' She'd written it in third year, when she was around fourteen, and had won first prize in school and the honour of being published in the local paper. She couldn't believe it had been on Johnny's fridge or that he'd even remembered it.

'I should have known you'd be editor of my favourite magazine...'

'Oh, but I'm not going to take it.'

'Why ever not?'

'I'm not qualified...'

'Of course you are! You're a published poet! And what are you currently doing?'

'I'm assistant features editor on *Irish Woman*...'

'Sounds like you are perfectly qualified...' He looked at her. 'Why don't you say yes? Take the risk?'

'It would be nice, I suppose, to have a short break from writing articles about ten ways to transform your life and variations on the theme.'

Johnny laughed. 'Wait, so you write articles about transforming your life? And you don't take your own advice? What's the worst that could happen?'

'I could fail?'

Johnny was still smiling. 'But what if you love it?'

She was just about to answer when Michael rejoined them, holding out two glasses, and then produced a bottle of wine from a pocket inside his blazer and began filling their glasses. 'Top-notch stuff,' he said, before producing another glass from inside his jacket. 'Dances on lips, toys with your tongue, sends a signal to your brain that you have entered another realm entirely. Makes life seem almost bearable...' He pressed his nose deep into his glass, his eyes closed. 'An aroma like *a bank where the wild thyme blows*... wouldn't you agree?'

Claudia nodded. 'It's delicious,' she agreed, but couldn't really taste much of a difference with the launch wine.

'Is it Blue Nun?' asked Johnny. 'Or Buckfast, perhaps?'

Michael pulled a face. 'Philistine,' he said. 'Next time, I'll buy a bottle of plonk for you and save the Montrachet for me and the discerning Claudia.'

Grace and Tom joined them. 'What are you drinking?' Grace said, her eyes narrowed. 'Don't tell me you have your own supply, Michael? Is my job-lot, bog-standard vino not good enough for you?'

'Sorry, Grace,' said Michael, airily, 'but my taste buds were destroyed by the last opening. It took a long time to restore my palate. I can't let that happen again. Grab a glass and you can have some of my Montrachet...'

Tom glowered beside her. 'I thought you weren't drinking this week?' he said. 'Aren't we doing Sobtember?'

'Sobtember?' Michael laughed. 'Is that a joke? Tom, we are drinking a divine wine, one that the Gods themselves would have drunk. Have a glass, stop this Sobtember nonsense... eat, drink, be so much merrier...' He produced another glass from somewhere, filled it and handed it to Tom. 'Johnny, you don't do Sobtember, do you?'

'If it is what I think it is, no. Definitely not. I'm an everything-in-moderation kind of person.'

They chatted together for a while and listened to one of Michael's involved stories about a French vineyard cycling trip where he and his friends had become so inebriated, they had forgotten how to cycle. 'In the end, we gave up,' he said. 'We just couldn't remember where our feet went and what they were meant to do. As for balancing on the thing, that just seemed an impossibility too far. We had to walk back to our hotel, pushing our bikes, and by the time we arrived, we were all stone-cold sober!'

When it was time to go, they stood outside saying goodbye. Claudia turned to Johnny. 'It was so lovely to see you again...'

He smiled. 'I was thinking that, as you're a journalist, you might take me on a walking tour... You know, the Ha'penny Bridge. Trinity College. Merrion

Square. Fitzwilliam Square... the nice parts of Dublin...'

Claudia laughed. A walking tour? What was he on about? 'I don't think you understand the definition of the word journalist...'

'It's just that journalists know things, secrets, they have insights and all sorts of things. And I'm back in town and everything's changed...' He looked at her for a moment.

Claudia was puzzled. 'But you're a local...'

'Yes... but...' He smiled at her. 'I'm a *returned* local. Need to find my Dublin feet again.' He passed her his card. 'My number.'

'Of course I can show you around...' It was nice to feel such familiarity for someone, after not seeing them so long. It was like being instant friends with someone, a half-stranger.

'Remember, what if you love it...'

Claudia laughed again. 'And what if I hate it?'

She left Sandycove feeling lighter and happier than she had in a long time. Probably the Montrachet, she thought. But there was something about the way Johnny looked at her, as though he knew her. And he did, in a way. He'd been her childhood friend and he'd known her father, whom so few people did these days.

But she also knew she was going to say yes to Foxy. There'd been a look in his eyes she recognised, he needed an ally and for some reason he'd reached out to her.

She *wasn't* going to love it.

But what if you do?

8

On Sunday, Claudia, Fiona and Patsy ate their Sunday roast, followed by Arctic roll, declaring it a culinary triumph. Patsy wasn't the world's best cook, she wasn't even the best cook in the family, but there was no one's cooking Claudia and Fiona liked more, especially her overdone chicken, the underdone roast potatoes and the packet gravy. Bad cooking tasted of home and was exactly the way Fiona and Claudia liked it. Claudia had decided not to tell her mother or Fiona about the job offer. As she wasn't remotely confident if it would work out, she didn't want Patsy worrying.

'So you went to the Johnny Hogan,' said her mother. 'You remember, Fiona, Johnny from next door. Grace's gallery is hosting his new exhibition. I must go in and see it. He always was a nice lad. Such a lovely family, the Hogans. His sister is running a café in Galway somewhere apparently.'

'Is he still wearing that leather jacket?' asked Fiona. 'Do you remember he used to mow our lawn? It was such a nice thing for him to do for us. We were useless at it, weren't we?'

'Pathetic.' The girls smiled at each other.

First thing on Monday morning, Claudia took the lift to the top floor of Hackett House, bypassing the second floor and the home of *Irish Woman*, hurtling up to the fourth, the executive level. She stepped out into the quiet calm of a long, carpeted corridor, past the metal-framed black leather chairs and a coffee table with a fanned selection of recent issues of Foxy Publishing's magazines and flanked by large ferny plants.

This was another world, far from the busy editorial floors with the constant hum of working life. Steeling herself, she walked past the open door of a large photographic studio, past the closed door of the boardroom, and ahead were two offices – one with 'Blake Moriarty, Chief Financial Officer' etched on a glass plaque, and beyond was Foxy's office.

Through the glass, Cian, Foxy's PA, looked up,

beckoning her in. From the large windows of the office was a view over the rooftops of the city, towards the beautiful Dublin mountains, covered at this time of year with swooshes of russets and brown, the colours of a science teacher's jumper, and above all of it was a vast expanse of silvery sky. Cian's desk was unfeasibly tidy, the only personal objects were a pastel-coloured Rubik's cube and a perfect bonsai, with a neat pile of files open in front of him.

'Morning, Claudia.' Cian had a slight frown on his face, as though he bore the weight of the world on his shoulders.

'Morning. How's it going?'

Cian sighed heavily, indicating towards the files in front of him. 'Just your usual common or garden legal nightmare. Anyway, I'll tell him you're here...' He stuck his head through the door behind him, murmured something and turned back. 'In you go... I hope you have good news for him...'

Behind Foxy were framed magazine covers of all his publications, and he stood, beaming at Claudia. 'Ah, Ms Kelly, how are you on this beautiful morning?' But through his smile, he also looked at her intently, as though masking the seriousness of their meeting. 'Do sit down, won't you?' He scooted his chair in closer to his desk, hands clasped in front of him. Claudia looked at the photographs on his desk, one of Foxy, his arm around a beautiful woman standing in dappled sunlight, both smiling, and then, in a small silver frame, a faded image of a much younger Foxy standing with the same woman on the steps of the Dublin registry office, a hand just appearing in the side of the image, throwing confetti. 'Cup of tea? Cian is remarkable in his ability to produce the most outlandish teas. I've had people request all sorts of things – peppermint, camomile... rooibos... I prefer plain old Irish breakfast...'

'Me too.'

'I knew you would!' He seemed pleased that they shared the same taste in tea. 'I used to like going to the old Bewley's café for a big tin, which would last me months and months. Going to Bewley's was always a treat as a little boy, we'd be brought in and allowed to choose a cherry bun.'

'My dad loved those...'

He paused for a moment. 'I'm rambling.' He smiled at her. 'Now, to your decision. What is your answer?' He looked alert, his head cocked, his eyes on her.

'I'll do it.'

He suddenly grinned, as though delighted, and for a moment she thought he was going to clap his hands. 'Well, this is marvellous... truly... wonderful. The best news I've had in a long time.' He stood and rushed to her side, clasping one of her hands in his. 'There's no time to waste. I need you in situ right away. Ready? You'll need to pack up your things at *Irish Woman* and bring everything up to *Irish Man*.' He was looking serious now, as though thinking and planning. 'Now, you're to do what you want to do with the magazine. Feel free to initiate and innovate. I'm very fond of the team but they might be little prickly to begin with, but I know your natural charm will win them over. I'll be popping in when I can and obviously I am only a text or a phone call away. Remember I am here to talk to, to advise, whatever you need. I live on Leeson Street, so never too far away. Now, what else do I need to tell you?'

Claudia couldn't think of a single thing. 'I'll just give it a go...' She knew she sounded feeble, but she had been struck with a slightly overwhelming sense of inadequacy. Foxy definitely had asked the wrong person. She gave it one last shot. 'Are you sure you want *me*, Foxy?'

'Quite sure.'

'Perhaps you have me mixed up with someone else?'

He shook his head. 'I definitely haven't. I'm

surer than sure. Now, best not to tell too many people outside of the magazines, just yet, if you wouldn't mind. Not with all the legal hoopla that's going on.' He sighed heavily. 'Right, there's no time to waste. I need you in situ right away.' He was looking deadly serious, thinking and planning, and Claudia was struck by this other Foxy, the decisive businessman.

'I have a couple of questions...' she said.

'Go on...'

'Why did the previous editor leave?'

'He'd had one run-in too many with my chief financial officer...'

'Blake Moriarty...'

'That's the fella...' Foxy looked at her blandly, giving nothing away.

'And tell me, the deputy editor...?'

'Mark O'Dowd...'

'He didn't want the job?'

Foxy shook his head. 'His heart isn't in magazines. He's a nice fella but is desperately trying to get back into academia or whatever it was he was doing before. He'll show you a few ropes, get you started, and he'll be delighted that there'll be someone else who's in charge. He hasn't enjoyed the last two weeks when we've been editor-less.'

'What are you looking for exactly? What do you want me to achieve?'

'Well...' He paused. 'Not too much. But I need you to freshen the editorial, a few new voices, make the magazine lighter, funnier, more modern. We've lost our way, I think, over the last few years. I've had my eye off the ball... and relied on others to take the reins. Feel free to initiate and innovate.'

Not too much? It was a complete Herculean overhaul.

'Now,' went on Foxy, 'remember I'm here to talk to or advise, whatever you need.' He stood up and flung open the door. 'Cian, Claudia's accepted my offer. Inform both teams? And make all other necessary arrangements, renumeration, contacts, etc. And send Claudia my number.'

After they had shaken hands and Claudia descended in the lift, Amanda was waiting for her. Knowing Cian's efficiency, the word had spread very quickly indeed. She had her arms folded, mouth pinched.

'I hear you're moving up in the world,' she said.

'Well, only a floor above.'

'You know what I *mean*.'

'It's just a few months. I'm not sure quite why...'

Amanda put up her hand to stop her. 'Nor am I.

Nor is *anyone*. I mean, you've been *promoted* over *me*. I told you Foxy wasn't all there and now this confirms it.' Amanda's eyes narrowed. 'Doddery. Mark my words.' She stepped to one side, to allow Claudia to pass and say goodbye to her old team. Carrying a large cardboard box filled with her notebooks and laptop, Claudia pressed the button on the lift again.

One and a half seconds later, Claudia was in another world – the world of man. *Irish Man.*

9

It was striking how quiet the third floor was, unlike the constant chatter that emanated a floor below. Her nerves multiplied, her stomach in knots. And then from around the corner appeared a handsome man with bouncy, artfully arranged hair, striped T-shirt, white jeans, no socks and loafers.

'You're here already! I was hoping to be your welcoming committee, but I see you've arrived to an empty corridor.' His blinding teeth matched his pristine jeans. He held out his hand. 'Jackson Moloney, executive PA to Blake Moriarty. He asked me to make you *extraordinarily* welcome to the third floor. My office is upstairs in C-suite, but I can be up and down and ensure your happiness. This is all so sudden!

Foxy doesn't *often* make executive decisions like this...' He laughed gaily. 'But, you know, he wouldn't be where he is today without having one or two maverick tendencies. Now, if there is anything you need just ask me, okay? I have all the goss, backstage info, who's hot, who's not, who's naughty and who's nice and who you can trust in this veritable nest of vipers. Come on, Claudy-pops – may I call you that? Well, Claudy-pops, let's go and see your new office and I'll introduce you to the *desultory* motley crew aka the *Irish Man* team. *Après toi!*' He swept his hand in a courtly way, ushering her forward, and they proceeded along the corridor towards the *Irish Man* office.

It was a similar set-up as that at *Irish Woman*: a rectangle of desks with laptops and phones, similar piles of files, books and old magazines. There were the usual empty coffee mugs and faded Christmas decorations which harked back to a happier time, but this office seemed plain, devoid of the plants, the books, the buzzy atmosphere which characterised her old office.

Four heads were down – three men and one woman – working in total silence. Claudia recognised Oscar de la Bournville, who was dressed in a fluffy black and white striped mohair jumper and a bandana around his neck, but the others she barely knew.

'The most miserable people in the world,' said Jackson, under his breath, and then louder, 'People, listen up! We have your new editor. Could everyone stop working and say hello to Claudia Kelly? What are you all doing? Updating your dating app profiles? Doing your online supermarket shop? Downloading content which violates company rules?'

One of the men, bearded and in a green T-shirt, gave a slight eye-roll and an irritated shake of his head. Oscar de la Bournville glowered at Jackson. 'Jackson, we're busy getting the next issue out. You know? The *magazine*. Our *raison d'être*?'

Jackson breezily ignored him. 'Right, who's first? I'll start with Simon Boyle, the designer...' Simon was the bearded, green T-shirted one.

Claudia held out her hand. 'Claudia. Good to meet you.'

'You too,' mumbled Simon, standing briefly to shake her hand before sitting down again.

'And this is Charlie,' said Jackson, as the young woman, dressed in a huge sweatshirt and jeans, her hair short and elfin, leaned over to shake Claudia's hand.

'Editorial assistant. I assist... editorially.'

'Unnecessary exposition, Charlie,' Jackson deadpanned.

Charlie laughed a little awkwardly. 'I suppose... you know... I just like to be clear... you know me...'

'And this is Mark, your deputy editor,' continued Jackson.

Mark didn't even bother to stand, just nodded moodily, holding out a hand and only allowing Claudia to grasp three of his fingers. 'How's it going...?'

'And this is Oscar de la Bournville, the fashion and arts editor,' said Jackson.

Oscar stood to shake Claudia's hand. 'Welcome to the world's happiest office,' he said, unsmilingly. 'A veritable treasure trove of sparkling delights, fun times and high jinks. We never stop laughing, do we, lads? It's just a rollercoaster of hilarity all day long.'

There was a flicker of a smile from Simon. 'Ignore him. He's just sad because he smudged his eyeliner this morning.'

'I *didn't* smudge my eyeliner,' insisted Oscar. 'It's *meant* to be like that. It's called smoky eye.' He turned to Claudia. 'You should know all about the smoky eye, Claudia, being from *Irish Woman*. They are all about the smoky eye down there. I tell you, if the smoky eye wasn't invented, then half the pages would be blank.'

Claudia laughed, but she was a little unsettled. She'd been warned that the team were difficult, but they were actually ice-cold and brittle, not like her lovely old team, a whole floor down. She wasn't going to last a week. Jackson was right. It was a nest of vipers.

'Your desk is over there, in the corner,' Jackson said. 'And I'll show you the kitchen, where this lot make their Pot Noodles every day.'

Oscar glanced up again. 'Gordon Ramsay over there dares to criticise other people's lunch choices... this is the man who is on a permanent juice fast.'

Ignoring him, Jackson led the way to the small kitchen. 'Aren't they all divine?' he said, when they were out of earshot. 'Charming, the lot of them. Now, Claudy-pops, have you everything you need? Let me know. And don't mind those lot in there...' He motioned towards the office. 'They're adorable, with their truculent little personalities and their terrible clothes. Now, you will be all right, won't you, Claudy-pops?'

Claudia was relieved that someone like Jackson would be around to hold her hand.

'By the way...' Jackson stopped. 'You're not *friends*

with Foxy or anything, are you? You can tell me, Jackson, your new BFF.'

'I only met him properly last Friday.'

Jackson contemplated her for a moment. 'So why...?'

'I'm not sure. He said he liked my writing...'

'So nothing else? You aren't *involved* with him?'

Claudia tried to laugh, surprised at how direct Jackson's questions were. 'Of course not...'

'His wife left him, you know that? No one raised an eyebrow. He's a workaholic, never left the place, no work-life balance. Obsessed with the business. He's going to have a heart attack or drop dead from stress one of these days. The poor lamb. You know he's losing his marbles, don't you, so we need to mind him, don't we, Claudy-pops? It's so good to have someone nice and *normal* on board. Unlike all those snakes that lurk in the grass.' He motioned again with his head towards the team. 'And, honestly, you can tell me anything and *everything*. I'm here to advise, soothe, be your listening ear. Remember, don't trust the nice ones...' He tapped the side of his nose. 'They're always the worst. Bye, Claudy-pops! Don't do anything I wouldn't do!' And he disappeared along the corridor.

Back in the office, only Charlie looked up and smiled. 'Everything okay?'

'Great, thank you.' Claudia went over to her desk and put her bag down. 'Perhaps we could have a meeting? You could all tell me what needs to be done?'

Oscar glanced up from the books he was flicking through. 'I can't. I'm off to meet Hélène Davenport at her *atelier...*'

Simon laughed. '*Atelier*? You mean her parents' spare room? And she was called Helen when I knew her. We grew up on the same road...'

'Why shouldn't she have an atelier? It might be in her spare room, but she's a wonderful designer.' Oscar stood up, swirled a coat around his shoulders and turned to go, barely glancing at Claudia.

Mark looked over, almost reluctantly. 'I can go through anything you need?'

Claudia nodded at him. 'Thank you, that would be great.'

She pulled her chair over to his desk, feeling a little ridiculous, and not remotely editor-like, as though she was on work experience and being shown the ropes.

'We're just finishing this month's magazine.' Mark explained that the issue would be in the shops by the end of the week and how many copies, something about problems in distribution and when the digital copy was released.

Claudia tried to look as though she was taking it all in, but she suddenly felt completely overwhelmed. She had allowed herself to take on a job for which she wasn't qualified, didn't want and wasn't going to be able to do.

Charlie and Oscar were chatting behind her. 'Did I tell you that Scooby wants to go away for a bit?' said Charlie. 'On his own. Without me. Or what he's calling an essential mental health break. He's been a little fragile lately.'

'Can't he have it at home?' asked Oscar. 'Far cheaper. Most people just stay in bed and eat toast. Or get into astrology or adult colouring books.'

Claudia tried to focus on Mark and finally he stopped speaking. 'So that's that...'

'Great... that was really great, thank you.' Claudia stood up. 'I think... I just have something I need to do.' Rolling up a copy of *Irish Man,* she thrust it into her bag and, muttering a goodbye of some sorts, she made her escape. Tomorrow was a new day, but right now, she had to work out how the hell she was going to survive this.

10

FOXY

Everything okay? See the office?
Any thoughts? Sorry for late text
as was in a long board meeting. I
believe in you. Remember, I'm
here to talk to. Any time. Will come
and find you tomorrow.

Claudia knew she *had* to come up with a plan to
manage this situation. If she could just cling on and
keep breathing for twelve whole weeks, that would
be a start. But she had to have a practical plan of
how not just to survive but to do her professional
best. That way, when it went wrong or Blake got rid
of her or whatever happened, at least she would

have tried. She sat up in bed, notebook open on her lap, and tried to focus. A list, of course, was what was needed, to plan her way out of this current nightmare.

Heavily underlined several times was the word 'breathe', and then 'remember, this is only for three months'. She had also written down everything she could possibly think of that she needed to either do or think about. What else could she bring to the magazine while she was there? That column remained blank.

She had gone through her copy of *Irish Man*, analysing and reading everything from the headlines to the contents to the captions. There was something lifeless and serious about it; it didn't reflect any of the lives or the humour of most of the men she knew. And there was nothing about the real world. The restaurant review was of Dublin's swankiest and most expensive place, there were articles about clothes most men would never be able to afford, there was none of the gossipy, chatty real life and, apart from the name, the magazine didn't even feel particularly Irish.

But how much should she change, should she just tweak or make radical cuts and alterations? She knew she could edit, she knew she understood magazines, but what about managing this unmanageable team?

* * *

Claudia left her flat just before 8 a.m. the following morning, determined to make up for yesterday's abrupt departure and try to at least face this challenge head-on. If she was going to fail, then she may as well fail trying. At Fitzwilliam Square, she lingered for a moment, looking through the railings and through the trees, to the patch of green beyond, the bandstand, the beautiful bird soundtrack in her ears. It was an oasis in the busy city and the sights and sounds galvanised her before facing the grumpy *Irish Man* team.

Bernadette was already on reception at Hackett House, looking her immaculate full-foundation and false-eyelashed self at this early-ish hour. 'Morning, Claudia. Getting ahead of yourself, is it? Have a good go of the day before the rest come in?'

'Something like that...'

'Very sensible.' Bernadette nodded approvingly. 'That's what I do. Up before everyone. Even Michael D, my Jack Russell. We both have a cup of tea, he loves his own cup. Always bone china. He is a dog

with notions, don't you know? And then half a grape-
fruit. For me. Not for Michael D. He does like a banana though. I've an extra banana here if you want
one and it's reached perfection in the old ripening. I
always think that bananas are a ticking time bomb.
You have literally a half-hour eating window before
they are reduced to a brown abomination.' She held
one up. 'Fancy it? Nice with a cup of tea. Versatility is
the banana's middle name. If it had a middle name,
that is.'

'I would love it, thank you...' Claudia reached for
it and was about to slip it into her bag.

'Hold it like a baby!' ordered Bernadette sharply.
'Remember, it may be versatile, but it cannot be
thrown around. We had a fella in the other day who
asked me to remove my banana from the desk area.'
Bernadette made a face. 'Snooty kind of fella...'

'Allergic?' The lift arrived, doors opened.

'Who knows? He just said that he has an issue
with bananas...' Bernadette rolled her eyes. 'He's on
the board... one of those plotters...'

Claudia turned around. 'Plotters?'

'Oh, you know... the *plotters* who are *plotting*.'
Bernadette eyed her. 'There are five on the board
and not a single one of them is on Foxy's side. They
all used to be a great group altogether, but then a

couple died. One on the golf course. Another eating a steak in Shanahan's. And then another retired and is currently in a motorhome somewhere up in the Slieve Bloom Mountains. So there's been a gradual shift in personnel. Not so person*al*. Or person*able*. One rotten apple and suddenly the whole barrel isn't so much cider as slurry. They've been influenced by...' She dropped her voice. 'I won't name names. Not here.' She looked around. 'Blake Moriarty is one of them and then this fella... the anti-banana man...'

Claudia suddenly felt sure she knew who Bernadette was talking about. 'What's his name? The anti-banana man?'

'Brian O'Brien. Silly name for a silly eejit. I mean, I don't know *everything* that's going on, but I'm careful who I talk to these days. You're all right, I trust you. If you're good enough for Foxy, you're good enough for me.'

'So this Brian O'Brien is one of the plotters...?' Claudia was whispering now, dreadfully aware of the silence in the reception, as though anyone could be listening in. But no one was around, there wasn't a sound in the whole building, and yet... Bernadette's entire demeanour had changed from relaxed receptionist to paranoid conspiracy theorist.

'He is indeed. And the whole board has been influenced by that supercilious tool, Blake Moriarty.'

Was she right? According to Jackson, the vipers were elsewhere. Perhaps Bernadette didn't know the truth and was slavishly supporting Foxy when, in fact, the business needed an overhaul. Even if Foxy wasn't doddery, perhaps he had just lost his edge?

'Anyway, there's to be a vote of confidence in the current leadership...' Bernadette had dropped her voice so low that she was speaking in an intense whisper. 'Poor Foxy is going to be outvoted, I know he will. This is happening in a few weeks, Foxy was saying. He got his lawyer, William Blake, but he's got as much get-up-and-go as a stalled car. But if there is this vote of no confidence then Foxy will be forced to sell his shares. I think, if I can remember what he told me, he's only got sixteen per cent shares. I said, well, that's stupid, isn't it? Why have you got so few? And he said, he gave them away in the early days to his friends and whatnot. He still has those friends – some of them anyway – but it still doesn't add up to a majority. And Mr Anti-banana man has his own shares, somehow, and when he turned up and announced he was entitled to be on the board, Foxy had no choice but to agree. It's all over for Foxy, I fear.' Bernadette fixed Claudia with a look. 'He's not the same Foxy I remember from when I started all those years ago. Full of life, he was. He lost the will to fight after Alison left...' She was whispering urgently. 'The plotters are going to win, I can feel it in my bones. The goodies don't always prevail, whatever those flash fellas in Hollywood would have you believe. I worry about him, I really do. Winter is coming.'

'It's only September,' said Claudia.

'I was talking metaphorically,' Bernadette explained witheringly.

The lift was still waiting patiently for Claudia, the doors open, and Bernadette had returned to her breezy, sunny self, as though one moment ago she hadn't been prophesying doom like an ancient crone. Claudia blinked, wondering if she'd imagined it.

She carried the banana carefully up to her new office, thinking over everything that Bernadette had told her as she made a cup of tea in the kitchen. What on *earth* was going on?

Simon had just arrived when she returned to her desk. He looked surprised to see her. 'You're in early...'

'Just hoping to... have a good go of the day... what about you?'

'Sending the issue off to the printers today, but I've been up since the early hours. Daisy was awake all last night... pacing around.'

'Your toddler?'

'Not quite. Daisy must be around ninety-five...'

'Your *grandmother*?'

'My rescue terrier who no one else wanted because she bares her teeth all the time, even when she's being sweet. Someone once said, one day you'll wake up next to someone who is completely obsessed with you. I do every morning. And it's Daisy.'

Claudia laughed. 'I could think of worse things to wake up to than a teeth-baring terrier.'

Dogs, she thought, the great leveller. The perfect conversational tool to tame even vipers. She powered up her computer, took out her notebook and looked at her list: <u>BREATHE.</u>

She did just that, reading the rest of her list.

'Morning...' Mark was next to arrive and only grudgingly acknowledged them, looking as though he'd rather be anywhere else. Either he was just miserable or perhaps he too was one of those plotters she was warned about by Bernadette and by the lovely Jackson.

Oscar was next to arrive. 'Thank you, thank you,' he announced loftily, his hands raised up in benediction, as though in receipt of an enthusiastic standing ovation. 'Thank you, you're all too kind. Please, please stand down. No, this is too much... too much.' He threw his bag onto the hooks and removed his scarf, which wasn't a simple process but more of an unwrapping. He caught Claudia looking at him. 'You like? It arrived yesterday. Straight from Antwerp. Fabulous it certainly is.' He powered up his computer, drinking his coffee and eating a croissant which exploded into a billion flakes of pastry, like confetti, settling on his mohair jumper. 'Feck's sake!'

Claudia focused on what she should be doing. She was in charge of a brand-new issue of the magazine and she could either keep it exactly the way it was or make a few tweaks. Nothing radical and nothing that couldn't be changed back again as soon as she would be gone. But there was little point in pen-pushing or coasting while she was here, she may as well be a little creative.

Charlie was next in. 'Morning. Everyone okay?'

Oscar piped up. 'I feel as though I can speak for everyone when I say we have all never been better and we are *all* absolutely thrilled to be here. In fact, I know for certain that we wouldn't want to be anywhere else.'

'What normally happens when the magazine is in the printers?' Claudia asked Mark.

'We plan for next week's magazine. Our freelancers have been sending in their ideas and we decide what we like.' He turned back to his screen. 'I have a few emails. Robert Dunphy wants to go to a new Michelin-star place. Wine guy Will Donnelly has a few choices of bottles at twenty-five euro... um... what else? There's an interview possibility with a new actor from a play at the Abbey Theatre.'

'Good morning, everyone...'

Mark stopped speaking. Oscar glanced up, his face passive. Charlie looked nervous.

A man stepped in. He had dark brown wavy hair, dressed in smart jeans, pale blue shirt and a navy gilet. He had a face that stopped just shy of being handsome as his nose was too small, his jaw too big, eyes slightly too close together, forehead slightly too expansive, his stubble looked as though it had been pencilled in by an overly neat artist.

He raised an eyebrow, looking straight at Claudia, walking straight towards her in two strides, hand stretched out. 'Blake Moriarty. Editor-in-chief and chief financial officer of Foxy Publishing.' His smile was perfunctory, his handshake had the strength of a chihuahua's paw. 'Good to meet you.'

Claudia smiled back at him. If she opened her mouth, she knew she was in danger she might say how lost she was and how little she knew and how being a sheep farmer in Connemara was preferable to anything in Hackett House right now. But after talking to Bernadette earlier and sensing the atmosphere from the team, she realised it was best if she played it cool.

Blake continued, 'Foxy informed me yesterday as to your... appointment and I'm only sorry I wasn't... more involved in the hiring process. But Foxy is a man who knows his own mind.' His eyes flickered over her, not in a predatory way, but as though he was assessing her or stalling for time. 'You've come from *Irish Woman*, I believe?' He looked as though she'd arrived from something so outlandish that it had nothing to do with editing.

Claudia felt a surge of defiance. She did know about magazines, she had always loved them. She could write and edit, but more than anything, she was willing to learn. She looked him in the eye. 'It's great to be at *Irish Man* and seeing what I can bring to the magazine while I'm here.'

'Is it now?' He looked straight back at her, matching her look. 'I'll leave you to it.' He swept out of the room, accompanied by the sound of a slight rustling from his waterproof gilet.

'Nice gilet,' said Oscar, which made Charlie and Simon laugh. 'I mean, why do finance bros have to announce they are finance bros simply by those awful, padded gilets?'

'He thinks it's like wearing a flak jacket, or body armour,' agreed Simon. 'I bet he was the kind of boy who liked to shoot people with a plastic rifle.'

'Oh God,' sighed Oscar, 'I lived next door to one of those. It was so tiresome, all he wanted to do was play war. I had to hide in our shed while he hunted me with his gun.' He paused. 'He's now the head of Greenpeace.'

11

Claudia could rattle off a 1,200-word article in an hour, could spot a misspelling in a darkened room and was able to write a listicle in her sleep. But actually publishing? Being the buck-stopping top dog? She knew less than zero.

As assistant features editor on *Irish Woman*, she hadn't had to worry about layout or advertising or the balance of content. There was so much she hadn't had to think about and all she had done, really, was write her own pieces, interview people she was interested in and commission some of the freelancers to write their articles. It had been, she now realised, a very comfortable job.

She had been in her new role for almost a week

and by Friday lunchtime she was aware of just how big a proposition it was. To their credit, her new team had answered her questions about who their readers were, the editorial tone, her endless queries about design and advertisers and what they felt worked and what didn't. She'd peppered them with questions about who each freelancer was, about the humour and style of *Irish Man* which gave it its personality. Claudia's hand ached from note-taking and she had taken home piles of back issues to plough through.

For a whole week, she lived and breathed magazine publishing, as though she was revising for an exam for which she had done no preparation or work or even turned up at the lectures. How did she not know all this? How had she loved and worked in magazines for six whole years and yet had given so little thought to the business side or their role in society or the relationship between them and their readers?

It was probably just as well that her new colleagues didn't chat convivially in the same way as her old ones, because she wasn't feeling particularly chatty, consumed as she was in learning as much as possible. She missed her old team and their easy working relationship. They had all used to gather in the kitchen at lunchtime, admiring someone's posh-looking sandwich or home-made soup. Questions would be asked about partners and children, but the most enthusiasm would be reserved for details about someone's dog – its general welfare, did it like its new bed, that kind of thing. But here, at *Irish Man*, the done thing seemed to be to affect a moaning attitude, as though they were all there under sufferance and would much rather be anywhere than in this office at this time.

Over the week, Foxy had made a few appearances, poking his head into the office. 'Everything okay, Claudia?'

'Grand, thank you.' She didn't have time to talk to him, as she'd just thought of another question for the long-suffering Mark.

Claudia became used to the silence and the rhythm of their day when each would disappear out of the office any time after 12 p.m. and return with a parchment-wrapped sandwich or a steaming plastic pot of instant noodles, to be consumed at their desks. Little would be asked about private lives, no questions about partners or even dogs. She did ask Simon about Daisy and he perked up momentarily to mention her most recent antics, as did Charlie when she enquired about her boyfriend Scooby.

Slowly, by the Friday, finally, there were a few signs of a slight thaw.

Mark was at his desk, eating a brown bread and cheddar sandwich, a textbook open in front of him. Claudia tried to see what he was reading.

'Mark's passion is ancient poetry,' called Oscar from his desk. 'He's *obs*essed...'

Mark looked up, irritated. 'Not obsessed. Passionately interested...'

'Same thing,' said Oscar.

Claudia was surprised. She hadn't thought of Mark being passionate about anything.

Mark sighed heavily, as though she'd asked him another question. 'If you must know, my degree and master's were in Medieval Manuscripts. I spent four very happy years in dark places wearing white gloves.'

'Were you a mime artist?' Oscar said. 'Did you wear a stripy top and have a white face?'

'As you well know, Oscar, I am referring to my work in the National Library.' Mark rolled his eyes. 'Magazines are so... ephemeral. Pointless, really.'

'Reassuringly honest as ever,' said Oscar. 'A man doing a job he hates.'

'I can't help it,' insisted Mark. 'I fell into this world and now I can't fall out.'

'Mark doesn't even pretend to enjoy being here,' remarked Oscar. 'I find *pretending* to enjoy work is necessary for the emotional well-being of my colleagues.'

'You're on the wrong trajectory...?' Claudia tried to encourage Mark to talk.

'Exactly. I'm living someone else's life. The National Library is my idea of heaven, except no jobs ever come up because no one ever retires. They just get older and older...'

Charlie was looking over. 'Scooby's the same...'

'A mime artist?' said Oscar.

Charlie laughed. 'No, of course not. But he feels his life is out there somewhere and he's not living it.'

Oscar looked at her. 'Darling, that does *not* bode well...'

'He's leaving for Greece tomorrow. To Hydra. He's managed to find a job as a goatherd.'

Oscar spat out his tea. 'A goatherd? As in a herder of goats?'

Charlie nodded. 'He wants to get away from the rat race for a while...'

'So he's joining the goat race?' said Oscar.

'Goats are very intelligent, apparently,' went on Charlie. 'Very intelligent... what are they? Mammals?'

'Ruminants?' suggested Claudia.

'So, he wants to ruminate with the ruminants.' Oscar looked at Charlie. 'It might be good for him, stop him being so despondent.'

She nodded. 'He has been down lately. It's just that I'll miss him. I don't mind him when he's down because I just like him however he is.' She turned away from them and focused on her screen.

Mark had been opening the day's post and held up a hardback book, a memoir of some sort. 'Do you like interviewing people?' he asked Claudia.

'Love it.'

'Good. Because I hate it. Would you interview Arnold Kennedy?'

Wasn't he one of Foxy's friends, the pundit of some sport? Claudia smiled brightly. 'I love him,' she lied, hoping he hadn't recently been released from prison or accused of sexual harassment. 'I'm a huge fan.' At least she knew how to interview, and it was nice to be able to do something which she definitely knew she could do.

'Rather you than me,' said Mark.

'Why? You're not a sports fan?'

There was a snort from Simon. 'Mark thinks Croke Park is a funeral home...'

'Whatever you do, don't ask Arnold Kennedy about his hair transplant,' said Mark.

'That wasn't him,' said Charlie. 'That was the other pundit. The one with the ears.'

'Then don't ask him about his affair...' said Mark.

'Again,' said Oscar, 'not him. That was the one with those awful ties. And the nostril hair.'

Just then, Foxy poked his head around the door again. 'Morning, folks. Enjoyed the last issue. I managed to catch up with it last evening. Read it cover to cover. Oscar, liked your piece on the resonance of ties. Surprisingly emotional. I wore my brother's tie for years... Anyway.' He cleared his throat, his eyes alighting on Claudia. 'You're all looking after Ms Kelly?' he went on. 'Showing her the ropes? Pointing out the secret biscuit stash, the fire escape...?'

'There's a fire escape?' said Oscar. 'No one told me. I always thought that in the event of a fire, we'd have to tie our clothes together and lower each other down from the window.'

'And there's no biscuits to be had in this office,' said Simon. 'Which is truly shocking and another reason why the Best Workplace in Ireland award will elude us yet again.'

Foxy laughed and then turned to Claudia. 'Time

for a word? Just see how you are getting on, that kind of thing?' He smiled at everyone in the office, as Claudia stood to gather her jacket, bag and phone. 'Oh, by the way, I was in my favourite stationers this morning... and I saw these wonderful new pens. Ballpoint, don't leak, but refillable. From Japan apparently.' He reached into his inside jacket pocket and produced a long, slim pen, handing it to Claudia. 'I thought you might like it. Blue ink? Do you write in blue or black? Although, I am not sure if those who write in black should be trusted.'

'Well, then, I'm untrustworthy,' said Oscar. '*I* couldn't trust someone who writes in blue. You need to be definite when you write, show you mean it. Black is the only colour.'

'Well, I like blue. And I love a nice pen.' Claudia took it from Foxy, feeling touched by this sweet gesture.

'Don't we *all* get pens?' Oscar was indignant.

'Sorry, Oscar,' said Foxy, 'but for some reason, I was only thinking about my new editor today. But next time I'm in the shop, I'll buy you all one. You've reminded me of something that Alison used to say, that it's the small gestures people value. She wanted the cup of tea together on a Sunday morning, the walk in the park, the night in front of the telly. Nothing fancy. It's all so obvious. Wish I'd learned it all years ago. Looks like I still need to be reminded.' He smiled at them all.

'Scooby says that the world is a grey place,' said Charlie. 'He says the joy has gone.'

Foxy looked concerned. 'The poor chap...'

'That's why he's gone to Greece,' explained Charlie. 'To take a break.'

'But you're his joy,' insisted Foxy. 'Does he not realise that?'

Charlie shook her head. 'Obviously not.'

'He prefers the company of goats,' said Oscar. 'But that won't last.'

'Not if he has any sense,' said Foxy. He smiled at Charlie and then turned back to Claudia. 'Ready?'

He chatted amiably as they walked towards the lift, pointing out some of the art on the walls.

'I bought that when I was young and frequented the junk shops. You'd find the most interesting things there. And that one... with the dog. Found that in the market in Aix-en-Provence.' In the lift, as they descended, he kept up the patter. 'So, how are things in Sandycove?'

'I live in town...' she said, wondering when she'd told him her mother lived in Sandycove.

'Oh, sorry, I'm getting confused. You're in that flatshare, aren't you? Flatshares are like Christmas, you can only endure them with people you like.' He smiled at her as the doors of the lift opened, and stood to one side, as Claudia stepped into reception. 'Morning, Bernie. Radiant, as always.'

'It's the rage. It shows on my face.'

He laughed and they exited the building and onto Baggot Street. 'Ernie's okay with you?' His voice was quieter now, as though the performance was over.

Claudia nodded and they walked quickly, towards the corner of Merrion Street, nipping down the lane and into the café.

'*Buongiorno*, Ernesto. *Come stai*? Two coffees, please.' He pulled out a chair at the table in the window for Claudia to sit down on, before slipping into one himself. His whole body seemed to change, as though he breathed differently in here, as though it was only here he could relax. 'Tell me, how are you getting on?'

'We're busy planning the next issue.' She took the coffee from Ernesto. 'Thank you.'

Ernesto smiled at her. 'Enjoying working for the big boss, yes? You like it?'

'I'm not sure yet,' she admitted.

'That's wisdom, is it not?' Foxy said to Ernesto.

'Never be sure of anything because that's when you fail.'

'But...' she began, and they both turned to look at her. 'The thing is, I'm still not sure why I'm there, exactly.'

Foxy smiled at her, his eyes gentle. 'It's never easy doing something new. Change and challenge are always difficult. But I know you're up to it. Now, tell me, how are you getting on with the team? They're wary, are they? A bit diffident?'

She nodded. 'I just can't quite get in there... there are moments when we connect, but it's early days, I suppose.'

Foxy nodded. 'They've been a little bit bruised. They're all a little unhappy and unmotivated...'

'You *know* that?'

'I like these people. A few of them talk to me, tell me things.' He tapped the side of his nose. 'Look, if you need me to talk to the team, let me know. Some of them I employed straight from college. Oscar was a skinny art-school kid, all lanky of leg and long of nose. He still spoke with his Roscommon accent and Simon arrived from some graphic design course with a very impressive portfolio. Look, Claudia, hang in there. You're there because I know you're the best person for

the job. Blake might not be too happy about it because he believes hiring and firing should no longer
be my job. But it's about time I got back to the roots of
the business and was more hands-on. And hiring you
is probably the best thing I've done in years.'

'Thanks, Foxy.'

'I'm here for you. It's the least I can do. I mean it,
it's the very *least* I can do.'

* * *

As they walked back to the office, it began to rain,
and then pour down, a Dublin monsoon. They shel-
tered in the doorway of SuperValu, watching the
street outside, people holding umbrellas over their
heads, cars splashing through the street, cyclists
swerving the potholes, the smell of damp and rain in
the air. The two of them looked out at the great sheet
of water, as though they were behind a waterfall.

Pedestrians dodged them, the city taking on a
frantic kinetic atmosphere as people rushed
through the rain, newspapers, briefcases held above
heads, vast golf umbrellas which bashed into people. A cyclist was the only person who seemed un-
affected by the rain, the rider calmly making his
way along. Foxy had noticed him as well. 'On a

bike, you dodge the raindrops. If you cycle slightly squiggly.'

Claudia laughed.

'I used to love my old bike,' went on Foxy. 'I used to peg around on it, an old black Nelly of a bone-shaker, but I so desperately wanted to look success-ful, so I sold it. I miss it. Do you know I haven't been on a bike in... I don't know... thirty years?'

'Mine's still punctured,' Claudia said. 'It's in the hall of my flat. I just haven't got around to getting it fixed. It would mean wheeling it to a bike shop and there's no bike shop for miles and miles. I would have to go all the way to Rathgar, I think.'

Foxy was looking across the road intently and Claudia followed his gaze. Under a huge umbrella which he used more as a battering ram was Brian O'Brien. Foxy stepped back a little, his eyes fixed on Brian O'Brien.

'You didn't want to meet Brian O'Brien, then?' said Claudia.

He eyed her, surprised she knew his name. 'No, not really. He's not my favourite person. He's trying to get rid of me. He's on the board and I'm in the way. But as I no longer hold majority shares, it's proving hard to cling on.' He spoke lightly, as though only half interested. 'How do you know him?'

'He was a friend of my father's...'

'Oh yes?' Foxy's eyes glittered.

'Before he died. They were in school together and... well... turns out he wasn't that much of a friend after all.'

Foxy didn't speak for a moment. And then, 'Wait here.'

He reappeared brandishing a small umbrella which he wrestled open. 'SuperValu's finest. Can't have my new editor getting wet, can I?' He opened it and handed it to her with a flourish.

Claudia felt incredibly touched. 'Thank you, Foxy. I'll bring it back tomorrow.'

'Keep it.'

Claudia turned to go, leaving him in the rain. 'Will you be all right?'

He waved her away. 'Rain is good for the brain. We had an aunt who used to say that. Auntie June. My brother used to call her Auntie Prune.' He paused. 'Safe home, anyway.'

'Thanks, Foxy...' And she began to speed up, hopping over puddles that were beginning to form, past the taxis and cars which sploshed their way through the rain-drenched streets.

12

On Sunday, Claudia and Fiona were both at Patsy's for lunch and were in the middle of their Viennetta when Patsy cleared her throat.

'I have something of an announcement.'

Fiona and Claudia put down their spoons.

'I've been on what I think might amount to... or at least has the appearance of being, or could perhaps be defined as...' began Patsy, looking nervous.

'Mum, what are you trying to say?' said Fiona, irritated. 'Spit it out!'

Patsy did as she was told, speaking quickly. 'I've been on a date. And I've agreed to another... it's with Alan. Dr Dunne from the practice.'

Fiona looked surprised. 'The socks and *sandals* guy?'

Claudia was less surprised, having witnessed her mother and Alan's interaction at the engagement party. 'Socks and sandals are ironically cool,' she approved. 'The fashion editor in work was wearing socks and sandals. Except his socks were gold and the sandals were fuchsia pink.'

Oscar had indeed turned up in such an ensemble, much to Simon's amusement. 'You don't think socks and shoes should be the least shouty of your outfit, Oscar?' he'd said. 'Not at all,' breezed Oscar. 'Nothing is off limits. You should see my underwear.' Simon had pulled a face. 'I'll pass on that, thank you, Oscar. Very generous offer though.' It was a moment when Claudia thought that perhaps the office was in danger of becoming actually friendly.

Here, at the family kitchen table, Patsy smiled. 'I don't think Alan wears his socks and sandals *ironically*. He's a very practical-minded man. And he's comfortable.'

'Practical is good, isn't it, Fi? If we are to have a new stepfather, then we need practical. And, best of all, he's a doctor. If any of us gets ill, we won't have to pay to see a GP.' Claudia winked at Fiona.

'I am *not* going to my new stepfather for medical treatment,' insisted Fiona, beginning to smile as well.

'Hold on,' said Patsy. 'Whoever said anything about a new stepfather? I've gone on a date. *One* date. For tea and cake. And it was very pleasant...'

'Did he pay?' asked Fiona. 'Because if he didn't, it's a red flag.'

'He paid,' said Patsy.

'Was he weird and fussy about his coffee?' went on Fiona. 'Did he insist on certain milk at a certain temperature, frothed in a certain way? Because...'

'Red flag,' said Claudia.

'He ordered tea...' said Patsy.

Fiona nodded. 'Thank God. What kind of cake?'

'A slice of fruit brack. With butter.'

Again, Fiona seemed mollified. 'He sounds eminently suitable. But you're sure he's not a cowboy coming and taking advantage and stealing all your money...'

'He's not a cowboy,' Patsy insisted. 'I don't think you can ride a horse in sandals, anyway. And I think he wouldn't be into horses and dust and things like that. He's asthmatic.'

'Ironic,' said Fiona. 'A doctor with asthma... you'd think he'd be able to cure it.'

'It's a lifelong condition,' explained Claudia.

'I know that, but it doesn't say much for his doc-toring skills if he's sickly...'

'He's not sickly,' insisted Patsy. 'He just has asthma. Anyway, this has got nothing to do with any-thing. I was just informing the two of you that I'd gone for tea and cake with Alan...'

'We'll be celebrating another wedding soon,' said Claudia, hoping to make her sister laugh again, but Fiona had stopped smiling.

'Will you girls please not get carried away?' Patsy went on. 'I'm *not* about to get married. And nor is Alan. He's a widower, as well, so we have lots in com-mon. His wife passed away more than twenty years ago now, poor thing. He's a very nice, decent and kind person. He makes home visits in his spare time, helps patients out to their car, rings to check on them, even picks up prescriptions and drops them in, that kind of thing. The other doctors don't do that.'

Claudia was nodding. 'He does sound nice...'

'You don't think *nice* is overrated, though?' asked Fiona.

'Nice is nice, is it not?' asked Claudia. 'You cer-tainly don't want horrible. Dom wasn't that nice, I now realise.'

Patsy was looking concerned, as she did whenever anyone mentioned Dom. 'I don't think nice is overrated, Fiona,' she said, firmly. 'It's a good place to start. Anyway, we need to help you choose your wedding dress. When do you want to do that?'

'Soon, I suppose...' said Fiona, without enthusiasm.

'Your father would have liked John-Paul,' went on Patsy.

'*Everyone* likes John-Paul,' Claudia agreed. 'But Dad always liked nice, decent men.'

'Well...' Fiona paused. 'Not always. After all, Brian O'Brien was his friend.'

They rarely spoke about him, not wanting to bring him to mind and the shadow he'd cast.

But Claudia suddenly felt she wanted to know. After seeing him so recently and after what Bernadette had said, perhaps it was time for some answers. 'What do you know about him, Mum?'

Patsy sighed. 'They were at school together and they'd been very close, they had a bond, I suppose. And boys in boarding schools are always especially close, growing up without family around. Philip was loyal to Brian, even though he knew what he was like. He felt sorry for him and I think he thought Brian was always on the outside of life. He lived with an aunt who wasn't interested in him, he had no one.

And then he was horribly bullied by a teacher. All of which would make your heart go out to someone, but for whatever reason, Brian decided the world owed him. Including your father. Back in school, he was apparently caught stealing a few times – money from the tuck shop, then money from a charity sports day. He was sent to the headmaster and Philip took the blame with him. And then, he did get expelled for stealing cigarettes and selling them to the boys. Philip always said that Brian was always looking for attention.'

'But what *happened*?' pressed Claudia. 'With Dad's investment?'

'Well, as far as I know, Brian was some kind of financial advisor and he came to Philip with an investment opportunity. And that was it. Philip gave him money... because, again, he felt sorry for him. It wasn't too much, I don't think. But the worst thing was that Philip had signed a clause which made him liable if the investment failed. And, obviously, the investment was a disaster and Brian kept telling Philip he owed money. I remember once, they almost came to blows about it.'

Claudia felt sick, as she always did when she thought about the last months of her father's life and the looming figure of Brian O'Brien.

Patsy continued, 'And then when Philip died, I was liable. And you know what happened. I gave him whatever we could, the repayment plan and he even wanted some of Philip's shares.' She paused. 'It was a terrible time.'

The three of them sat in silence and Fiona reached for her mother's hand across the table. 'But we survived. We got through it.'

Patsy closed her eyes for a moment. 'Your father was too trusting. Naïve in a way... two sweet for this life.'

'I hope I never meet Brian O'Brien ever again,' said Fiona.

Claudia said nothing.

'I think it's the end of him.' Patsy smiled at them both. 'The debts are paid off, finally. And the three of us are happy and healthy. And we have a wedding to look forward to. John-Paul reminds me of Philip, a kind, gentle man. You've chosen very well.'

'John-Paul's *not* like Dad,' insisted Fiona. 'I am *not* marrying my father.'

It was only later, when Claudia was back in her box room, did she remember that she hadn't told Fiona and Patsy about her new job. But hadn't Foxy told her not to spread it around?

13

The following week, Claudia began her day earlier than everyone else and stayed late into the evenings, reading previous issues, talking to freelancers, commissioning articles, chatting to PR and agents, trying to bag the best interviews and, more than anything, trying to understand the magazine.

At the end of the month, a brand-new issue of *Irish Man* would be out and she wanted to be proud of it. Everyone in the office was busy. Oscar was writing about 'how socks maketh the man' and Mark was writing up his interview with chef PJ Doyle. 'He's such a narcissist,' he commented, as he typed away. 'He said he didn't trust a man who couldn't make a decent Béarnaise sauce.'

Oscar looked up. 'Why *make* a sauce when you can open a bottle of ketchup?'

Simon agreed. 'That's why God invented the squeezy bottle with the flip-cap. So no one had to simmer a bloody sauce over a stove ever again.'

As picture editor, Charlie's job was to make sure all the images which had been taken for that issue were in, as well as sourcing others. Simon was designing the magazine from cover to cover, importing the ads and placing every article, every piece of text, every image.

On Wednesday evening, Claudia headed again to Sandycove for Celia and Michael's dinner party. Johnny Hogan was going to be there, she remembered, feeling a lift of excitement. She had been so busy with work that she hadn't thought about him and now she realised how much she was looking forward to seeing him.

Clutching a large and exuberant bouquet she bought in the little flower shop outside the train station, Claudia walked quickly across the village to Celia and Michael's house. In the middle of a large and very beautiful terrace of red-brick houses, it was set back from the road with steps running up to the front door, two topiaried bay trees on either side.

Grace and Tom had been just about to ring the

bell when they spotted Claudia. She waved and hurried up, while Tom gave a supercilious smile. Grace had always had dubious taste in men, going back as long as Claudia knew her. There was Jim in college who drank three litres of milk every day and tried to get everyone to call him 'Jimmy Boy'. It didn't catch on. Or there was Arthur who only wore black and said he was a relative of Vlad the Impaler about which no one could tell if he was joking or not. And then there was Peter who never showered because he claimed he didn't want to destroy his microbiome with chemicals but reeked of body odour so badly that Grace finally pulled the plug. Something he should have done after a daily bath. So far, Grace had always eventually seen the light and Claudia hoped she soon would with Tom.

'Isn't this nice?' Grace hugged her. 'And don't you just *love* the trees. Like little leafy sentry guards. And the door, painted in... what colour would you call it?'

'Aquamarine?' suggested Claudia. 'Or Aegean blue?'

Tom sighed. 'It's just *blue*. Honestly, why do people want to complicate colours? They are either light or dark. Some people try so hard to be different.'

'Tom, you're being rude,' said Grace, with a

smile. 'Claudia works in magazines and knows about colours and things like that and I work in an art gallery...'

Tom sighed. 'It's just all so unimportant...'

'It may be but it's nice, isn't it, Claudia?' Grace pressed the doorbell. 'When I grow up, I want to be Celia, elegant and beautiful and desirable...'

'Desirable...' snorted Tom. 'This is a woman who relies on bay trees to show the world how exquisitely *tasteful* she is.'

'Tom!' Grace giggled and gave him a swipe on the shoulder. 'She *is* exquisitely tasteful. She has an art gallery after all. And she's my boss. Behave yourself!'

'What?' Tom was looking hurt. 'I'm only wondering...' But he stopped because the door was opening and there was Celia looking even more magnificent than she usually did. Dressed in cream wide-legged trousers, a cropped cream jacket over a white top and a large pearl necklace, Celia was almost ethereal, one of those people you couldn't imagine ever crying or anything bad happening to her. She breezed through life, buoyed up by natural beauty and effortless style.

'Grace!' Celia kissed the air beside Grace's cheeks, her hands lightly on her shoulders. 'My favourite person. And Claudia! How simply wonderful to see you. I said to Grace that we must invite you to our little dinner for Johnny. We adore him, don't we, Grace? And, Claudia, apparently you know him?'

'He was my...' began Claudia, but Celia had already turned her attention on Tom.

'I've been ignoring Tom. You have a very ignorable face, Thomas. The kind of face that makes people appreciate their own husbands.'

Grace let out a peal of laughter. 'You tell him, Celia. He's being especially obnoxious lately.'

Tom affected a smile. 'And you, Ms Desmond, are the kind of woman who makes husbands remember their wives.'

Perhaps Tom and Celia loathed each other, thought Claudia. And this was their way of pretending it was harmless banter.

Celia laughed. 'Touché, Tom! Now, all of you, come in and see lovely Johnny, who's in the drawing room. Darling Michael is doing battle in the kitchen, doing whatever it is one does with chicken and garlic, or perhaps he is feeding his sourdough. I told him I am feeling a bit left out these days as he used to say how much he loved feeding me, but now it's a little bubbling pot of sourdough starter.' She laughed again. 'He wouldn't accept any help from me. Said I would only burn everything. Which of course I do. I can't even cook cheese on toast. Michael always says I have two talents. Running the gallery and the other...' She trailed off. 'Well, the other doesn't matter...'

'What is it, Celia?' asked Grace.

'Well... Michael, being a sweetie, says my other talent is to look beautiful.' She giggled. 'Of course he's short-sighted, so I take his compliments with a pinch of salt.'

'But you *always* look beautiful,' Grace said, slavishly. 'I wish I looked as effortlessly gorgeous as you.'

Tom was studiously silent, Claudia noticed, probably disapproving of Grace's adoration. She handed over her bouquet. 'It's so lovely to be invited...'

'Oh, divine!' Celia thrust them under her nostrils briefly before abruptly discarding them on the hall table. 'Come through to the drawing room and say hello to Johnny. Tom, will you take Grace and Claudia's jackets and leave them in the cloakroom, please?'

Tom, to Claudia's surprise, did exactly as asked. As Grace and Celia talked briefly in the hall waiting for Tom, Claudia went into the living room, which she'd been in before with its too high ceiling and red sofa so large you could only perch on the edge. On the walls were huge terrifying canvases of abstract red and black, the kind of things that Claudia imagined haunted Michael's dreams.

But there was Johnny, standing and opening his arms to hug Claudia. 'How's it going?' He looked at her, smiling. 'By the way, you didn't call me for our walking tour.'

She laughed. 'I didn't know you wanted me to.'

'I said I needed to be shown around... Have you any idea how many new buildings there are in town? I look around for a landmark and there's some big gleaming edifice blocking my view. So I need a guide.'

She was smiling at him. 'Okay. I'll bring you on that walking tour...'

'I can't wait. Now, tell me, did you take the job?'

She was surprised he'd remembered. 'Yes...'

'And? Do you *love* it?'

Claudia laughed, shaking her head. 'Not remotely.' For the first time in over a week, she could perhaps see that there was a funny side to this hellscape.

Celia interrupted them. 'You two can discuss whatever it is you're discussing later but we first need some drinks. Gin and tonics? I have a lovely bottle of Sandycove Distillery. It's superb. There is the slightest hint of saline and locally grown herbs.'

Tom stepped forward and saluted. 'Anything else

you need, madam? Am I to be on drink-making duty as well?'

'You don't think you came here to be wined and dined, did you, Thomas?' said Celia. 'Yes, *of course* you're on drink-making duty. You know I couldn't make a glass of water!'

He and Celia walked over to the large Chinese cabinet within which were antique glasses and bottles of every kind of alcohol, from posh sherry to expensive vodka, jars of Luxardo cherries and a bucket brimming with ice.

'Tom's gin and tonics are to die for,' said Grace, joining Claudia and Johnny. 'He's quite the expert.'

Over at the drinks cabinet, Tom said to Celia. 'You see, ice in first... two fingers of gin...'

'Try three,' Celia was saying. 'Go mad...'

'You need a perfect ratio,' Tom was explaining. 'You can't just lash it in, that's where you're going wrong.'

'Story of my life,' tinkled Celia, 'always lashing in the gin.'

Claudia glanced at Grace, who was smiling happily back at everyone. 'He truly is an expert. At everything!'

14

Claudia was busy arranging her face into something neutral, when Grace dropped her voice. 'Poor Tom needs a great deal of praise lately, so do lavish it on him when you get your drink. He's feeling a little out of sorts. Working too hard, I think, and feeling a little overwrought. You see, as a therapist, it must be so hard not to take on other people's pain. I've tried to help and advise, but he's the kind of person you can't tell what to do. And I completely understand. People either don't take advice or they resent the person who's given it... and so if it all goes wrong, then you're to blame. No one likes advice,' Grace went on. 'They might pretend they do and encourage you to tell them. But all people want to be told is that whatever they are currently doing, then they are right. Our job as friends is to reassure and to be there for the good times and then when it goes wrong.' She gave another light laugh.

Claudia nodded, realising she was right. We all had to make our own mistakes, which was why Grace had no idea just how insufferable Claudia found Tom.

Johnny caught her eye and smiled. 'I think,' he said, 'the key is to decide *who* you want to take advice from. My mother, obviously. My sister, sometimes...' He laughed. 'My agent, always. Some of my closest friends.'

Grace nodded, and turned to Claudia. 'I *wanted* to tell you that Dom wasn't right for you...'

'Why didn't you?'

'Because you wouldn't have listened...'

Claudia nodded. 'I know...' She grinned at Grace. 'I had to go through being all heartbroken, before I realised he was wrong for me...'

'Heartbroken?' Johnny looked at her with concern.

'Not really *heartbroken*,' said Claudia. 'A bit disappointed. For whatever reason. But I'm over all that now.'

Johnny was listening. 'Why did your boyfriend end things?'

'He said he wanted space,' interrupted Grace.

'Space?' Johnny pulled a face. 'What a cliché.'

Grace nodded. 'He already has all the space he needs. Between his ears. And in his heart. He's the only person in the world who didn't cry at *E.T. or Schindler's List...*'

'He's just not easily moved to tears...' Claudia tried to be fair to Dom.

But Johnny was looking at her. 'You know, we probably learn more from the end of relationships than the thing itself...'

'I did, actually,' agreed Claudia. 'I learned that I wasted too much time on him. Should have cut my losses long before... only...' She paused. 'Only, I really liked his flat. It had a balcony!' She winked at Johnny to make sure he knew she was joking. Well, *kind of* joking. That flat *had* been really, *really* lovely.

Thankfully he laughed. 'I once went out with someone for six months too long, because I liked her dog so much. He had allergies and I was really invested in getting him better. Turned out I liked him more than her.'

Now Claudia laughed. 'I went out with someone once at college because he had a car...'

'Oh, we've *all* done that,' said Johnny. 'The power of the four wheels. The biggest aphrodisiac for young people since the birth of the alcopop.'

'Are you single, Johnny?' asked Grace. 'I would say the women of the art world are throwing themselves at you, do you have a muse in a garret somewhere?'

Johnny shook his head. 'I don't go in for muses. I've been single for a while now and very happy. I go to the cinema on my own or to a restaurant with a book for company.'

'But you don't have anyone to watch television with or go on minibreaks...' persisted Grace.

'When was the last time you went on a minibreak?' asked Claudia.

'Three months ago,' said Grace, her words faltering. 'To Drogheda. A psychotherapy conference. So not a minibreak as such. And I had to go and find an off-licence and sneak a bottle of fizz back into the room because the bar closed at 9 p.m. and the minibar was pure extortion. Five whole euro for a bag of crisps! And then Tom was so tired from speaking all day, he fell asleep so it was just me watching television, drinking the Prosecco. And then I spilt a brimming glass all over me because I was lying down. And there were crisp crumbs in the bed, embedding their evil little shards into me all night long. So I didn't sleep. And everything was sticky from the Prosecco. Honestly, you need paint stripper to wash that off. And so... yeah... it definitely was *not* the minibreak of dreams. But...' She brightened. 'My point still stands.'

'I think we need to redefine the minibreak,' said Johnny, fixing Claudia with a look. 'Adventures can be found on your own doorstep.'

'Claudia's not into adventures,' announced Grace. 'She's decided to have a manless existence. Dom put her off the whole *species*...'

'I'm not off the *whole* species... just enjoying being single. Like Johnny.'

Johnny seemed amused. 'I think being manless is an appropriate response. It doesn't have to be forever...'

'I was the same,' said Grace. 'I'd given up, and then I met the love of my life.'

On cue, Tom appeared carrying a tray of drinks towards them. 'Here we go... best gin, best tonic, limes... lots of ice.'

Celia was behind him, already sipping her own. 'Oh, *divine*... Tom, you really are the best cocktail waiter in Ireland. If you ever give up the therapy, you could always take up bartending. I can see you in a little bow tie, a little apron.'

Grace laughed. 'So can I!' she said, eagerly. 'He looks so handsome in a bow tie.'

Managing not to roll her eyes, Claudia turned to Johnny. 'So, you're happy to be home?' She sipped her gin and tonic. It was decidedly ordinary, not the earth-shattering, mind-blowing experience she had expected.

Johnny nodded. 'When I was in London, I got so homesick and missed everything. Obviously my mother. My friends. Irish food, chatting to a complete stranger at a bus stop, that kind of thing. And now I can go into any shop in the country and buy a bag of Tayto. Same goes for Barry's Tea. Or Jacob's Mikados. I can say something and the person will get it and not think I'm a lunatic.' He paused. 'And obviously, it's beautiful. Not that I'd forgotten but I'm renting a little cottage at Bullock Harbour. This morning I opened my front door and I could hear this sound, like a cow mooing or lowing, or whatever they do...'

'Both, I think...'

'Strange, I thought. Cows in the city? But then I saw these heads in the water. Soft brown heads.'

'The seals?' Claudia used to walk early in the

mornings and there they'd be, sitting on rocks, their bodies submerged under the smooth surface.

'It's like singing. Tuneless, obviously. Bit like me.'

'They wouldn't win a talent show...'

'No.' He smiled at her. 'Except for swimming. They're pretty good at that.'

'You can't be good at everything.'

'How is your gin and tonic, Johnny?' interrupted Celia. 'Give Tom your feedback.'

'It's excellent. Thank you.'

'I'd say making gin and tonics is one of Tom's best talents,' said Grace, laughing, but Tom looked puzzled, as though hurt.

'What makes you say that?' he said.

'I was just pulling your leg,' said Grace, hastily. 'You're so good at making drinks and *so* many other things.'

'Well, I try to be a jack of all trades,' said Tom. 'Cocktail making, therapy... my meatballs are incredible. If I do say so myself.'

'Oh, they are!' said Grace, fervently.

'And hanging pictures,' said Celia, a look on her face Claudia couldn't quite work out. 'But the gin and tonic is very good. I'm better at drinking them than making them.'

'I can't even make a cup of tea. It's always too

weak,' said Johnny. 'Sometimes, when I go to someone's house, they make me a cup of tea and it's delicious and I ask them to write down the recipe. But asking for a recipe for a cup of tea is like trying to find the pot of gold at the end of the rainbow. It's impossible. Tea just happens.'

'Alchemy,' said Claudia, nodding.

'The mystery of tea,' agreed Grace. 'Other nations don't understand why we are so evangelical about it.'

'Exactly,' said Johnny. 'It's magic...'

Tom looked puzzled. 'What are you three going on about?'

'Small talk,' said Johnny, smiling broadly. 'Just chatting.'

'Right...' Tom had a look in his eye as though he thought they were stone mad. 'I'm not very good at small talk... I prefer big talk. Life, the universe and all that...'

'Aha!' Celia's husband, Michael, roared from the doorway, wearing a large navy and white striped apron tied around his waist. 'The revellers are gathering, the chicken is roasting, the pavlova is pavlovaing...' He walked over and embraced Grace. 'Darling Grace, so lovely to see you... and Johnny, looking magnificent...' He grasped Johnny's hand firmly. 'And beautiful Claudia.' He kissed her hand. 'So good of you to bestow your presence on us.' He turned to Tom. 'And the psycho...' – his pause was infinitesimal – '*therapist.*'

'Michael, darling,' said Celia, 'would you like one of Tom's delectable gin and tonics?'

'I would.' Michael slapped Tom on the back, making the ice leap in his glass. 'What's your secret, Tom?'

'No secret,' said Tom. 'Just gin, Michael, and tonic. It's about ratios. It's science. No magic or alchemy at all.'

'Well, then, what are you waiting for?' boomed Michael. 'Make me one of these scientific marvels.' Tom went to make him a drink and Michael looked over at Claudia. 'Last time our paths crossed was at Johnny's opening. We were discussing the merits of art, weren't we?'

Claudia laughed. 'We were, Michael. Both of us really knew what we were talking about.'

'Michael may not be the world's greatest art expert but he is the best at buying presents...' Celia said.

'I have to be,' agreed Michael. 'When you're married to an exacting woman, who expects only the very best, you have to up your present-buying game.

Celia likes pure silk...' He looked across as her as she laughed, tinkly and teasingly.

'Oh, Michael, you'll never let me forget that one. Well, when we first met and Michael was wooing me...' She placed her long-fingered hand on Michael's arm. 'He turned up at my little flat in Mount Street with a box tied with the most glorious ribbon. So I guessed lingerie... because there is nothing I like more than beautiful, expensive, pure *silk* lingerie...' She pronounced it in an overly florid French way, *lahhngheriee*.

Tom was looking over from the drinks cabinet, listening, probably sneering at Celia, thought Claudia.

'So, darling Michael turned up with this exquisite box... and I'm thinking a little lacy camisole, a silk playsuit, French knickers... but you'll never guess what it was? A pair of *flannel* pyjamas...' Celia laughed as though this was the most amusing thing she'd ever heard.

'You'd complained of being cold at night,' explained Michael.

Celia was still bubbling over. 'But I had *you* to keep me warm.' She batted her eyelashes as her husband gazed lovingly back at her.

Celia's eyes remained fixed on her husband's

face, smiling adoringly, throughout their dinner of smoked salmon, roast chicken and the raspberry pavlova.

Michael, like most barristers, dominated the conversation. 'So there I was,' he was saying, 'stumbling backstage at the 3Arena at the Bruce Springsteen concert... a couple of brandies to the wind, all gratis from the VIP bar... Anyway, I was trying to find my way back to the gang and I pushed open a door and immediately fell over something... it was the strangest sound, my head seemed to be exploding. I thought perhaps I had died and these were the hounds of hell, howling and barking as I descended...' He looked at the faces of his rapt audience. 'And then I realised that, far from dead, I was very much alive and had stumbled upon the side of the stage, my ear pressed to some ginormous amp thing. And there is the roar of the E Street Band, Bruce himself giving it socks. So, I'm about to crawl away before security throw me off, but Bruce, being Bruce, sees me and drags me up. Right into my ear, he yells, "Stay there!" And the band begin "Dancing in the Dark" and he dances with *me*! The whole crowd were cheering... and me and Bruce waltzing on stage.'

Everyone laughed. 'I hope that story is true,' said Grace. 'Because I am going to tell it to everyone.'

'Cross my heart and hope to die,' said Michael. 'I'm a barrister and we don't tell lies. We tell stories.'

Over dessert, Johnny and Claudia began talking, just the two of them.

'I was thinking about your dad today,' he said. 'I was remembering when he taught me to ride my bicycle. I had one, a small little thing, and I was only seven or eight, and he held the back of it and ran alongside over and over, every night for a week. And then, one day, I took off, raced down the road and I thought, I don't know how to stop! And your Dad was shouting, "The brakes, Johnny, pull the brakes!"'

'It's nice to hear stories about him.' She smiled back at him.

'And your mother is doing well?'

Claudia nodded. 'She announced the other day she is going out with someone, a doctor at the surgery. Alan Dunne...'

'I know him! I went to school with his son Paul. He's a doctor in Australia now. Very nice guy. His dad would pick us up after football practice and buy us a bag of chips because we were all starving. "Now, boys," he used to say, "don't tell the medical council I am buying chips for children or I'll be struck off." He was very kind to us all.' He paused, looking at Claudia. 'Your mother had a difficult time when your dad died, didn't she? I mean, of course she did, but wasn't there an issue with a debt? I remember Mam saying something about it. She was so worried about Patsy.'

Claudia nodded. 'Dad left everything in a complete mess, financially. He owed money because he'd invested in a company, a friend of his from school, and there was a clause to say that if the company failed, he would be liable for debts. Poor Mum had to work overtime at the surgery... evenings, weekends... I don't think she ever completely recovered from the shock. The sudden death, compounded by the huge financial stress, would have been too much for anyone to deal with.'

Johnny was taking it all in. 'Wow. That's a lot. Your poor mother.' He smiled at her. 'By the way, I bumped into Fiona the other night. She was with her fiancé...'

'John-Paul? Isn't he lovely?'

'John-Paul?' Johnny was shaking his head. 'No, definitely Cameron.'

He must have misheard, Claudia thought.

'More pav, anyone?' Michael stood up, platter in one hand, brandishing the cake slice. 'Pass your plates.'

Grace handed hers over and he dolloped another slice on. 'It's delicious, Michael. Isn't it, Tom?'

Tom looked half asleep as he was leaning slightly back in his chair, probably the effect of those quite ordinary gin and tonics. Just as Claudia handed her plate to Johnny to pass along, her cake fork fell to the ground, and she ducked under the table to retrieve it. But just as she was about to bob up again, she saw Celia's leg was stretched out under the table, her foot resting in Tom's crotch. Claudia slipped upwards again, not knowing what to do.

15

What on earth did Celia see in Tom? Did she actually find him attractive? Or was it a case that she was just playing with people and toying with them? Luckily, Grace was entirely oblivious, laughing away, listening intently or joining in the chat. Horrified, Claudia tried her best to look neutral. Her eyes flickered towards Celia's, who smiled back, as though life was one big game, and she knew she was winning. Surrounding Claudia, the conversation continued, and she concentrated on pushing her pavlova around her plate.

'Everything all right?' asked Johnny, quietly.

'Grand... grand... you know...'

He looked briefly over at Celia, making Claudia wonder if he had guessed or seen something as well.

Celia was no longer quite so ethereally glamorous; all her beauty and affectations were now nothing but grubby. As for Tom... Claudia could barely formulate her thoughts. All his posturing, his put-downs and supercilious manner, and he was just as base and basic as anyone else. In fact, he and Celia deserved each other. They were all surface.

Urgghh, she shuddered. She had totally misread that light banter before dinner, believing it to be Celia playing games with Tom and now she realised that it was nothing but flirtation.

Should she tell Grace? Didn't Grace say no one actually *wanted* advice? Would she just end up hurting Grace, the idea of which was awful? Perhaps she should just chat to Grace later, ascertain how she was and take it from there. If she seemed upset, then she would speak. If not, she'd keep schtum.

At the end of the evening, Celia and Michael stood, their arms wrapped around each other, waving them all off.

'Thank you all so much for coming,' Celia was saying. 'We loved it, didn't we, Michael?'

Michael nodded. 'Great company, great wine and incredible food...' He patted his belly. 'I make a good pavlova, if I must say. Not as good as my dear old mother's, but not too shabby.'

They all waved from the bottom of the steps, standing on the street. Claudia could barely make eye contact with Grace, racked as she was with what she had observed.

'I can walk you to the station, if you like?' said Johnny to Claudia.

'Oh, do,' said Grace. 'Be a gentleman, Johnny...'

Tom's usual supercilious expression now had taken on a darker meaning. 'Oh, yes,' he said, 'we can't have Claudia stumbling around, after all that wine...'

'I'm fine,' Claudia insisted.

'It's no bother,' said Johnny, affably. 'Just to make sure you're okay.'

Claudia hugged Grace goodbye and gave Tom a perfunctory wave, trying to smile and act normally, and then she Johnny set off towards the station.

'Did you notice what I noticed?' he asked, as soon as they were out of earshot.

Claudia eyed him suspiciously. 'It all depends what exactly you noticed?'

'Well...' He cleared his throat. 'Perhaps you didn't... I just thought that...'

'Does it involve our host and the male guest who was not you?'

'Yes... and the weird vibe between them...'

'And her foot...'

'I didn't see the foot...'

'Under the table?'

'Gross...'

'I know. And I don't know what to do...'

He shook his head. 'Not sure...'

Just ahead was the glow of the train station, just a few late stragglers arriving home. Claudia would have to hurry because the last train going into town was due in three minutes.

'We can talk about it again,' said Johnny. 'When we go on our walking tour...'

Claudia laughed. 'You're not going to let me get out of it, are you?' She smiled. 'What about this Saturday afternoon? One o'clock and we'll meet outside the Shelbourne Hotel.' She had to be gone by 5 p.m., however, for the wedding dress fitting. But it wouldn't take that long to walk around town with Johnny. Perhaps they would run out of things to see or talk about and it would dwindle after an hour or two.

'What's your number?' he said, tapping away at his phone as she told him and then, at the turnstile inside the station, he waved her off. 'See you Saturday! Do I need to bring sandwiches? Or one of those sticks that turn into a stool, just in case we get tired? What about waterproofs? A thermos?'

Claudia laughed. 'Make sure you tell a responsible adult where you're going, just in case we don't reappear after dark.'

Johnny gave her the thumbs up. 'I'll bring my compass and torch!'

Claudia had to run then, because the train was pulling in, and she ran down the steps thinking how lovely it was to see him again and how it was as though there had been no time in between and their friendship had just carried on and grown up with them. Of course, despite how attractive he was, she wasn't going to have romantic feelings for him, despite the excitement bubbling away. This was just a very nice thing indeed. A new-old ready-made friend. The only dark cloud was Tom. And poor Grace. And awful Celia. She shuddered again. What on earth was going to happen?

16

GRACE

Wasn't it a lovely night? Everyone was in such good form and wasn't Johnny so charming? He's a dote, isn't he? Celia adores him and he adores Celia. But who wouldn't? Didn't she look divine last night? And Michael's cooking was incredible. That pavlova was to die for!!!!

CLAUDIA

It was amazing. Loved the pav.

GRACE

And isn't Celia and Michael's house so amazing? I was telling Tom how much I envied them… who wouldn't envy Celia? He said she has a very inflated idea of herself!!! Tom can never just relax and be happy!!!

A brand-new bride and groom had just arrived at the Shelbourne Hotel on Saturday afternoon. The bride's veil caught on the breeze as she exited the car, her groom reached out his hand and took hers, kissing her briefly.

Johnny was already waiting outside the front door when Claudia walked up.

'Is the wedding the first part of the tour?' he asked, giving her a quick hug.

'Yes, I arranged it specially.'

Over the last two days, she had wondered what to feature as part of the walking tour and where to bring him. Tourists were usually ushered towards Trinity College or Temple Bar and around the Georgian Quarter of Dublin but her only plan was to play it by ear.

'I thought we'd begin with a wedding and end with a…'

'Not a funeral!' He laughed. 'I mean, I know we Irish pride ourselves on our ability to hold a good funeral, but do we have to?'

'I was going to suggest a pint,' explained Claudia. 'You said how much you've missed a proper Dublin pub since you've been away.'

He nodded. 'They do have pubs in London, very nice ones as well, but there is nothing like an Irish pub. You can't recreate it properly no matter how much people try.'

The sky was blue, with a few clouds.

'I'm disappointed it's not raining,' said Johnny. 'I've been back a month now and the weather has been far too good.'

'It rained the other day...'

'Yes, thank God. I took a photo and sent it to my friends abroad. Irish rain, I told them, the very best kind.'

'I love your evangelism for Ireland,' she teased him.

'It's the curse of the returned emigrant. Everything's rosier in the place you've just left.' They turned into Kildare Street towards the vast buildings of the Irish parliament, once the private mansion of the Earl of Kildare, where a low black car pulled up to the security, gliding past the small protest group who shouted at the car.

Claudia and Johnny ambled along, taking back-streets and shortcuts, both of them being a tour guide to the other, Johnny pointing out places he knew and Claudia the same, the city acting as a memory map.

'We went there for my foundation year gradua-tion,' said Johnny, pointing at Kennedy's pub. 'And later, we crashed the Trinity College Ball.' They peered through the railings. 'I think I remember giving my friend Micko a piggyback across the cricket pitch. In the end all the Trinity students joined in, ball gowns and black ties. I think us art school kids won.' He shrugged faux-proudly, making Claudia laugh again.

They stood outside Oscar Wilde's house on the corner of Merrion Square.

'Favourite Oscar Wilde quote?' she challenged.

'Oh... I suppose, *we are all in the gutter but some of us are looking at the stars...* Can't beat that one. Or perhaps, *always forgive your enemies; nothing annoys them so much.*'

Claudia laughed. 'My favourite is, *be yourself; everyone else is already taken.*'

Johnny smiled at her. 'You win... it's the best.'

They crossed the Liffey on O'Connell Street, and walked along the Quays towards the Ha'penny Bridge, a small and beautiful pedestrianised crossing which spans the river and features in postcards and on the camera rolls of anyone who was ever in Dublin. Right in the middle, Johnny stopped, the Liffey rushing below them.

'We need a selfie,' he said, taking out his phone. 'Come on.' He pulled her in closer as he snapped them both grinning. 'I'll send you a copy.'

They walked along the other side of the Quays to Usher's Island and then headed up and away from the river, past the old Viking settlement and up towards Thomas Street where the art college was. They stood outside the main doors, looking in. 'I spent two very happy years, doing my foundation course,' said Johnny. 'It was possibly the best period of my life. We were all just so happy, can you imagine? No worries, nothing to do except create and have fun. I'm still friends with everyone from my year.'

'Well, I never,' said a voice. 'And what is the great Johnny Hogan doing in our midst? Do we have a superstar here with us?'

A small man with a white beard and large square glasses and a corduroy suit was beaming up at Johnny, who was smiling.

'Hello, Professor Jellett.'

'I heard you were back in town,' said the professor, 'and it's a funny thing but I was thinking I should ask you to come and meet our students sometime. Perhaps give them a talk?'

'I would be honoured...'

The elderly gentleman smiled at Claudia. 'We're all very proud of him, as we are of all our students. But he was always someone we knew would go on to great things.'

'It was being here that gave me the confidence,' said Johnny. 'My amazing teachers for one thing...'

'Ah, well, we're just here to water you a bit, make sure you've got the right soil and a bit of fertiliser...' He paused before taking Johnny's hand. 'I'm so pleased for you,' he said, earnestly. 'Really very pleased indeed. I saw the exhibition in Madrid. Sublime, it was.'

'Really?' Johnny was almost blushing. 'That is so kind of you to say, Professor Jellett. It means the world to me...' He glanced at Claudia for a moment, as though to apologise for keeping her.

'Now, you're to give me a call,' went on the professor. 'And we'll set up that talk. Come in anytime, for tea. We're all still there. A few new faces among the faculty, but us oldies are still around.'

They walked back towards the city centre, past the great spire of Christchurch, through the medieval streets, and cutting across Dublin Castle, weaving Temple Bar and past the stags and hens drinking outside the Oliver St John Gogarty pub, a facsimile of an Irish band playing inside. And then it was back to St Stephen's Green where people were enjoying the late-summer sunshine in the park.

'Right,' said Johnny, 'you promised me a pub.'

'I did,' she agreed. 'Doheny and Nesbitt's?'

'One of my favourites.'

'I can't stay long because I am meeting Fiona and my mum for a wedding dress trying-on session at 5 p.m.'

She found a small table in the snug at the front of the pub, screened off from the rest of the room, and Johnny returned from the bar with two pints and a packet of Tayto cheese and onion.

'Thank you for being my tour guide,' he said, holding up his Guinness. 'I loved it. Here's to old friends and neighbours...'

She realised she didn't want the afternoon to end. Far from wanting to cut it short, it was a day you wished would go on forever. But duty called and when they finished their drinks, Johnny walked her across town to Beautiful Day! – the wedding dress shop.

17

Just as they were saying goodbye, Claudia spotted her mother coming towards them.

'Well, Johnny Hogan,' said Patsy, 'you're very welcome home, back from London, so I hear. And all well with you, is it? I was in the gallery in Sandycove and saw your beautiful paintings. Stunning.' She turned to Claudia. 'Aren't they just?'

Claudia nodded, as Johnny smiled. 'That's so kind, thank you...'

Patsy looked at Claudia. 'Did you just bump into each other?'

'Claudia was giving me a guided tour...'

'Actually, we guided each other...' said Claudia.

'And we had a pint in the pub,' said Johnny.

'You don't want to join us, Johnny? We are choosing a dress for Fiona. I would say, being an artist you have a good eye...'

Claudia laughed. 'Mum! Johnny doesn't want to choose wedding dresses...'

'He would have a good eye, though,' insisted Patsy. 'And I think Fiona might listen to him.'

Johnny was smiling. 'I don't think I'd be good at wedding dresses and it sounds like a family day out, you don't want me there.' He smiled at them both. 'I'll say goodbye.' He turned to go, giving them both a wave. 'Thank you for a lovely afternoon, Claudia.'

'Bye, Johnny,' called Patsy. 'Tell your mother I'll be down to Galway to see her one of these days...' She turned back to Claudia. 'We'd better be quick. Fiona's in there on her own and she's already texted asking where we are.'

They were placed on a white sofa while Fiona struggled in and out of wedding dresses, behind a white curtain. From time to time, the curtain was whipped aside, as though it was a magic trick and Patsy and Claudia obediently oohed and cooed, making all the right noises.

Fiona was behind the curtain again; this time being tied into a corset-style white dress. The sales assistant was pulling on the strings as hard as she could. 'Just a bit more,' she was saying, breathless with the effort. 'We could knock at least another inch off your waist...'

'Did you do any of this trying on and everything when you were getting married?' whispered Claudia.

'Oh God no... I mean, we didn't have the money. You've seen the photographs. Your father asked me, I accepted, and we only had a month to get everything ready. There was a cancellation at the university church on St Stephen's Green and we decided there was no time like the present. If you know, you know.' Patsy smiled at Claudia.

Claudia was thinking of Dom and how much she had hoped the search for one's life companion was over and they could just get on with life together. Except deep down she'd always known that he wasn't the *one*, she'd just been scared to be on her own. Relationships were a ready-made life, giving you an identity, a purpose, and someone to do things with. But Dom wasn't much of a doer. He hated the cinema, didn't really like going out for dinner and wasn't particularly sociable. Being single was so much better than being with the wrong person. After a while, you felt utterly invincible.

'How's Dr Alan?'

'He's fine... we've gone on another date. We had a

charcuterie board...' Patsy pulled a face, as though they were living the high life, and Claudia suddenly felt suffused with love for her gorgeous mother who deserved fun and romance and charcuterie boards.

The curtains of the dressing room were suddenly pulled apart again and Fiona was revealed in the hideous corset dress. Her arms and shoulders were bare, her hair in a kind of white headband, her waist so small that any residual flesh she might have, along with her breasts, was forced out over the top. It looked like something the bride of Frankenstein might have worn. Or a reality television contestant at some awards show.

The sales assistant was beaming valiantly. 'Doesn't she look fabulous?'

Patsy looked startled. 'Yes.' There was no other answer. 'Like a princess...' Her voice had a robotic quality to it.

'Yes, beautiful,' echoed Claudia, obediently.

'I don't,' said Fiona. 'I look ridiculous as though I've taken leave of my senses.' She pulled off the headband and handed it to the sales assistant. 'I can't. I just can't... the dress is lovely. For someone else. *I'm* the problem...'

'But you look lovely,' protested the assistant. 'Like a princess! Your mother said so.'

Strangely, Fiona seemed emotional, nearly in tears. Claudia couldn't remember seeing her cry for years. Obviously when their dog Petal died, the three of them sobbed in the vets, mopping their eyes, remembering all the wonderfully sweet things Petal had done for them.

'But I don't want to be a princess. I never have,' said Fiona, furiously, tears pooling in her eyes. 'Would you mind undoing the thing at the back? I think my lungs are going to collapse.'

The assistant was horrified. 'Jayzus, quick, Maureen! Get the scissors!'

The dress removed and Fiona's lungs saved, she, Patsy and Claudia escaped to Bewley's, the legendary café on Grafton Street in the centre of Dublin, a place where they'd all been coming all their lives. They sat beside the stained-glass windows and ordered tea and cherry buns. Tensions dissipated and Fiona seemed to relax a little. Both Claudia and Patsy sensed it was best to stay away from all talk of weddings and even of John-Paul. Perhaps, like many brides-to-be she was finding it all rather overwhelming. Claudia attempted a topic which didn't feature wedding dresses or anything which might upset Fiona further.

'Tell us more about this date,' she said. 'Fiona,

did you hear, our mother is ordering charcuterie platters?'

Fiona smiled wanly as Patsy laughed. 'We're going to the cinema tonight. The Mary Robinson biopic.'

Patsy seemed so happy and excited, exactly the way you are meant to be when romance is in the air and life glows in pink. Claudia hadn't felt that pinky-glow for years. Not even with Dom. He had never inspired that feeling. It was funny, but today had felt glowy, even if it was just with her old neighbour Johnny. It was almost as though they had floated around the city.

When Patsy nipped to the loo, Fiona turned to Claudia. 'Would you come with me to John-Paul's parents' anniversary meal next week? I'm dreading it. I just wouldn't mind some moral support... basically I need emotional backup. I was going to tell them you're lonely and miserable and need to leave the house otherwise you'd spend all evening watching terrible soap operas.'

'It wouldn't be *totally* untrue...'

Fiona nearly smiled. 'I just can't face them. I need someone on my side. Like an emotional support dog.'

'What's happened?'

'I just need...' Fiona paused. Neediness was usually anathema to her. 'I need moral support. And you know how much they like you...'

'Do they?'

'They do! The *love* you...'

'I don't think they even know my name.'

'Look, please come. It's in town, so it's easy for you and they are bringing us to Rénè's.'

Rénè's was the least fashionable and most expensive restaurant in Dublin with a menu featuring grey vegetables in aspic or flambéed bananas and Claudia would rather stay in and eat microwaved baked beans but this was obviously an emergency.

'Will there be a dessert trolley?' Claudia asked.

'There might be...'

'Do they serve nuts with your drink in the bar?'

'Hopefully...'

'Will there be chips on the menu? Proper ones, thin and crispy?'

'Perhaps...'

But it wasn't just the chips or the siren call of a dessert trolley which had persuaded her, it was Fiona's tone of voice. Claudia couldn't remember hearing her so desperate for a long time, perhaps not since that year when Fiona wanted a Huggy Monkey for Christmas, the kind with long arms which Velcroed around you. And thankfully Santa came good that year: Fiona was attached to Huggy Monkey – or rather it was attached to her – for the whole of the following year.

'Then I'm coming.'

'You are?' Fiona sounded relieved and happy. 'Oh, thank you, Claudia! I'll see you next Wednesday, okay?'

What on earth was going on?

Later, when Claudia arrived home, letting herself into the communal hallway, her bike wasn't where it normally was – leaning against the stairs, a pile of dusty letters on the saddle – but was just beside the door. And it was gleaming. Dusted down and cleaned; the saddle polished; the broken clasp on the strap holding the front basket repaired. And the puncture was fixed. She took the handles of the bike and pushed it up and down, staring at the tyre. There was the sound of footsteps coming in behind her. It was Leesha and her constant companion, Roger, who she insisted was just a friend. Roger was the kind of man who had a face too big for his eyes, a fringe which clung to his forehead as though afraid of being blown off, and he tied his pastel jumpers around his shoulders. He was also only too pleased to be at Leesha's beck and call. 'Oh, hoi there, Cloidia,' he said, in his nasal voice.

'We're going for sushi,' said Leesha. 'Your bike's been fixed then?'

Claudia nodded. 'But I don't know by whom...'

'Some old guy in a boiler suit and pork pie hat came around earlier and rang the bell... said he'd been sent by someone...' Leesha turned to Roger. 'What did he say his name was?'

'Doggy? I think,' said Roger. 'Or Piggy... something loike that.'

'Foxy?' suggested Claudia.

'Foxy!' Leesha laughed. 'Yes, it was Foxy.' She gave Roger a playful slap on the shoulder. 'Piggy! What are you like? Anyway, you can cycle again, although I don't know why you'd bother when you can Uber. See you later, Clauds...'

Claudia felt incredibly touched that Foxy had done such a thing. It gave her a lovely feeling that there was someone who cared enough to fix her puncture.

18

Claudia spent most of Sunday consuming everything she could about Arnold Kennedy in preparation for her interview with him the following morning. She had vaguely known who he was: formerly a rugby player who'd been injured young and set up his own management consultancy, as well as being a household name – at least in rugby-loving households – due to his role as a TV pundit.

She had read the proof copy of his autobiography, learned more about rugby than she ever wanted to, was fascinated by the story of how he met his wife – a doctor who patched up his knee all those years ago – and absorbed his philosophy of life. Arnold was a believer in getting on with things, limiting introspection and not looking back. She liked the sound of him, even though he was obviously very much a lad's lad, the kind of man who would hold court at the bar of the Old Spot after a game at Lansdowne Road. From his memoir, she learned that the only time he ever cried was when he was stretchered off the pitch, aged twenty-five, knowing his international career was over. 'It wasn't a good day,' he had written in his spare prose. 'In fact, it was a very, very bad day.'

His office was on the top floor of one of the houses on Merrion Square. Claudia stood in front of a glossy red door with 'Kennedy Consulting' on a mirror-shiny brass plate. She was buzzed in – 'Top floor, Claudia,' the voice said – and she began her ascent, springing up the sweeping, curlicued stairs. By the second floor, she was feeling less energetic and peered up through the centre of the staircase heavenward. *This is what mountaineers must feel when they look up towards Everest*, she thought, before ploughing on, her legs wobbly like a newborn foal's. She reached for the curve of the bannisters to steady herself. Perhaps she had entered the world of sport, and they deliberately situated their office on the top floor of a four-storey building and engineered precipitously steep stairs just to sort out the ones who could power up them from those who couldn't. She definitely couldn't.

When she eventually made it to the top floor, she contemplated falling to her knees and lying, face down, for as long as it took to recover. Weeks, if necessary. From behind a desk, a young man in a Hawaiian shirt was looking over. She tried to breathe normally, hoping they wouldn't think she was having a panic attack and panting like a greyhound spotting a Bichon Frise.

'Claudia from *Irish Man*?'

She nodded and began to hobble over to him when, from behind her, she heard a booming voice.

'Someone looks as though they are in need of a sit-down!'

Turning around, there was a grinning Arnold Kennedy in front of her, a bear of a man, dressed in navy trousers and white shirt, red socks and trainers. He had the kind of shoulders that could break down a door or carry you from a burning building.

'Arnie Kennedy,' he said, his hand outstretched, studying her intently. 'You are very welcome, Claudia Kelly...' He said her name carefully, as though trying it out. Shaking his hand was like placing it in a vice and tightening the screws and when he released her, her poor hand throbbed.

'Thank you, Arnold...'

'Call me Arnie,' he corrected. 'All my friends do. Now, let's go into my office.' He led the way, calling over his shoulder. 'Gavin, two teas and an entire packet of biscuits for Claudia, please. She looks in need of some sugar.'

The thought of a biscuit propelled her as she limped along in the great man's wake.

His office had two windows overlooking the green square below and Arnie sat down in his large cream leather chair. 'Do you know I was in the very first issue of *Irish Man*?' He nodded. 'I was in Hackett House in those early days... but we can get on to that. That was after my rugby career...'

'Tell me about your father... you write that he didn't approve of who you were...'

'*Approve*? He *hated* me doing this...' He waved a hand around. 'He was almost angry with me when I got injured, thought I should have done more rehab, never given up until I was back on the pitch.'

Gavin entered the office carrying a tray of tea and biscuits. 'Thanks, Gav,' said Arnie. On his desk were family photographs, the whole family in a rugby strip, another of them on a yacht, squinting into the sun. He reached forward and took a biscuit. 'Don't tell my trainer, right?' He winked. 'He says I'm getting a bit of a middle-aged spread...'

'Tell me more about your father. Was he ever proud of you?'

'Only because my success made him look good. I think he only liked me when I was scoring points.'

This was an entirely different Arnie to the one in the book. He hadn't gone into much about his father, instead he had concentrated on his days playing schoolboy rugby and being chosen to represent Ireland aged only seventeen. Today he was opening up to her, as though he trusted her on sight. And he was ready to talk and all she had to do was ease the way, ask a few gentle questions.

'I had a love-hate relationship with being a professional player... hated it. I was living my life for other people. My father, for one. My teachers in school. My coaches. None of them cared about the boy I was, the man I was becoming. Who I was, was something I had to discover for myself. And it's a big lesson to learn how quickly the crowd can turn. One moment you're their hero, the next their villain. You start to lose yourself in all that. I had to fight to reclaim who I was.'

'How difficult was it to give up rugby?'

'Hard. Initially. It had shaped and defined my

life. I didn't know who I was if I wasn't splashing across a muddy field, clutching a ball, a dozen Neanderthals in heavy pursuit. You can't explain the thrill of that, the primal adrenaline, the feeling that this is what life is all about, thousands of people cheering you on, an entire country behind you willing you on. You're a rock star, effectively. You're the person that everyone watching at home or from the stands is relying on to bring home glory. You're part of a tribe, you, the team and the fans. It's un-fecking-believable. You think you're invincible. You begin to think that the sun shines out of your arse. You believe the hype. You believe it when someone writes in the *Irish Times* that if you lose, everyone is going to fall into a national depression last seen in 1845, you know? Someone actually wrote that shite.'

He shook his head, remembering those days.

'But I was the one waking up on a Monday morning, bruised, aching, alone. And wondering what was all that for? What was the point? It was, I suppose, an existential crisis. And it became harder and harder to put on the green jersey, to psych myself up, to see myself as a latter-day Cú Chulainn or whichever hero you want. Because that wasn't me. I began to walk around in a daze, training and trying to eat steak and all that, and waiting for Saturday, match day. And that was just the season. The rest of the year, I had to try and remember who I was, when I wasn't playing rugby. Only I had no idea. And then I got injured. And I met my wife, Annette. Doctor in Vincent's Hospital and she'd never watched a rugby game in her life. And I thought to myself, this is where I need to be, right here, with her.' He smiled at Claudia. 'It was like being born again.'

'And you started your consultancy...'

'Yes. We were a few lost souls on that top floor of Hackett House. Lost souls who were finding ourselves. Me, Foxy, Ernesto and Toby Rabbitte...'

'The bookmaker?'

'The *multi-millionaire* bookmaker...' Arnie laughed. 'That's right. But he wasn't anything like that in those days. We were just renting desks and phones and went to Doheny's for drinks and it was a support group. We made mistakes, talked about them and learned lessons. Hard ones. We lost money, bailed each other out and then, eventually, we all found success. Ernie's property empire is huge. His café... you've been in it? That's what he does for fun. I wouldn't have made it without those men, we're there for each other, to advise, to listen.'

'Foxy mentioned you were friends.'

Arnie smiled. 'Those were good days. And great

craic. Going to Doheny's after work to discuss everything, help each other out, troubleshoot. None of us had any money but we were a gang, you know? All on our own. No family to help us. Toby had grown up in various foster homes, Ernie had run away from Italy. God knows what from. We never asked. And Foxy's parents couldn't have been more disinterested...' He paused a moment, perhaps wondering how much to divulge. 'We've all seen each other go through hard times, we've celebrated the good times. And you know, you're never out of the woods, there is never a time when you think, I've made it, I'm okay because there's always something around the corner, ready to catch you out. That's the beauty of business. You are always on your toes...' He paused. 'Foxy is going through it right now.'

They talked for the next hour about everything he knew about life and some very personal subjects which caused Arnie to stop speaking for a moment and gather himself. But he knew exactly how to bring it back to humour and told some funny stories including one about when he was on TV and there was a large fly which kept buzzing around. He ignored it, but it kept flying around and was so large that it was perfectly visible to the viewers at home.

'The producer was saying in my ear that it looked

like it was trying to make an emergency landing in the middle of a hurricane. I was trying not to laugh and then it landed on the bald head of the fella next to me. So I stood up and thought I would quickly launch the fly into space with a flick of my hand, but then the guy moved and I ended up belting him across his ear.' He guffawed. 'Try explaining *that* live on TV. Luckily he is an ex-player so had a head like a cabbage. Just like me. So my swipe didn't hurt him.'

Eventually, it was time to go. Claudia stood up, feeling grateful how much he'd opened up. She held out her hand. 'Thank you...'

He looked at her for a moment. 'Foxy's a good man, you know that...'

She nodded. 'I mean, I don't *know* him that well...'

'Do you know the value of trust? Because trust is everything. It's one of the most important parts of any relationship. And that's what's going wrong at Foxy Publishing. There are people in there, determinedly undoing all the trust, creating division. It's made for a difficult atmosphere, I bet...'

'Perhaps...' Claudia stood up, tensing her muscles in preparation for his vice grip. Somehow, this time it felt a little less bone-crushing.

'Good to meet you, Claudia... say hello to Foxy, won't you?'

'Thank you, Arnold...'

'Arnie!' He grinned at her.

'Bye, *Arnie*.'

By the time she was running downstairs, she felt she might actually have a good interview.

19

Claudia and Grace sat in the corner of Luigi's, a flickering tea light on the table in front of them. Claudia watched Grace carefully, assessing her mood, trying to ascertain if there was anything which might have dislodged her blissed-out, loved-up self.

But no, all seemed well, as the majority of her chat focused on Tom as usual.

'What would you recommend for male pattern baldness?' asked Grace.

Claudia laughed. 'I haven't a clue!'

'I thought because now you are on *Irish Man*, you might know this kind of thing? Poor Tom is losing his hair. He keeps looking in the mirror and lamenting how much he's receding and he doesn't like me to touch his head because he says that will just hasten the follicular decline, as he calls it. He cheered up a bit when I told him how sexy bald men were.' Grace picked up another breadstick. 'God, these are delicious. You know, I need to stop eating bread. Celia says it creates inflammation.'

'Inflammation? Where?'

'In the body. Not sure where, exactly. Or what exactly inflammation is but she says she has so much more energy since giving up bread.'

Claudia was sure she did. 'But you like bread.'

'I *love* bread. It's my favourite thing. But think what I could gain? The energy levels and radiance of Celia Desmond. No more jowly puffiness.' Grace clutched at her jaw, like a basset hound tugging at its pendulous face. If basset hounds could indeed tug.

'You don't have jowls.'

'I will if I don't give up bread.' Grace nibbled on another breadstick. 'I'm just like one of those people who are looking at all the beautiful people all the time...'

'Try working on a women's magazine!'

'No, I'm serious. I'm the kind of person that beautiful people like to be friends with so they feel better about themselves.'

'Grace... come on... that's silly...'

'I know it is. But I can't help it. And I really don't mean you. You're my best friend but it's everyone else. Celia. And even Tom. He's out of my league. He's better-looking than me.'

'I *really* don't think that's true.'

'And Celia... I know she doesn't mean to but she patronises me a little. Like I'm her younger sister. I think she only hired me because I'm not glamorous.'

'But you are glamorous! And anyway, that's not important. You're brilliant at your job, managing and organising, you're charming...'

'Not like Celia...' Grace said gloomily.

'*No* one's like her...' Claudia rolled her eyes.

'They're all on another level, talking about things I don't understand. Jokes and references. It's this verbal volleying all the time...'

'Between who?'

'Tom and Celia. Every time he comes into the gallery, between seeing clients, he takes things that are simple and complicates them. I used to think so clearly and rationally. I think I might be going mad. Tom says I should go for psychotherapy.'

'You? You're the most sane person I know!'

'Sometimes I feel emotionally filleted, my bones picked apart by his therapist's brain.'

Claudia nodded sympathetically. 'It sounds exhausting.'

'I need to be better.'

'But what if you do know it all and he doesn't?'

'But he went through six years of three-times-a-week psychotherapy, plus the degree...'

'*Diploma...*'

'The *certificate* to prove he is cleansed of trauma...'

'What was his trauma exactly?'

'Terrible teenage acne... um... he didn't get a Raleigh Chopper... his mum worked outside of the home and he was a latchkey kid...'

'That's *it*?'

'I think his dad shouted a lot. But Tom doesn't go into that very much, probably because he's so cleansed. He doesn't need to bang on about it.'

Claudia hid her inner rage, while wrestling with her dilemma. 'Grace... What would you do if Tom was having an affair?'

Grace stared at her. Her face still, eyes suddenly icy. 'What did you say?'

'*If* Tom was having an affair...' Claudia stumbled on, half wondering if she could change tack and double back. '*If* Tom was having an affair, what would you do?'

'Is he?' Grace was still staring at her.

Claudia swallowed. 'I was just thinking... *if* he was...'

'Is this research for an article?'

'Something like that...' But coward as she was, she couldn't do it. Not to lovely Grace.

'Well, I'd kill him,' said Grace, happily. 'And her! And anyway, it's not going to happen. Tom is too good. He's got a PhD in being good...'

'Diploma...'

'WHATEVER!' Grace glowered at her for a moment. 'Well, if I hear that Tom is having an affair, I'll let you know and you can quote me for an article.' She smiled back at Claudia. 'But I fear you're going to be waiting a long time. I've met Mr Perfect, you see. Mr Squeaky Clean!'

Claudia was going to have to leave it. But she was sure that, sooner or later, Grace would learn the truth about Tom, and Claudia would be there.

20

All week in work, Claudia felt a surge of power, as though she had finally learned to ride a bike or was a pilot who had perfected a loop the loop. She knew what the magazine was and what it needed and it all seemed so enjoyable, so satisfying. She commissioned amusing articles, she asked a comedian to write a piece on the perils of trying to look stylish on stage, she asked a Nigerian-Irish chef to write a food column, and there was a new small piece called 'a walk to a pub' detailing a beautiful hill ramble that led to a cosy pub.

At quiet moments, she felt her mind drift back to Saturday afternoon and her walk with Johnny. It had been one of those days which come out of nowhere, which involve no planning or anticipation and just unfurl themselves in the moment. You didn't get many days which were a surprise, like that. She hoped they would be good friends forever. She googled him and looked up his exhibition in Madrid and read some of the reviews. She was in danger of becoming a little too interested and she reminded herself that they were just old friends.

On Wednesday morning Claudia was making herself a tea in the shared kitchen in the office and, as the kettle was boiling, she felt someone come in behind her. It was Blake Moriarty.

'Ah, Claudia,' he schmoozed. 'How are you?' His smile looked as though it had hung around too long and was fading, as though he'd been posing for photographs and his lips were tired.

'I'm fine, thank you. Just making tea...'

'I can see that... How are you getting on?' Blake continued. 'Finding it all a bit of an uphill struggle? A bit much for you?'

'Not at all...'

He wasn't listening. 'It's not easy starting a job when you aren't...' He paused, as though trying to think of a word that would cause the least offence. '...experienced.'

'No...' Claudia faltered. 'It's not...'

'As you know,' Blake went on, 'my office door is always open. Anytime you need advice or support... just ask me. And I know you and Foxy are close but I feel it's my duty to warn you that he's a little...' He searched for the word again. He obviously wasn't very articulate.

'Doddery?'

'Yes! Yes, that's it. Doddery. The poor man. He's not what he was. A cognitive decline. It happens to the brightest of men, they are masters of their universe and then... it's tragic, really, then they just lose it, like air seeping from a balloon.'

'I've seen no evidence of that,' said Claudia, firmly, looking him straight in the eyes. 'None whatsoever.'

'But you said he was doddery...'

'I suggested it was the word you were looking for...'

He pulled a face. 'Well, he *is* on the decline, whether you have seen evidence of it or not. He is able to mask it and perhaps with some more... impressionable staff, they choose to see what they want to see. But we have to take care of him. He gave me my first job in media. I was working for a big insurance company, loving life, and then I saw that Foxy Publishing needed someone to modernise and develop, to stay relevant. I met Foxy and he gave me the job on the spot. I felt as though I'd found a father, you know? He's an inspiring guy, right?'

Claudia nodded.

'It's sad, that's all, to see him deteriorate and lose his grip. It's why his wife left. She'd had enough of trying to shield him. But I'm not giving up on him. I'm going to take care of him. So, remember, my door is always open. Anytime. Or...' He paused. 'Talk to Jackson. My PA. He and you get on well, he said.' Blake eyed her. 'You can confide in him...' His smile curdled on his face.

Claudia turned back to the freshly boiled kettle as though it needed immediate attention, just so she didn't have to look at Blake again, and she felt him leave the room. So Jackson was one of the vipers, she knew immediately. All that Claudy-pops nonsense. She knew who she liked and trusted and it certainly wasn't Blake or Jackson.

21

Just as she was stirring her tea, Charlie came into the kitchen. 'Is there any milk for my hot chocolate? I'm in need of something sweet.'

'Are you okay?' Claudia handed over the carton.

'Bloody life and everything about it.'

'Work or home?'

'Both.'

'Tell me about work first.'

'It doesn't matter...'

'No, go on...'

'Well... it's just a bit... well, not boring but...'

'Not exciting?'

Charlie perked up. 'It's definitely not *exciting*.'

'What do you think would make it more exciting?'

'I would like more of a creative input, I suppose. All I do is look for stock images to match the articles. I would like to commission artists, bring in cartoons, drawings... and more interesting photographers.'

'Okay then. Why don't you make a few changes? Be inventive. No more boring stock images.'

Charlie nodded. 'Are you sure?'

'It's a no-brainer. I can't believe that you *didn't* think you could do that.'

'I think I lost confidence in myself. I studied visual journalism in Liverpool. I used to produce my own magazine. And then... I don't know... when you're working with editors who don't want you to do what you want... you lose a little hope.'

Claudia understood completely. 'You need to be encouraged. And tell me, what about home?'

The smile was gone. 'Oh, just missing Scoobs. He's still finding himself and herding his goats. He's gone native. I could barely hear him with the sound of the bleating goats behind him. And he is always running out of battery on his phone or barely has a signal. He's even bought himself a special little mouth whistle yoke to call to them. But apparently they don't respond to his whistle, not like they do when Giorgos whistles for them. And I think he only called me to tell me to check in on his mam and make sure she's okay because it was her birthday.' Charlie sighed.

'You miss him?'

Charlie's eyes were suddenly filled with tears. 'Yes, but I can't tell him because I don't want to worry him. I told him to go because it was good for him. But now I want him home again.'

Claudia smiled at her. 'The least we can do while he's gone is make work a little more interesting, okay?'

Charlie smiled back. 'It's really nice to have another woman around. I mean, I like the lads, they're grand. But it's not the same, is it?'

* * *

At lunchtime, after a morning of writing and finalising that month's edition, she stood up. 'I'm going for something to eat,' she announced. 'Anyone want anything brought back?'

'Crisps,' said Oscar, immediately.

'Sweets,' called out Charlie.

Simon looked up. 'Where are you going?'

'Simon only likes sandwiches from the hot deli counter in SuperValu,' explained Oscar.

'It's true,' agreed Simon. 'Ham, egg mayonnaise and cheese in a baguette. Mustard *and* chutney.'

'A Simon Special,' said Oscar. 'It's his invention.'

Simon seemed almost animated as he spoke about this sandwich. 'If I was hit by a bus tomorrow, at my funeral, people will remember me by my sandwich... it's the most incredible combination.'

'Really?' Claudia was sceptical. 'I think it sounds a bit much.'

'But that's the beauty of it,' said Simon. 'And if you're feeling really decadent, like it's a special occasion, your birthday or something or Christmas...'

'Or Easter,' suggested Charlie.

'Or St Patrick's Day,' said Oscar.

'...then you can shake over a few crisp crumbs, a kind of dusting of cheese and onion...' Simon looked proud of this gourmet twist.

'I have to admit it's a good sandwich,' said Oscar. 'Simon let me have some of his once when he felt sorry for me. I was having a bad day.' He turned to Claudia. 'Hangover, obviously. A raging one. Like my insides were waging a war against me. Me! Without me, they are nothing. Such ingratitude. Anyway, I was begging to be put out of my misery and just be left alone to die in the corner of the office when Simon let me have the rest of his sandwich. He didn't *buy* me one, of course.'

Simon stood up. 'I'll come with you, Claudia, and we'll buy a round of my incredible invention.'

Everyone stood up and immediately began passing over ragged five-euro notes or taking out phones to send Simon money.

As he and Claudia took the lift downstairs, Claudia – being the incisive journalist she was – asked him the origin of the Simon Special.

'My dad used to have a pub in Raheny,' he explained. 'And he'd make egg mayonnaise and ham sandwiches for the regulars on a lunchtime. And then when I was old enough, it was my job. I'd rush back from school at lunchtime and get to buttering the bread and mashing the eggs. It was my genius move to add the cheese and my other additions. Everyone went mad for it, all the old fellas almost lost their lives in the excitement...'

Claudia laughed. 'And it's still your favourite combination?'

'It reminds me of Dad,' he said. 'And it brings me right back to that dark bar, where I'd be paid in bottles of 7Up and bags of Tayto. And I'd eat the crisps sitting on the orange velour sofa in the back room and then I'd be allowed to have a game of pool. You know, it's still my dream to have an orange sofa and a pool table...'

They had entered SuperValu and took their place in the deli counter queue.

'I was just wondering, how you were getting on,' Claudia said. 'In work.'

'Fine...'

'I wondered if there was anything you needed?'

'Like a pool table and an endless supply of crisps?'

'Yes... but that's for your home life but what about your working life?'

Simon shrugged. 'It's all been a bit... I don't know...'

Claudia waited.

'It's been a bit challenging,' he admitted.

'In what way?'

'Oh, editors, managers, control. We're all a little beaten down, I think. The creativity has gone. No one is interested in that. It's all about selling ads but it'll all be gone soon. You know the board is going for a full takeover. They don't care about the magazine, they want to buy the company and have control of all the magazines but I think once they take it over, they will sell off each title. Lease out the building. I don't know. But I think Foxy's days are numbered.'

'I hope not. But while we are here, is there anything we can do to improve things for you? How can your work be made more interesting?'

'Well...' He looked at her. 'I'd like to be allowed to get on with it. To be a little bit more adventurous with the design, try out a few things. Just trust me.'

'Okay,' she said. 'I trust you.'

Simon smiled. 'Thank you.'

'As long as...'

'What?'

'You teach the team how to play pool. I want us all to go to a pool club and you show us all.'

'A night out?'

'A staff night out. All of us. It will be fun.'

'Fun?' A smile was beginning to curl around Simon's lips, as though the idea was taking root.

'Yes, fun. *Organised* fun. And we're going to love it.'

22

On Wednesday afternoon, Claudia was busy typing up her Arnie interview when her phone rang. 'Claudia? It's Johnny...'

'Hello, Johnny...'

She was conscious that everyone in the office was pretending not to listen.

'Uh...' he began. 'Look, maybe... I don't know... are you free for dinner tonight...?'

'Dinner?' She felt herself smiling. 'I'd love to...'

Oscar looked up from his desk, giving up all pretence of getting on with work.

'Who are you talking to?' Oscar hissed loudly.

Claudia smiled and waved him away. She wondered why Johnny was asking her. Was he at a loose end? Did someone else cancel?

'We could go for a drink before dinner?' he went on. 'What about we meet in the Merrion Hotel and I could book Roisín's Supper Club? It's new, apparently. Modern Irish cooking.'

'Roisín's? We have a review of it in this month's issue.'

Oscar loomed over her desk. 'It's meant to be very good,' he said in a stage whisper. 'Who are you going with? May I come?' Claudia swivelled in her chair, blocking him out.

'So 6 p.m. in the Merrion bar?'

'Sounds good to me.'

She put the phone down, ready to face Oscar's probing. 'So, this date? Who with?' Every other face in the office was looking up at her.

'It's definitely not a date,' insisted Claudia. 'So don't make it awkward.'

'Claudia, you're talking to your pal Oscar,' said Oscar. 'I make everything awkward. It's what I do. Now, this date. Who is it with?'

'It's just an old friend being nice to me. And he might be looking for advice after moving back to Ireland.'

'It sounds like a date from where I am,' said Oscar. 'Doesn't it, Simon?'

Simon half nodded, unsure on whose side to land.

'Or it could just be *dinner* with an old friend,' said Charlie, smiling at Claudia. 'You do know, Oscar, that it is possible for men and women to be friends, without everything having to have a romantic implication?'

'Is it though?' Oscar looked sceptical.

'It's rare,' conceded Simon.

Oscar drew his chair closer to Claudia's desk. 'Now, tell Uncle Oscar everything. Who is he? Because he'd better be good enough for our Claudia...'

Our Claudia. It felt like a term of affection.

'It's not a date, it's dinner with an *old* neighbour.'

Oscar looked disappointed. 'An *old* neighbour? That doesn't sound exciting. I thought you might be embarking on a passionate love affair. But no, just dinner with an old neighbour. But where is this *old* neighbour Johnny taking you?'

'Merrion for a drink, followed by Roisín's Supper Club.'

Oscar whistled. 'That sounds like a date. How old is this Johnny? Over eighty?'

'No... he's thirty-five...'

'Then it *is* a date!' exclaimed Oscar.

'It *isn't*. I promise. I think he must need something... contacts, that kind of thing...'

But Oscar and Simon looked unconvinced, sure that it was a date and they wouldn't be persuaded otherwise.

'We met the other Saturday for a walk around town,' said Claudia. '*Also* not a date.'

'Uh... that was a date,' said Oscar firmly. 'Oh, Claudia, how naïve you are...'

It wasn't a date, she thought. But... it would be nice if it was. But then again, if it was, she'd be too scared to go and would definitely turn him down. But this was just two friends and that, however attractive he was, made it easier.

'I haven't had a nice date for decades...' said Simon, gloomily. 'Feels that long, anyway. Why is meeting someone so difficult?'

'*You* should find it easy,' mused Oscar. 'You're not under-represented in the brain area, you're handsome-*ish*, you have a surfeit of what one might call Dublin charm. *Some* might consider you a catch. There is no reason why you, being of sound mind and body...'

'Body's a bit ropey,' admitted Simon. 'Mind not the best either...'

'Okay, so you being of ropey mind and body, should and could meet someone nice.' Oscar drummed his fingers across his cheek. 'Claudia, Charlie and I will find you someone, won't we?' He turned back to Claudia. 'If this *thing* you're going on *isn't* a date, then have you considered our Simon?'

'Oscar, shut up.' Simon threw a furious look at him. 'Sorry, Claudia. The man's a fool. Don't listen to him.'

'What if you have a partner but he would prefer the company of goats to you?' asked Charlie. 'Scooby is Greece's newest goatherd and doesn't seem to miss me at all. Just goes on about the goats every time he calls. Which isn't very often. Says he can never get a signal.'

'I think a man who prefers goats to you, Charlotte, needs his head examined,' said Oscar. 'Unless they are particularly amazing goats. Like, do they dance? Or able to do long division or know the lotto numbers?'

'No, they're just goats.'

'Well, then, he's having some kind of midlife crisis. He needs an intervention. Let's leave now. Swim or whatever across the Aegean and rescue Scooby.'

'He doesn't want to be rescued,' went on Charlie. 'Says he was born to be a goatherd.' She started to tear up. 'And so Scooby won't be home next week like I thought he was going to be. He's gone native. Stopped wearing shoes and says he feels more at home with the other goatherds than he does with anyone else...'

'The wild man of Hydra,' said Oscar. 'He'll come home, when the goats' charms have worn off. He'll have to learn all about traffic again and what baked beans are and why underwear is essential.' He looked at Charlie, kindly. 'If he has any sense, that is. There's only so much conversation you can have with a goat.'

Charlie nodded. 'I just miss him, that's all. It's like only half of me is here.'

'Scooby will definitely be home soon,' Claudia said. 'He'll miss you too much.'

Charlie had brightened up. 'It's Christmas in a few months and he loves Christmas. He can't miss it.'

'Goats don't celebrate Christmas,' said Oscar, wisely. 'They don't hang up stockings or drink hot ports.'

Charlie was smiling again. 'You're right. Thank you.'

'I know I'm right, or my name isn't Oscar de la Bournville...'

Everyone in the office laughed. 'Your name *isn't* Oscar de la Bournville,' said Simon. 'Weren't you born Thomas Devlin?'

'I might have been,' said Oscar, loftily. 'But my name is now Oscar de la Bournville. Don't I look like an Oscar de la Bournville?'

They all nodded, agreeing.

Oscar gave an expressive shrug. 'Anyway, that's not relevant right now. What is relevant is that *our* Claudia is going on a date...'

'It's not a date...'

But no one in the office was prepared to believe her. Later, when they were all getting ready to leave for the day, Claudia was about to go to the bathroom to spruce herself up.

'Do you need to borrow some clothes?' said Oscar. 'Or make-up? I can touch you up... a bit of my Victoria Beckham *guy*liner...'

She allowed Oscar to spruce her up, and even did as she was told when he sprayed a cloud of perfume into the air and made her walk into it. 'It's so *common* to spray it onto the skin,' Oscar explained. 'You have to make a perfume rain-burst...'

Claudia dutifully walked into the perfume shower while Oscar was studying her face. 'You know something, Claudia? You don't need my help. You are looking radiant...' He turned around to the rest of the team. 'She's looking lovely, isn't she?'

Simon, Mark and Charlie all nodded, and suddenly Claudia felt quite emotional.

'Thanks, everyone,' she said. 'And I think you're all looking lovely too.'

Simon seemed pleased. 'I haven't looked lovely for years.'

'I've *never* been lovely,' said Mark.

'I need Scooby to tell me I'm lovely,' Charlie said mournfully.

'And I,' announced Oscar, 'I is lovely all the time. Just ask my mam, the one who called me Thomas. Still does, by the way. Refuses to call me Oscar.'

There was almost a waving-off committee as she left for her non-date at the Merrion Hotel.

'Bye, honey,' said Oscar. 'Don't do anything I wouldn't do. All I have to look forward to is a bowl of cereal, on my own...'

Charlie was having none of it. 'Would you get out of that, Oscar. You're off to an opening at the National Gallery...'

'It's a fashion show, actually,' said Oscar. 'I'm in the front row, naturally...'

The lift doors closed as Claudia was still laughing. She dared not say it out loud, but she was actually beginning to enjoy herself. In fact, she was *loving* it.

23

Claudia was early to meet Johnny so she sat herself down by the crackling turf fire in the comfortable surrounds of the Merrion Hotel. The low armchairs were soft and yielding, there was the sound of ice being shaken from behind the old oak bar, the tinkling of a piano from the lounge and soft lighting from the Waterford crystal chandeliers, the rest of the world only just visible through the large sash windows. She felt herself relaxing as she sipped her posh gin and tonic, riffling through a bowl of Japanese bar snacks, looking for her favourite green ones.

'Well, hello, Claudia...' It was Foxy, standing in

front of her, a glass of whiskey in his hand, smiling down at her.

'Foxy, I haven't had a chance to thank you for fixing my puncture... it was such a wonderful surprise...'

He waved her gratitude away. 'It's nothing. That was Paolo, who does odd jobs for Ernie. Used to work as a mechanic on the Giro d'Italia, so knows his way around a bike. And he's only delighted to get his hands on bikes, gives him a break from plumbing...' He paused. 'How is everything? All quiet on the *Irish Man* front? Shall I sit down for a moment?'

'Of course.'

Foxy slipped into the chair beside her.

'Is this another of your secret non-offices?'

He laughed. 'I suppose it is. I was just meeting my lawyer, discussing a few things. Thought I'd just have a quick drink before heading home.' He smiled at her. 'What about you?'

'I'm just meeting a friend, an old neighbour, actually... Johnny Hogan...'

'The artist?' Foxy looked impressed, before turning to catch the eye of the waiter. 'Another of whatever this young lady is having and another Midleton for me... thank you. Oh, these things,' he said, delving into the Japanese snacks. 'I like those strange little orange balls.'

'They're very good,' agreed Claudia. She felt a sudden pang for Foxy, the stress of work, perhaps he was lonely, having a whiskey at the end of a long day. He did look tired and his brow was knitted, as though he had a great deal to think about. 'How was your meeting with your lawyer?'

His face changed, and he tried to smile. 'Great... great... productive. Things are progressing. Building a case, that kind of thing. He's trying to see if there is any precedence about maintaining control of your company if you own it but aren't the majority share-holder, that kind of thing.' He pressed his lips to-gether, making a huge effort to sound bright and breezy. 'It was my fault, he was saying, because I cre-ated the shares way back, when I needed extra capi-tal. I was trying to buy the building and then went mad handing out the shares. I gave some to Ernie and other pals, Toby and Arnie... and... well, a chunk to... others... and that's... that's been my undoing, it seems.'

Foxy took the ice-cube-clinking, frosted glass of gin and tonic from the waiter and placed it in front of Claudia, and then his crystal glass of whiskey.

'Thank you,' he said to the waiter. 'And some

more of these delectable little nibbly things.' He turned back to Claudia, eyebrows raised. 'I do like a posh snack to have with a drink. Obviously, I am also partial to a Tayto crisp or a packet of dry-roasted peanuts, but sometimes it's nice to be exotic.' He smiled. 'Alison used to always tease me. Said I had pretensions, but I was still an ordinary lad from...' He stopped suddenly. 'I've been trying to keep Alison's houseplants alive. Have you any expertise? I've been reading books and watching videos. Late at night, I find myself watching a video of how to repot an orchid and making notes. Honestly, what have I become? Alison wouldn't recognise me. The same with emptying the dishwasher or laying the bed. I used to think that cushions on the bed were a tremendous nuisance, but Alison always liked a pile of them, all arranged. I now know which order they should be placed in and why she liked it so much. Because it shows you love your home, that *it's* important. That this place, the bed, is where you begin and end your day, and it shows that you think it and *you* are important enough to do something which doesn't matter. It's a simple thing. But I suppose it's taking care.'

'Self-care?'

He nodded, almost embarrassed. 'Exactly. I'm

learning a lot these days. But that's essentially what it is. Same with houseplants. To nurture something small and beautiful, something that brings actual life into your home, which grows and produces flowers and trembles in the breeze from the back door and looks beautiful. I know I sound mad, but to be in a quiet house, with no one to talk to or to eat with or with whom to watch television, you tend to appreciate the little plant which is growing towards the light, or the orchid which is flowering on the windowsill or the fact that the fern needs to be close to other ferns in order to thrive. Well! I'd never thought about them before like that. I've learned a lot about life from those plants.' He lowered his voice. 'I know, I've gone completely doolally, but I don't care. Or rather, I *do* care. But these days about the right things, which is our home.' He picked up his glass and Claudia did the same.

'Here's to homes,' she said.

'Homes and all who live in them.' He smiled at her. 'How is your flat?'

'It's fine... just would like to have my own place one day.' Foxy was so easy to talk to, she thought. It was like being old friends.

'Renting is hard, after a while.'

'Everything I have is in boxes. I had to leave my

own plants behind when I moved out of my ex-boyfriend's place. I just couldn't bring twenty-five plants with me. When I buy my own flat, I'll buy some again.'

Foxy looked appalled. 'That's terrible. The poor plants.'

Claudia laughed, for the first time not being agonised by the thought of her plants surviving – if they were – without her. 'I'll get new ones. One day.'

'You will. You and your plants will rise, or rather grow, again.' He looked at her. 'So, tell me how's everything at the magazine?'

'Good... good... it's all coming along. I've commissioned a few new people to write columns, I have asked our freelancers to write articles, we're changing the tone a little. And I like it.' She paused. 'Actually, I *love* it. It's the best job I've ever had.' As she spoke, she realised how much she was loving it, the challenge, the learning curve, the ability to shape an entire issue. Even the team. Actually, *especially* the team. 'It's been wonderful.'

Foxy nodded, smiling. 'I remember the first few years of the magazine how excited I was all the time. I'd lie in bed thinking of ideas for what we could do. I'd wake up every morning with these kind of butterflies in my stomach, just so happy about what might unfold over the day. That lasted for years, really, until things started becoming stressful. When you are building a brand and working hard, it's exhilarating. Success is the challenging part.' He laughed, shaking his head. 'I am a victim of my own success.' He paused. 'Thank God Alison isn't here to hear me say that.'

Claudia was about to say something when she saw Johnny walking towards them. He'd left his leather jacket behind and was wearing a navy blazer over his jeans and T-shirt. He smiled when he saw her. 'I'm not late, am I?' She stood up to greet him and he hugged her, before noticing Foxy. 'Hello... Johnny Hogan.'

Foxy stood and introduced himself, shaking Johnny's hand. 'Good to meet you. When Claudia mentioned she was meeting Johnny Hogan, I wondered if it was you. I heard you were back in town. My wife and I are big admirers of yours. We saw your exhibition at Madrid the year before last.'

'Thank you... that's very generous of you. And you're the great managing editor of *Irish Man*? I took out my first subscription when I was fourteen. It was the mix of articles and politics... and I learned so much. And there was art and fashion...'

Foxy shrugged, but seemed touched. 'That's nice to hear,' he said.

'There was nothing like it at the time... the humour, the stories...'

'We've lost our way a bit,' Foxy went on. 'It was always meant to be the reader's best friend... or big brother...' He glanced at Claudia. 'But I think this young woman has a vision and is bringing it back to its original premise...'

'I always loved it,' said Johnny. 'I remember needing a big brother, a guiding hand, and it seemed to have all the answers. There was a big article on the benefits of going to art college and what you need to get in and what the best ones are... I must have read it a hundred times. And I remember there was a feature on leather jackets. Something about Marlon Brando, I think...' He laughed. 'God, what an eejit I am, but I remember thinking that's who I want to look like, that's who I am... and I went to the market and bought a cheap jacket and I've been wearing a variation of it ever since.'

'I remember you coming home in your new leather jacket and asking me what I thought of it... it squeaked...' said Claudia.

'I was probably trying to impress you with how cool I was,' said Johnny.

'You *were* cool,' insisted Claudia.

'No, I just learned it from *Irish Man*.'

Foxy laughed and seemed pleased. 'Ah, thank you. That means a lot. Look, I'll leave you both to your evening.' He turned, holding his hand in the air in a quick wave, and walked away.

Johnny sat down in the chair Foxy had just vacated. 'Well, this is swanky...'

'You suggested it!'

Johnny looked around the room. 'I'd forgotten what a beautiful hotel it is.' He smiled at her. 'And you look nice.'

'So do you...'

'Thank you. I was hoping you would reciprocate the compliment. It's the only way to get people to say nice things to you, if you say them first.'

He did look nice, though, she thought. And brought a decidedly cool element to this grand room. He ordered a drink and Claudia carried on sipping hers.

'How is your job, which you love so much?' he asked.

'Very good...' She smiled back at him. 'So what about you? What have you done today?'

'I've been looking at new studios. Now I'm back, I need to get my working space up and running. I love being home. I've missed it far too much. When I was living in New York and then London, I got so homesick. I'd miss everything – Irish food, Irish radio. Our brilliant television. Just talking to someone at a bus stop, that kind of thing. Obviously my mother. My friends. All that. But I convinced myself that it was just homesickness talking, putting gloss on it all, making me forget the bad bits... and I don't know. Maybe I'm getting old or something, but it wasn't a homesickness gloss. It was real. I'm where I'm meant to be. Every day, without fail, someone has said something which has made me crack up. And, of course, it's where I belong. I think it's time I settled down.'

24

At Roisín's Supper Club, they ordered different things from the menu so they could try as much as possible, as well as chips for the table and a bottle of delicious Riesling. And, best of all, they didn't stop talking, catching each other up on the last few years, and veering into favourite books, best films, politics and everything in between. Johnny even told her about his last relationship, which had ended some time ago.

'Since then,' he said, topping up their glasses with red wine, 'I've been just focused on work. So it's been good for me. Just quiet time, painting in my studio and not really worried about anything else. It was when I thought about coming home to

Dublin, did I realise that five years had gone by and I hadn't really done very much except work. Even this... going to restaurants is a novelty. And I am loving it.'

For a moment, Claudia wondered if he'd only asked her out to dinner because he just wanted dinner, not to see her. But that was okay, wasn't it? Why wasn't he allowed to call an old neighbour and go out for a catch-up dinner? And wasn't this nice, having an old friend who just happened to be male? Wasn't it something of a relief that there was nothing between them, except a platonic shared history? Being manless actually made your life bigger, because in the old days, she'd be worried about if he *liked* her or if she *liked* him or keeping an eye out for red flags or signs of toxic behaviour. Now, she was focused on just having a nice evening.

They shared a chocolate mousse with Irish sea-salted shortbread for dessert, and a glass of syrupy, unctuous amaretto, both poking their spoon into the bowl and scraping the sides. The mousse was one of the most delicious things Claudia had ever eaten.

'Chocolate mousse should be used for its therapeutic purposes,' said Claudia. 'Feeling down, chocolate mousse. Feeling happy, chocolate mousse... and so on.'

'It's ridiculously good,' agreed Johnny, going in again with his spoon.

Claudia looked around the restaurant. They were surrounded by couples, all doing something similar to her and Johnny, sharing a dessert or clinking glasses in celebration, or talking in low voices over the flickering flame of a candle. If anyone looked at them, they would assume they too were a couple and for a moment she imagined what it would be like to be here with Johnny under different circumstances, one with a romantic hue.

The notion wasn't *abhorrent*. If she *had* to break her manless pledge, Johnny wouldn't be the worst person in the world to become romantically involved with. And actually, the fact that they had known each other as children and now here they were, grown adults with *certain desires*, it didn't suddenly seem so outlandish or even wrong to cross the Rubicon to something else. She looked at Johnny while he chatted amiably away, thinking how handsome and what easy company he was. Perhaps, he could be her plus-one at Fiona's wedding. She could see them now, Claudia on matron-of-honour duties, sexy Johnny standing by, waiting for her, everyone in the registry office wondering who that handsome man was with Claudia. '*Johnny Hogan,*' she would tell them all, airily, as though she was used to going out with gorgeous men who had international professional reputations. *He's a famous artist you know...*

'Claudia?' Johnny was speaking to her.

'Yes, sorry... I was miles away...'

'Have you talked to Grace?'

'Do you think I should?'

'I don't know... Perhaps it's just a moment and they are both regretting it. Perhaps it won't happen again.'

'That's what I was thinking... hoping...'

'Just be there for Grace when it all goes wrong.'

'It might not. She worships Tom to a ridiculous degree.'

Johnny nodded. 'I feel a bit sorry for him...'

'Him?'

'Yeah... it must feel awful to be like that, to be so emotionally immature that you have to try to prove how right you are and psychologically superior... He must be desperately insecure.' He smiled at her. 'People are complicated.'

'Some are more complicated than others...'

'And those are the ones to avoid. Problem is, complications are like icebergs. You just don't know how big they are until you have invested too much time.'

With the bowl scraped, the final coffee drunk,

the bill paid by Johnny, they headed out into the night.

It was warm and moonlit, the city was quiet, the sounds from inside the pubs of voices and singing, the shops dark, the street lights glowing. Claudia knew that they'd never do this again, probably. They would say goodbye and she would go home and perhaps they might run into each other again at some point, but this lovely evening was over.

'Well... thank you for a really nice evening...'

He smiled. 'Would you like me to walk you home? I could do with stretching my legs... I wouldn't want you falling over after all that amaretto.'

She laughed as they began walking together into the night, resuming their easy conversation. Who knew that just talking to someone about life, the universe and chocolate mousse could be so fascinating and absorbing? It didn't matter if they never did this again, Claudia told herself, it had been lovely.

In Fitzwilliam Square, they paused at the railings to the park, peering through. There was a patch of moonlight on the grass, the bandstand illuminated like a stage.

'It's my favourite square in the city,' Johnny said. 'I used to have a friend who lived in one of the top-floor flats. We used to spend summer evenings sitting on these little rickety camping chairs until it was pitch-dark.'

'I love it too.' Claudia had her hands on the railings. 'It's amazing how night makes everything mysterious. The most ordinary places are transformed.' She'd drunk too much, she realised. As had Johnny, who was actually currently scrambling over the railings.

'Come on,' he was saying.

Before she knew it, Claudia was being pulled up by Johnny. 'Is this technically trespassing?'

'We'll just trespass for a moment. I promise.'

The moon fluttered behind a cloud, the bushes and trees inside the square loomed like a vast forest and Claudia found herself being lifted up, before landing in a heap on the other side.

'I think every bone in my body has been broken. I need to be winched to hospital.'

But Johnny was already pushing his way through the foliage and onto the grass on the other side. Strangely, perhaps it was the spotlight made by the moon or perhaps it was the amaretto, but Claudia found herself prancing around on the grass like a show pony.

Once upon a time, back in her childhood, she

was able to perform cartwheels and she chose this moment to see if she still could. She took a run at it, imagining her body twisting, her hands pushing up from the grass, as she turned into a graceful mid-air arc, but as she tried to twist, she realised she was folded over, her arms weak, useful only for typing and putting food in her mouth and incapable of supporting an entire human body. She crumpled into the ground, and rolled to a standstill. Breathing heavily, she looked up at the stars above, the grass cool beneath her, her arms outstretched, and began to laugh. Somewhere, she could hear Johnny laughing too: deep, big belly gasps for breath. He was on the ground too, crawling towards her, shouting inaudibly, something about that being the funniest thing he'd ever seen. *Ever*. And then, the two of them staggered to their feet and tried more cartwheels, attempting parabolic perfection, but each time falling to the ground accompanied by continued paroxysms of laughter.

In the middle of the park was a bandstand and, next, they danced around it, Johnny taking her in his arms, and singing waltzing music, and they spun around, both singing louder and louder, and laughing. Eventually, they collapsed on the steps of the bandstand. The moon appeared from behind the cloud and the whole park was suddenly revealed to them, bathed in this night-time glow.

'This is why I became an artist,' said Johnny, 'to capture moments like this. To try to preserve a feeling, an atmosphere... to prolong the ephemeral.'

'I like the ephememereral,' said Claudia, making Johnny laugh. 'And has being an artist been everything you have wanted it to be?'

He nodded. 'To have somewhere to go, something to do, a place to be at peace, and to create and all that... well, it's been my saviour.'

Claudia thought about this for a moment. 'Why is life so hard?' she said.

'It is sometimes,' said Johnny. 'But it's not always. And if we didn't have the hard bits we wouldn't have the good bits.'

Claudia nodded. 'I think this is the most beautiful park in the world.'

'The *whole* world?'

'Absolutely! The whole world!' She realised that she was a little drunk but she didn't care. She was happy and relaxed and all was well.

Johnny laughed. 'It's very nice, I'll give you that. I wouldn't mind living in one of those houses and coming here every day, without having to climb over the railings.'

'I would climb over the railings even if I had a key,' insisted Claudia. 'It's the only way to enter Fitzwilliam Square if you want a magical evening. It's like Narnia and the wardrobe or Hogwarts through the platform thingy.'

Johnny smiled at her. 'It is magical, isn't it?' He paused. 'I was worried about you, when you said you were heartbroken. I remember thinking how could this incredible woman be heartbroken... she is too amazing... and who does the man who broke her heart think he is?'

Claudia smiled at him, feeling touched he'd felt so defensive of her. 'Actually, I wasn't actually heartbroken... just a little bruised,' she admitted. 'I was just being dramatic.' Thinking back, now, a year on, she was surprised how little she thought of Dom. Her bruised heart had healed far better and far quicker than she had thought. 'You know when something bad happens...'

'Yes...'

'You know it takes time to recover...'

'Yes... been there, worn the T-shirt...'

'Well, you know life can beat you up and you think it's an awful thing, and you are just existing. Well, that's you recovering. That's part of you getting your wings back.' She looked at him. 'When you are able to bring your bad feelings along with you but you are still doing all the things you are meant to be doing like working, or seeing friends, or cooking dinner. You have to bring the bad feelings with you because they're just as scared as you. Your feelings need to be minded. And you have to show them you're in charge and they don't have to worry. Do you see what I mean?'

'Kind of.' He was smiling at her, amused.

'I think I might have had too much wine to explain myself properly. But I mean that the bad feelings are as important as the good feelings. You have to say to the bad feelings, you're right to be there now, but soon you will go away. That's recovery. That's when your phoenix feathers are beginning to grow again.'

'I know what you mean.' Johnny laid his head back against the bandstand. 'I've been there when the bad feelings were taking over and then, somehow, you get stronger, and they lose their power.'

'And your wings are growing and then you take off again,' said Claudia, far too earnestly. 'It was like that when Dom finished with me, told me there was no future and basically he didn't love me and I had no home and no future.'

'I hate him,' said Johnny, with feeling.

'Well, he doesn't matter any more,' said Claudia. 'Because I am like a phoenix from the flames!' She stood up and started flapping imaginary wings and began running around again. Johnny started laughing and began flapping his own wings and running around, both of them laughing. And then she tripped and fell and lay on the ground.

'I'm done for it,' she shouted. 'You go on without me! Save yourself!'

Johnny flopped down beside her, laughing, unable to breathe.

'No, really,' insisted Claudia. 'You go and save the world... I'll just wither away here...'

Johnny was now gasping for air, rolling onto his back, and so did Claudia, the two of them looking at the stars and laughing.

'You know... you know,' she began, 'when your power is taken away from you? It's probably not the same for men...'

Johnny made a shrugging, non-committal movement.

'But you know when a man...' she looked over at him, 'has taken away your power...'

Johnny rolled onto his side, his hand supporting his head, looking at her, suddenly serious. 'Not Dom again... I thought we were done with that eejit...'

'No, not Dom. I'm done with Dom... it's Brian O'Brien...'

'Who's he?'

'My family's nemesis,' said Claudia, earnestly. 'He was a friend of my father's and he was the one who persuaded my father to invest and Dad was liable for debts... and I don't know if the stress killed my dad, but all I do know was that he died knowing he owed all this money.'

Johnny was listening. 'And you want revenge?'

'No... I can't get revenge. It's all done. I just want to know why. He was friends with Dad, I want to know what happened. It still hurts me. And Fiona. And Mum.'

'So, why don't you talk to him?'

'Fear...'

'You? Fearful?' He smiled at her.

'Yes...' Claudia rolled over to face him, her hand under her head. 'I need to pluck up the courage to talk to him. Just a conversation, that's all. I am a journalist, after all.'

'You might find that there is a perfectly reasonable explanation and your mind might be put at rest.' He was lying on his back, looking at the stars. 'You know,' he said. 'I think I met him once. It was just after your dad died and I remember walking home and I was thinking of you all... we all were. The whole street was so worried about you and Patsy and Fiona, my mother and all the other neighbours were discussing what they could do to help... but anyway, I remember this strange man was there one day, standing outside our house. And he looked as though he might topple over, he seemed unbalanced somehow, his feet were too small... He was dressed all in black, like Gomez Addams, and had black hair...'

'Sounds like him...' Claudia was staring at Johnny.

'He was staring at our house and I asked him was he looking for us. And he said was I Philip Kelly's child, and I said no, that Philip Kelly had two daughters and anyway that Philip Kelly was dead. And off he went, kind of tottered off. He had a weird way of walking, as though his feet didn't touch the ground.' Johnny shook his head. 'I remember your dad dying. He was the first person I'd ever known to die.'

'Me too...' She smiled at him, sadly.

'It must have been so hard on all of you...'

'It was. Awful. But you get through. There was so much for Mum to deal with and it's only now that I can even begin to appreciate her grief.'

'I actually remember they always went for an evening walk together.'

Claudia smiled, nodding. 'Always. After dinner and everything was cleared away, off they'd go.'

'I used to really like that and I remember thinking that if I ever got married, I wanted someone who would walk with me in the evenings.' He laughed. 'If I ever get married, I want a walker...'

'I've got to go home,' said Claudia, suddenly. 'I've got to be up for work in six hours!'

Somehow, they scrambled back over the railings and Johnny walked her and her bike home, waiting while she fumbled for the key.

'I hate my flat,' she whispered loudly. 'It's so messy and dirty. Plates everywhere. Mouldy mugs. It is like living with someone determined to die by E. coli.'

'What a way to go,' said Johnny, almost wistfully, making Claudia laugh again, as she slipped the key into the lock. 'Claudia?'

She turned around.

'If you'd like someone to come with you when you talk to that man... Barry O'Barry...'

'*Brian* O'Brien...'

'I'm volunteering... just... if you need me.'

'Thanks...' Claudia waved and disappeared inside.

25

Oh God.

Groaning in self-loathing, Claudia lay in bed in the horrors. Had she really flapped her wings and pretended to be a phoenix? Had she *really* done a cartwheel and fallen inelegantly to the ground? What about singing and coming out with all sorts of shite about God only knows what? How unutterably, excruciatingly embarrassing. Mortifying. A lovely evening with an old friend, ruined by her flapping her arms and talking utter bollocks?

But the worst thing was, she couldn't blame the drink. She'd always been the one person in the group dancing or singing or being a fool. When she'd met Dom, she'd put all that to one side, maturing and behaving herself more. Dom wasn't one for acting the maggot and he'd tamed her, made her behave herself, her silly side expunged. But it had obviously been – to her shame – lying dormant. She dreaded imagining what Johnny now thought of her. He was probably blocking her number right this moment, hoping never to be exposed ever again to any more of her crackpot theories on life, the universe, or her dancing and skipping around one of Dublin's nicest and most salubrious parks.

Thank God it was Friday and she just had to get through one day before she could spend the weekend in a darkened box room, reminding herself she should never drink again.

At Hackett House, she crouched behind her desk, sipping her coffee, wishing it was socially acceptable to wear sunglasses indoors. But she wasn't light-sensitive and she definitely wasn't Anna Wintour. There was nothing for it, but to erase all memories of the previous evening and hope she never bumped into Johnny Hogan ever again. Not that he would have called her, anyway. He'd been his friendly, making-contact and being-polite self. But duty done, he could go back into his world, and she to hers. Except hers was agonising.

She needed a biscuit, she thought. What this office lacked was sweet things. At *Irish Woman*, there were constant supplies, but here there was nothing.

Oscar turned to Claudia. 'I forgot about your date!'

'It wasn't a date...' She slunk further down in her chair.

'Well, your not-a-date date, then. How was it?'

'It was a nice evening with an old friend...'

'Ah, yes, your young old neighbour... and?' Oscar cocked his head. 'Did sparks fly?'

Claudia groaned. 'It wasn't a date and if it was, it was terrible.'

'Terrible?' Oscar propelled himself over to her on his wheely chair. 'In what way?'

Everyone in the office was listening in. 'Well, it was very nice, and we had lots of good chats...'

'And was he attractive?'

'He was, yes, but that's not relevant... because he's just an old neighbour.'

'A *young* old neighbour. Yes, you told us.' Oscar was smiling. 'But he was attractive.'

She nodded, because he was undeniably so, not just the way he looked or his cheekbones when he smiled or the way his eyes followed hers when she was speaking or how he fell about laughing as much as she did, matching her energy... 'But it's just platonic,' she insisted. 'He's just an old friend.'

'A *young* old friend,' repeated Oscar.

Simon was nodding. 'I'm fed up of platonic. Yes, it's nice to have friends, but sometimes you want to be more. And they don't. And then you can't be friends.'

'It's a sad fact of life,' agreed Mark.

'I would say this Johnny is into you,' said Oscar. 'How could he not be? With that face. And that hair. And the brains.'

'And personality,' offered Charlie.

Simon obviously felt obliged to offer something. 'And your Birkenstocks. They are a tick in my book.'

Poor Mark was obviously racking his brain. 'And your skills as an editor,' he offered.

They were all looking at Claudia, as she squirmed in agony. It was just platonic, of course it was. And okay, so she found him attractive, but she couldn't be thinking along those lines. She was just a little vulnerable after a year alone. And this was sent to try her, to test her resolve. 'It was just a nice night out... and I think I may have been a little too talkative...' To put it mildly, she thought. 'But it doesn't matter in the least.'

'Talkative is good,' said Simon. 'Imagine if you hadn't been.'

'Yes,' agreed Oscar. 'To *not* be talkative should be outlawed. I was on a date once and he didn't talk once. Just yes or no or maybe. I think I elicited a "perhaps" at one stage. But after half an hour, I made my excuses. Even if there is no chemistry, then at least you can have a good chinwag.'

'But I got a bit drunk,' she admitted. 'Not *terribly* but enough to skip around Fitzwilliam Square...'

Oscar laughed. 'No way...'

She nodded, ashamed, aware the team were looking at her. Even Mark had stopped working to join in. But she may as well tell them about last night as she needed to unburden herself from the shame.

'We've all been there,' said Simon, kindly. 'I mean, not that I've skipped around Fitzwilliam Square but variations on the theme.'

'I ended up in a wheely bin in Holyhead harbour once,' admitted Oscar. 'God knows how I got there. I vaguely recollect a ship of some kind.'

'I once got lost in York, dressed as a monk,' said Mark, shamefaced. 'It was a conference on medieval manuscripts and there was a cosplay monk thing going on and I just became too enthusiastic.'

'I don't drink,' said Charlie. 'So I can't join in.

However, I once cycled into the Royal Canal after being chased by a swan.'

They all agreed that Charlie's experience was the most horrific. Claudia was feeling a little soothed and touched by the kindness of the team. 'Has anyone got anything sweet to eat?' she asked.

They all searched their pockets and rucksacks and piled their findings on her desk. It didn't amount to very much – half a tube of Polo mints, some chewing gum, an individually wrapped Biscoff biscuit from Simon. 'I was given that with a cup of tea the other day. It's been in my pocket for a week.'

'You're not saving it?'

'I was keeping it for an emergency, which this obviously is. You have it.'

Claudia was feeling slightly better after the bolstering from her colleagues and the five of them settled into their morning's work, with just the sound of the biscuit tin being regularly opened, fingers hovering over the contents while difficult decisions were being made.

And just as she had managed to push all thoughts of Johnny Hogan to one side, her phone vibrated.

Thanks for a brilliantly fun night!
Have a good day today and best
of luck with finishing the magazine.
And seeing Brian O'B… remember,
I'm available to accompany you.
Just say the word. J.

She stared at the text for far too long, thinking about the myriad different meanings and whether he was mortified on her behalf or not. She couldn't quite guess. But she found herself smiling. Perhaps he wasn't quite as repulsed by her as she had imagined. Or perhaps he was just incredibly polite. But still. It was kind of him to remember what she'd told him about Brian O'Brien. And perhaps he wasn't embarrassed about her behaviour. Perhaps he'd genuinely enjoyed himself. The idea was a radical one… if one went through life not being embarrassed by one's behaviour, then essentially you were freeing yourself.

'What are you smiling about?' asked Oscar.

'Nothing…'

'You're staring at your phone. Did you get an intriguing text?'

'Might have done.'

'Ah…'

'Ah what?'

'Just ah...' He nodded his head, musingly. 'I like texts which make people smile. Whoever sent it is obviously a good person.'

'He is, I think.'

Oscar smiled at her. 'Good. Sounds like a keeper, as my auntie Eileen used to say. But bear in mind she didn't ever take her own advice. Husband number one, alcoholic. Number two, on the run. Number three, layabout.'

'She didn't keep any of them, though, did she?'

He chuckled. 'No, you're right. Good old auntie Eileen.' He looked heavenward. 'If you're listening, Eileen, you were right all along. She gave up on men then, spent the rest of her days line dancing. Had the hat and the boots and everything. Think she was my first fashion icon, actually.'

'She sounds fabulous.'

'You know something, she was. Just like you.' He paused. 'And this old neighbour of yours has obviously put a smile on your face.' He looked at her, an eyebrow raised. 'We all need someone who makes us smile.'

26

Foxy came into the office. 'Time for a quick catch-up?'

She nodded, grabbing her bag. 'Mark, will you make sure the copy from David on the best local breweries has been delivered, and Charlie, keep a lookout for the photographer to send in the shoot. We need to approve them by 6 p.m. this evening... and Simon, will you have the proofs ready for me?'

She caught a look being shared between Foxy and Oscar. They both had a similar expression on their faces: a half-amused, half-something-else look.

'She's doing pretty well, don't you think?' said Oscar. 'Not bad for a newbie.'

'I'm telling you,' agreed Foxy, 'I know talent when I see it.'

Claudia felt herself blushing, wondering if they were teasing her or if they actually meant it. She looked at the others in the office, Simon had looked up and was smiling as though what they said wasn't a total joke.

'But do you, Foxy?' went on Oscar. 'You did employ a certain Mr Moriarty, did you not?'

'We all have our off days, Oscar. We're all allowed to make mistakes.' Foxy winked at him. 'I'm finding my groove again, trying to fight back.'

Claudia wondered if there was an article in that, about rediscovering your midlife mojo that didn't involve sports cars or dressing like a teenager. She immediately thought of their freelancer list, working out who might be the best person to write it.

She followed Foxy to his office. 'I don't have time to go to Ernie's,' he explained. 'Nor do you, I imagine?'

She shook her head. 'It's full on. The next issue is coming together and I have a meeting with the sales team to discuss the advertising and all that later.'

They sat on either side of his desk, and Cian brought them both a cup of tea.

'Now, anything you want to discuss? Any worries, concerns, thoughts?' asked Foxy.

'What are you going to do about Blake Moriarty? Why can't you just sack him?'

'Believe me, I've thought about it. I've dreamed about it...' Foxy kept his voice low. 'But I've had my lawyer look into every permutation. Getting rid of someone when they are in the middle of a five-year contract is extremely difficult. It would cost a great deal of money.' He paused. 'That might have to happen. But first, I'm going to fight.'

'Good.'

They looked at each other for a moment.

'I'm glad you're on board,' he went on. 'I'm glad you're doing so well.'

'I haven't done an issue yet. But it's coming together.'

'You like the team?'

'I love the team.'

He grinned at her. 'They're a good bunch, I have to say.'

'By the way, Arnold Kennedy says hello...'

'You met Arnie?'

'He told me all about the early days. He said you were a group of lost souls here in Hackett House at the beginning...'

Foxy laughed. 'That's one way of putting it. We never got lost on the way to Doheny and Nesbitt's though. Back then, Arnie was starting his communications business, he'd just retired from rugby and the poor man was recovering from his third knee operation and he could only hobble around. But that lift was always breaking down in those days and he couldn't face the stairs. So we all carried him down. You know the size of him? The size of a milking parlour? Jayze, I don't know how we did it, but we managed to stagger straight into Doheny's, sat him at the bar and lined up a row of nice cold pints. Vincent, who used to run the place, said, it's not often we see men staggering *into* the pub.' He chuckled to himself. 'They were good days, they really were.'

He seemed much cheered when he walked her back to the lift and reached to press the button for her. He caught his watch just as it was about to fall off his wrist.

'I have to bring it to the jewellers. I must have changed the strap twenty times over the years. And it's kept going. I've just had to change the battery every now and again.'

It was a simple Timex watch, with a white face and Roman numerals. Most men of Foxy's age wore big, expensive things or had the latest fitness watch, but this was simple and unpretentious.

'Family heirloom?' Claudia asked.

'Something like that. Ah, here's the lift now. Mind yourself, Claudia. You're doing great. Keep going.'

* * *

That evening, she was cycling home when she saw Johnny Hogan walking along the street with a glamorous blonde woman in a smart navy trouser suit and briefcase.

The bike wobbled for a moment, but Claudia pressed on, hoping not to be spotted.

'Claudia!'

Too late.

She pulled in.

Johnny was smiling at her. 'I was wondering if I would bump into you,' he said. 'Being so close to your office...'

She smiled wanly, aware that her hair couldn't have been flatter and that today, for some unearthly reason, she'd actually *chosen* to wear an old cardigan, which she loved but had caught Oscar giving it a not-impressed once-over. 'Are you in your bobbly cardigan era, Claudia?' he'd said, loftily.

'Obviously,' she'd responded. 'And I love it.'

'But it's not enough to love something,' said Oscar. 'It has to love you back. Clothes are like people. It can't be unrequited.'

She'd laughed but Charlie had stuck up for her. 'It looks cosy and comfortable.'

'Oh, please.' Oscar had tossed his head, witheringly. 'You'll be telling me your underwear is decades old next...'

Simon had made a coughing sound, which had made Charlie and Claudia laugh.

Now she wished she wasn't wearing this old, beloved cardigan which she'd bought years before from Brown Thomas and had still been expensive despite being in the bargain bin at the end of the January sales. It was ready for the recycling bin now. But Johnny, not being Oscar, didn't give it a glance.

'Claudia, this is Alejandra Montez, she runs the gallery in Madrid where I had my exhibition last year.'

The woman had the most beautiful skin, her hair was pulled off her face and tied in a high ponytail. She shook Claudia's hand.

'Welcome to Dublin,' said Claudia. 'I'm so sorry about the weather.'

'I love bad weather,' insisted Alejandra, charmingly. 'Ireland's weather is famously bad, we don't come for the sun. That's why you come to us.'

'I'm in need of a holiday,' said Johnny. 'Wouldn't mind a bit of sun.' He smiled at Claudia. 'How was your day?' He quickly explained to Alejandra. 'Claudia is one of the country's best magazine editors.'

'Just for a bit,' Claudia said quickly. 'It's just a temporary thing.'

'Claudia and I grew up next door to each other,' went on Johnny. 'We're old neighbours.'

'He's the boy next door?' said Alejandra. 'That means you're ordinary, yes?' She was flirting with him, Claudia realised and either Johnny didn't realise or he didn't mind.

'Technically yes to being the boy next door. And definitely yes to being ordinary.'

Alejandra placed a hand on his arm. 'We should go, yes? We have a reception at the Spanish embassy and it's not the kind of thing you can be late for.'

'Alejandra is famously punctual,' said Johnny. 'She never arrives a minute too soon or too late.'

'I arrive on time.' The beautiful Alejandra shrugged. 'Is there another way to arrive?'

'In Ireland, you can't arrive on time,' explained Johnny. 'That's rude. Nor can you be early or actually late. There is the perfect sweet spot of arrival time that you have to be Irish to understand.'

'Well, I'm Spanish and it's time to go.' Alejandra smiled gorgeously at Claudia. 'Good to meet you, the girl next door.' She now had Johnny in a grip around his upper arm. '*Vamos*, Johnny.' She yanked him away, leaving Claudia standing, holding her bike.

'Enjoy the reception...' she said.

'I'm only going for the *jamón*,' he said, over his shoulder. 'I'll text you.'

27

On Wednesday evening, Claudia stood up from her desk, about to leave for the anniversary meal for John-Paul's parents. Oscar looked up. 'Off home?'

She shook her head. 'I'm going out for dinner. My sister's future parents-in-law's wedding anniversary.'

'Sounds exceptionally dull. Why on earth would you do that to yourself?'

'Fiona needs moral support.'

Oscar gave it some thought. 'Sisters should be supported,' he agreed. 'Mine needs regular pep talks, rallying cries. Says I'm her personal life coach. You wouldn't think she was a power-suit-wearing, ball-breaking senior partner at PWC?' He smiled at Claudia. 'Where are you going?'

'Rénè's.'

'Rénè's?' He looked almost faint. 'I thought it had closed down years ago. It should have done, anyway.' He surveyed her. 'What are you wearing?'

'This. It's all I have...' She was in her slim jeans and puff-sleeved black top and a pair of ballet pumps. Her old bobbly cardigan was consigned to the back of the chair, strictly to keep her warm but not to be seen in public in.

'Wait. Just. There.' Away Oscar swept and, from a far office, she heard sounds of banging. Oscar returned, holding up a black suit carrier. 'I knew we had this somewhere. It was left over from our Power Broker's issue and we had some women models.' He unzipped the bag. 'It's not Chanel,' he said, pulling out a small black jacket. 'It's Dior... they never rang to pick it up and I never bothered my ample...' He gave Claudia a look. '...My *glorious* arse to send it back. But this jacket, like Cinderella, will go to the ball. Now, put on some more make-up, do your hair and...' He looked down at her shoes. 'You don't have any others, do you?'

She shook her head. 'Anyway, I'm not the centre of attention.'

'But what if you meet the love of your life? You have to be ready. When mine walks in that door, and our eyes meet, and hearts are all around and the birds are singing, I'll be ready. As should you.'

Claudia slipped the jacket on, it was beautiful, the lining was a smooth satin, the outside a heavy black wool.

'Off you go, Cinders,' said Oscar. 'Have a wonderful time! Give my love to your sister!'

Hoping it wouldn't rain and destroy the borrowed jacket, Claudia walked across the river, over O'Connell Bridge and towards the Ha'penny Bridge, to Rénè's, where a top-hatted doorman waved Claudia down the steps to the cellar restaurant. She was shown into a small bar, which was a sea of peach velour and large Lumière candelabras and a tinkling piano.

Fiona's face brightened when Claudia appeared, which was both flattering and worrying as Claudia couldn't recall the last time Fiona's face brightened when she saw Claudia. Fiona mouthed something which Claudia couldn't quite get and then she heard Robert whisper loudly, 'What's the sister's name again?'

'Claudia,' said Josephine, equally loudly. 'Or

something like that. She's DEPRESSED. Bored and lonely. Only watches television.'

'Watching television is *why* she's depressed,' said Robert in a flat voice.

Claudia wondered whether she should keep walking towards them or delay her arrival, tie her non-existent shoelace or stop to smell the artificial flowers.

'*Or* the fact she's single,' went on Josephine. 'One minute they are young, the next old with nothing to show for it, except a wardrobe full of clothes which no longer fit them.' She looked up just as Claudia arrived to stand in front of them. 'Fiona was telling us you're in a sad place at the moment. She said you *still* hadn't found a man and so I think you should put an advertisement in the *Irish Times*. It worked for my good friend Sandra Cecily-Byrne. She was looking for a companion and was very fussy. Yes, so she *happened* to be looking for a dog, but it's the same point. She was inundated with emails from people offering their pedigrees.'

Fiona didn't say a word. It was left to John-Paul to rescue Claudia. 'She's fine, Mum. Stop fussing.'

Josephine drew back, pursing her lips. 'I was just being friendly to the friendless,' she said in a low but very audible mutter.

Claudia decided that it was best to try to pretend this was all entirely normal. After all, she was here for Fiona. 'What a lovely place... it's just so... so...'

'Peachy velour...' said Fiona.

Claudia was aware that every time Fiona spoke, Josephine turned slightly murderous, narrowed eyes on her, staring at her as though she was plotting her downfall.

'It's very kind of you to invite me,' said Claudia.

'Oh, it was a voucher that Robert won at some quiz at the golf club...' Josephine rolled her eyes. 'He's always winning things – bottles of whiskey, boxes of chocolates, tins of biscuits and then this voucher. We had *no* idea what to do with it and then John-Paul suggested we use it for our wedding anniversary. *Not* that we celebrate. Why bother? I mean, we celebrated the engagement of John-Paul and Fiona, but I have no idea why.' She glared again at Fiona, who was now busily searching for something in her bag, as though trying to escape into it.

'Would you like a drink, Claudia?' said John-Paul, trying to smile.

Claudia glanced at Fiona. 'White wine,' said Fiona. 'Is what I'm having.' She sounded as though she might have had a couple already.

John-Paul nodded to the waiter. 'Another white wine, please...'

Fiona said something which sounded like 'and vodka' but only Claudia could hear.

'Wine *and vodka*?' Claudia mouthed at her.

Fiona's eyes were wide. 'It's actually helping,' she mouthed back.

'Your jacket,' said Josephine to Claudia. 'It looks expensive. You young women spend all your money on clothes and nothing of value.'

'It's actually borrowed.'

'Oh, the perks of working for a women's magazine,' Josephine said, resentfully.

'I'm on *Irish Man* at the moment, but I'll be going back to *Irish Woman* soon...'

Fiona looked at her, indignantly. 'You didn't tell me.'

'Oh, it's no big deal. It's in the same building, the same company... just a... kind of break...'

'I'm in need of a break,' said Josephine. 'Dublin has terrible weather and *terrible* people.' She glared at Fiona again. 'I was trying to park the Hyundai today and someone gave me the two fingers.'

'I hope you gave them it back.' Robert was momentarily roused from indifference.

'Well, anyway, happy wedding anniversary,' said Claudia, accepting the glass of wine from the waiter.

'Forty long years,' Robert deadpanned. 'Every one better than the one before.'

Fiona had downed her wine in one impressive swig and was now giving her empty glass to the waiter. 'Line them up,' she said to him, meaningfully.

'My mother *warned* me not to marry Robert.' Josephine's voice was full of venom and seemed equally possessed with the need to drink heavily. 'Not only is he boring, she said, but he will love himself more than he will ever love you. She was right.' She paused to knock back her glass of wine. 'The last thing she ever said to me was, I told you so.'

Finally, they were shown to their table and the stilted, angry monologue continued.

But it was when they were eating dessert that Josephine, who had by now downed a whole bottle of the Portuguese wine by herself, said, in a slurring voice, 'What does everyone think of the *tart*?'

'Very nice,' said John-Paul.

'Delicious,' said Claudia, balancing a berry on her last forkful.

'A bit sour,' said Robert, looking straight at Josephine. She ignored him.

'It's funny,' Josephine went on, 'some people like

tarts. I can't stand them. They are the kind of things I would like to give my own two fingers to.' She looked pointedly at Fiona and, for a moment, the two women met each other's gaze. 'So, our son is getting married. What a catch for any *deserving* woman.' She gazed at John-Paul.

'Thanks, Mum.' John-Paul looked back at her nervously, a look on his face last seen on that of a citizen of Pompeii.

And then the eruption.

'Yes, it's a time of great happiness and celebration.' Josephine's face flashed to fury. 'Or rather it would be... if this woman... this THING!' She turned to Fiona, eyes aflame. 'If this harlot hadn't been conducting a treasonous tryst with John-Paul's best friend!'

Fiona had her head in her hands. John-Paul was frozen in the blast of his mother's fury. Robert mildly topped up his wine, his eyes half closed. Claudia tried to work out what she meant.

'Mum,' said John-Paul, 'we've agreed not to talk about this. You promised you wouldn't mention it again. We all make mistakes...'

'We do, John-Paul,' said Josephine. '*Mine* was marrying your father. Yours will be if you marry this... *this*... woman!'

'Mum,' pleaded John-Paul, 'how are we going to move on if you keep bringing it up? You shouldn't have been listening at doors. I've told you before.'

'Well, Fiona the tart shouldn't have been carrying on with Cameron! God only knows what he was thinking. I always thought of him as such a nice boy. But he was led astray by this... person.'

Claudia reached for Fiona's hand under the table, squeezing it.

'Mum,' said John-Paul, with studied calmness. 'This is between Fiona and me. She's my fiancée and we love each other. We're going to work it out and it has nothing to do with you. I have forgiven Fiona and Cameron. It was a moment of madness...'

'Moments,' said Fiona, quietly, her face white and scared. 'Momentssss.'

'Yes. Okay. But,' went on John-Paul, 'however many times it happened, *we've* been together for a long time and *we* will get over this.'

Fiona was near tears. 'I'm sorry,' she whispered. 'I really am.' She stood up, pushing her chair back. 'I think it's best if we go...'

'John-Paul's not going anywhere,' thundered Josephine.

'I meant, Claudia and me,' said Fiona, pulling at Claudia's hand. 'I wouldn't dream of coming between you and your son, and I am grateful that John-Paul has decided to forgive me, and although I wish...' – she threw Josephine a look – 'you hadn't been listening at doors and snooping, it's out in the open now. It happened. And I'm sorry...'

Robert was looking up, finally interested in the proceedings. 'It's quite all right. Things happen. I remember when... Ow!'

Josephine had flung her arm at him. 'Do me the favour of shutting up, Robert,' she commanded. 'Immediately!'

'We're going to go,' Fiona said. 'Thank you for dinner. Thank you for letting me invite Claudia. I'm going to go and stay with Claudia for the night. Bye, John-Paul, Josephine, Robert...'

'Yes, thank you.' Claudia got to her feet, placing her folded napkin onto the table. 'Thank you for a lovely evening.'

Fiona made eye contact with her, at the absurdity of the use of the word 'lovely'.

John-Paul was on his feet, following them out. 'Ignore her,' he was saying to Fiona. 'She's just upset and angry, that's all.'

'Those awful girls,' they heard Josephine say. 'So plain and wan, both of them.'

Fiona had begun to cry, as they stood at the

bottom of the steps leading to the street outside. 'You're too good for me... you're too nice...'

'Ah, don't say that. I don't have to be nice.'

'Nice is good!' said Fiona, as though trying to convince herself. 'Nice is the best.' Tears were running down her face. 'Nice is nice... I'm not good enough, I'm really not.' She slipped her arm through Claudia's and pulled her up the steps, from the cellar, to the pavement. 'I'll call you tomorrow. I'll be sorry for the rest of my life...' And they left poor John-Paul behind and walked back to Claudia's flat, Fiona weeping by her side.

28

'There's no one I love more than John-Paul,' explained Fiona, as they walked through the city. 'He's my best friend, my soulmate... but... oh God. Cameron.' She paused, almost trembling, her tears suddenly dry, her eyes shining. 'He's... he's... I can't put it into words. But he was *all* I could think of. I became obsessed. But I've stopped that now. So has he. It was a moment of madness...'

'Moments,' said Claudia. 'Plural.'

'Yes, plural moments of incredible madness. I mean, *marrying* someone like Cameron would be insane, so I just need...' She stopped. 'I need *both* of them. John-Paul *and* Cameron.'

Claudia gazed at her, almost mesmerised by the

sight of her pulled-together, controlling sister who was now, apparently, falling apart. 'How complicated do you want your life to be?'

'I don't care,' Fiona said, passionately. 'I mean, I want complications more than I want boredom. I want confusion and crazy more than I want quiet and calm...' She raised her eyes to heaven. 'And then that old bat tonight. Josephine. God. And I'm going to be forced to endure her for the rest of my life...'

'Well...' Claudia pulled a face. 'Not if you don't want—'

But Fiona was on a roll. 'God, why did *she* have to find out? John-Paul and I were arguing in their garden when we were over there trying to discuss the wedding and the old boot was in the shed, her ear pressed to the wall, listening through a jam jar.'

'What did she hear?'

'She heard me grovelling and promising never to do anything like that again. Oh, *Cameron*...' Her voice had the plaintive note of a country-and-western singer. Until this moment, Claudia would have sworn on Petal's life that Fiona did not have a passionate bone in her body, but here she was trying to breathe and talk and focus. 'He's just so interesting,' she went on. 'Everything he says, I just feel like my synapses are straining, trying to take it in. He will talk about something that's in the news, and it's as though he's turned it upside down and said something entirely new and different. I feel like my nerve endings are on fire, every cell in my body is vibrating. Just the sound of his voice...'

Claudia had never seen Fiona look quite so alive. 'So, be with *him*?'

'How can we? Poor John-Paul. What we have done is truly terrible. The kind of thing that is a highway to hell, a path to perdition, a road to Damascus... or whatever... Honestly... we just can't. John-Paul is the kind of man every woman should marry. He should be cloned or give TED Talks about how to be the perfect man. If he did, the world would be a much better place. There'd be no wars, I'm sure of it. And anyway, I love him...'

'You *love* him?'

'Yes, I love him...' Fiona seemed sure. 'Who wouldn't?' She paused and looked briefly hopeful. 'Unless you would love him? You could...?'

'Fiona!'

'Sorry. It's just that would be the perfect solution...'

'Stop it.'

'You're right. I've lost my mind.'

'You really have.' Claudia looked at her older sister, this person who she'd known forever, who had never caused any worry, who had worked hard and ticked every box and done everything right, and who was now going off the rails. It was almost thrilling. 'So what are you going to do?'

'Marry John-Paul, of course! He's the best human being I've ever met. And forget Cameron...' She gave a guttural cry of anguish. 'But...' She stopped in the middle of the pavement.

'But what?' Claudia turned around.

'Do you think that this has anything to do with losing Dad?'

'What? You're *blaming* Dad?' Claudia laughed and began pushing her bike again as Fiona ran to catch up.

'I don't know... I'm just trying to find a reason why I'm so self-destructive? Why I am hell-bent on ruining my life. Other people can be normal, but to me it feels like driving a car with the steering all wrong. It's so hard to keep it all straight.'

'Has it always felt like that?'

Fiona nodded. 'Always. I had to do everything right and now all my badness is spilling out of me. Your life is so much easier than mine. I've always had so much responsibility... you're the youngest, you haven't had to worry about anything. It was me who had to worry about Mum and the debt, make sure she wasn't lonely, went off to college so I could get a job which paid well enough to support her...'

'*Do* you support her?'

'No.' Fiona shrugged. 'But if she needed me...'

Claudia rolled her eyes, choosing not to say anything else. They had reached the flat and Fiona helped Claudia carry her bike up the steps.

Inside, Fiona picked her way through the piles of clothes, boxes and dirty plates. 'How do you live like this?' she whispered.

'I don't,' said Claudia. 'I just come here to sleep and to eat.'

Her sister wrinkled her nose. 'It's vile. You need to find somewhere else.'

'I'm trying!'

'You should have done what I did, and do something with your life that actually pays well, and not mess about with the arts. And then you might have a flat of your own.'

Fiona, who had been *sleeping* with her fiancé's best friend, was lecturing *her*!

'Well, maybe *I'm* doing everything *I* can to be normal?' said Claudia, passionately. 'And do you know something, I want to love my life. I want to love what I do. You have to take risks because what if you love it? If you don't take a risk, you risk not realising you love it. If you see what I mean?'

'Not really,' said Fiona infuriatingly, deliberately not understanding.

'I don't want to be like you, avoiding the things I love because I want to be normal. Feck normal. I want to be happy... I want to be in *love* with my life...'

'And are you? Are you in *love* with your life?'

'I know I'm more likely to love my life this way than if I was doing something entirely wrong for me.' She glared at Fiona. 'At least I am not denying who I am!'

Fiona was silent for a moment. 'You're right. I'm sorry. What the hell do I know about anything?'

Claudia smiled at her. 'No, *I'm* sorry. I haven't a clue about anything.' She paused. She was about to tell Fiona about Johnny and how they danced in the moonlight and flung themselves around and how he was the one who had said 'what if you love it' and how she kept thinking about him and those blue eyes of his and the way he smiled at her and his lovely voice. 'Anyway, it doesn't matter. Why don't I make us both a cup of tea and we'll drink it in my room? At least it's tidy in there.'

When they were ready for bed, teeth brushed, make-up removed, Claudia's borrowed Dior jacket hanging up, they sat on the bed, backs against the wall, mugs of tea in their hands.

Fiona smiled at her. 'Thanks for tonight and for being there. I couldn't have faced it on my own.'

'Any time.' Claudia paused. 'By the way, talking of affairs...'

'*Et tu*, Claudius?'

'No, Grace...'

'Grace?' Fiona looked shocked.

'No, her Tom...'

'That idiot! Not remotely surprised. With whom?'

'Grace's boss. Celia...'

'Oh God, that woman loves herself.'

'Yeah, she does... and so does Tom.'

'Am I the Celia in this scenario? John-Paul is the Grace?'

'No, you're the Tom, I suppose...'

'Thanks.' Fiona fell silent.

'All I mean is that relationships are complicated,' said Claudia.

'But they shouldn't be. I just don't know why I am making it complicated for myself. Why exactly am I sabotaging my nice relationship?'

'Maybe you don't want nice...'

'Who *wouldn't* want nice? What sane, rational, normal person wouldn't want a nice partner?'

Claudia shrugged. 'You, obviously...'

She waited for Fiona to get angry, but she didn't. 'You're right,' she said, after a pause. 'I think there must be something wrong with me.'

'And me,' said Claudia. 'At least you have someone...'

She and Fiona sat in silence for a moment.

'Do you ever think about that man...?' said Fiona, eventually.

Claudia instantly knew who she was talking about. 'Brian O'Brien?'

'Yeah... him.' Fiona looked at her. 'What happened? Why was Dad so stupid? Why were they friends? He wasn't like all of Dad's other friends. They were nice. Like proper dads.'

'I've seen him recently...'

Fiona had been slowly slumping down the wall, pulled by gravity and too much alcohol, but she was now sitting up, alert, like Frankenstein brought to life. 'You have?'

'A few times now... he's been going in and out of my office. He's on the board, I think...'

'The *board of what*?'

'Foxy Publishing. They're plotting against Foxy...'

'Wait. Have I just entered a spy novel? Who is

plotting? Who the hell is Foxy? Are you sure you aren't working for the Irish Secret Service?'

'It's Foxy's company,' explained Claudia. 'He's in charge of all the magazines.' She was trying to keep her mind straight about who and what and why and when everything was going on. 'He started *Irish Man...*'

'And you work for *Irish Woman...*'

'No, I work for *Irish Man...* I have been doing it for the last few weeks. I work with men... a whole team of them. And Charlie, except she's not a man. But they've all been really unhappy and there's this man called Blake Moriarty... he wears a gilet...'

'Oh God...'

'I know! And he's on the board and I think there's some kind of takeover going on and Brian O'Brien is one of them.'

Fiona blinked at her. 'A couple of things,' she said, politely. 'Firstly, I hate my future mother-in-law. She will be my cross to bear. Not that I could lift the old heffalump and those bloody kaftans would probably wrap around my neck and strangle me. Which is probably her plan all along. But secondly, you should have told me about Brian O'Brien. And thirdly, whose side are we on? This Foxy person or the board's?'

'Foxy's, of course!'

'Why of course?'

'I don't know... I just like him. You'd like him too. And I don't trust Blake. Or Jackson.'

'Who's Jackson?'

'Blake's familiar... his dogsbody...'

'Ah,' said Fiona, understanding immediately. 'Anyway, it's business. Be careful who you trust.' She paused. 'Does Brian O'Brien know who you are?'

'Hasn't a clue.'

'You're sure?'

'Sure.'

'And you want to ask him about what happened?'

Claudia nodded. 'I just wish I was brave enough.' She would never talk to him, she knew that, because whenever she saw him, she was transported straight back to being the girl who'd just lost her father.

'You've always been braver than me. Always. Anyway, I think I've officially reached a crisis in my life.' Fiona looked up, eyes gleaming. 'I've never had one before. It's quite exciting. And I'm almost sorry that it's over. And I'll marry John-Paul and we'll carry on living together and I'll do my boring job and try not to crack up.'

'So you're *definitely* forgetting about Cameron?'

And suddenly Fiona smiled, as though Cameron

was the magic word, but then the look faded. 'I can't think about him,' she said, giving her head a shake. 'It's so hard because Cameron works in the same building, that's how it started, really.' Fiona was lying down now, her eyes closing, in a reverie of her own. 'I'm in love with my fiancé's best friend and I've messed everything up... But I'm going to marry John-Paul. I'm going to make this work. He wants to... and so do I... so do I... so do I...'

Fiona's breathing turned deeper and longer and Claudia remembered those years of sharing a bedroom and it was as though no time had passed, listening to her big sister falling asleep.

She closed her eyes and finally fell asleep but it was a vision of Brian O'Brien which danced in her dreams.

29

The following day, Claudia and Oscar were on a lunch run, but on the threshold of SuperValu, Oscar hesitated, hands shielding his eyes. 'I just can't...' he said in a horrified tone. 'It's the overhead fluorescent lighting.'

'You're epileptic?'

Hands removed, Oscar blinked like a post-hibernation squirrel. 'No, it's just so unflattering.'

Claudia laughed. 'Could you possibly bear it for the pleasure of scoring a Simon Special?'

He sighed. 'I am starving, so on I will have to go.' They pressed forth, into the floodlit shop, Oscar shuddering. 'It's like having the big light on. Claudia, please tell me you're not a *big* light person?'

Claudia found herself giggling. 'No, don't worry. I'm a lamp person.'

'Oh, *thank God*. Otherwise we could never be friends.'

Claudia felt a glow of a small, unobtrusive lamp.

They shuffled along in the snaking queue for the deli counter, behind office workers, men in high-vis and teenage girls bunking off school.

'The deli counter is one of those uniquely Irish places that you would never find in the tourism ads,' observed Oscar. 'I wonder if any other country in the world provides such an array of possible sandwich fillings? You could create an infinite number of combinations. I might write a piece for the magazine on the joys of the deli counter.'

'As long as the lights are dimmed, of course.'

Oscar smiled conspiratorially at her, and she felt that little glow of acceptance again. 'So, tell me your midterm report on *Irish Man*. Are you enjoying yourself?'

'*Enjoying*?' she teased. 'That might be too strong a word.'

'You're right. *Enjoying* work. What was I thinking? An oxymoron if I ever heard one.' He paused. 'But you're coping?'

'Trying to, anyway.' They shuffled forward a step. 'What about you? Are you *enjoying* work?'

He shrugged. 'Well... I've been style editor for ten years. I suppose I am a little bored but also scared of doing anything out of my comfort zone.' He looked at her. 'I think I am waiting for Blake to sack me. It's not as though anyone *cares* about the magazine any more. Foxy still does because it's his baby, but he's been pushed up to such a point where he doesn't have anything to do with the running of the magazine.'

'So you care about the magazine?'

He nodded. 'Of course. I wouldn't be here otherwise. Well, I *would*. I mean, I need the job. A mortgage on a studio flat in Ranelagh doesn't pay itself. But I wonder who does still care about the magazine? Mark doesn't. He came in for a summer and has stayed for five years. Hates every second, the poor man. He's just angry he's not fulfilling his true purpose. Simon cares, I suppose, but he's not allowed to do anything creative and I think is a little worn down. Charlie is a sweetheart and very good at her job. Probably could do with more responsibility and I think she's always been treated as not that important and therefore her career hasn't flourished.

It's Blake...' He eyed her as though gauging how much to say.

'What about him?'

'He came in all sweetness and light but turns out, cue baddie music, he's bone-chillingly ruthless. His background isn't magazines. He doesn't love them the way we do. To him, it's just another commercial enterprise. Initially, I think Foxy was pleased to have someone who wanted to grow the business and advertising revenue and all that, and Blake's role, from what I can tell, was to position Foxy Publishing for a new generation. But he hasn't done that. Instead, he's just been focused on changing the leadership, bringing in new members to the board. Poor old Foxy has watched his power being taken away, bit by bit. And these people don't love any of the magazines. They just love the profits and there's this one total weirdo who claims to have a whole raft of shares...'

Claudia felt her skin prickle. 'Brian O'Brien?'

'You *know* him?'

She shuddered. 'In another life... Don't worry. We're not friends. Not at all.'

'How do you know him?'

'A long time ago, he involved my father in some kind of dodgy business. And... well, it went wrong.'

'Of course it did. The man's got a brain the size of one of those sweetcorn kernels in that tub there...' He motioned towards a vat of yellow behind the glass of the counter. Oscar eyed her curiously. 'And what happened? Are they still friends?'

'I doubt they would be,' explained Claudia. 'Dad died when I was fifteen. We didn't know about this investment until the week of his funeral which was when...'

'When Brian O'Brien sauntered up to collect his money? Am I right?'

'Exactly right.'

They shuffled forward again. 'I've been in the magazine for a long time,' went on Oscar. 'At the moment it's like fecking Narnia, forever winter.'

Despite herself, Claudia laughed. 'We need Aslan to come back.'

'Exactamento. Whither Aslan?' Oscar paused, contemplating Claudia. 'Maybe *you're* Aslan?'

She laughed again. 'It's the hair. It needs a cut.'

'I will say this, everyone was very surprised that Foxy hired you. An unknown. We couldn't work it out... but perhaps this is him fighting back. A small snowdrop in this permanent winter. I can't work it out. He must have been desperate.'

'Thanks a lot!' Claudia thought for a bit. 'You said you were scared about leaving your comfort zone...'

'I might have said such a thing, but show me someone who isn't...' He sighed. 'I'm stuck. In a rut. I write the same articles every month. I bore myself.'

'How can we help you not be bored?'

'Fire me. That will sharpen me up. Throw me out on the street. Make me fend for myself. Light a fire under my ample arse.'

Claudia laughed. 'You *want* to be fired?'

He nodded. 'Please. I need to be forced into an *uncomfortable* zone.'

'Well, I'm not going to do that. But I will force you into an uncomfortable zone. I want you to stop writing articles about clothes men will never wear and write articles about clothes they do want to wear. Make it practical. Give them solutions, advice, make it normal... but...' She searched for the word.

'Elevated?' Oscar suggested.

'That's right.' She smiled at him.

He was silent for a moment. 'Are you suggesting perchance I write about... sportswear? About the hideous garment known as the polyester GAA kit?'

'Perhaps. But elevated.'

'A Herculean task, beyond my capabilities. I think I would have preferred to be sacked.'

'And write a piece on the joys of the deli counter and the perils of the big light, okay? You're a very funny person, and we need more humour. And Oscar?'

'Yes?' He eyed her suspiciously.

'Your arse is not remotely ample.'

He clutched his chest. 'Oh thank you! That's the nicest thing anyone has ever said to me.' They had reached the front of the queue and he looked up, beaming at the hair-netted, plastic-gloved woman behind the counter. 'Five egg mayonnaise, ham and cheese baguettes, please. And five packets of Tayto.'

* * *

Back in the office, Simon was ready with the kettle on the boil and the teabags in the mugs and as soon as Charlie announced Claudia and Oscar had returned, he quickly made the tea and carried it into the office on the lid of a box of photocopier paper. They sat around, drinking the tea and eating the sandwiches, including employing Simon's Michelin-level crisp crumb sprinkle. Their chat naturally developed into a meeting, an excitement had all infused and enthused them, as though they were all falling back in love with their jobs. Apart from Mark, of course. But that was okay. Every office needed one person who didn't quite fit in.

'I've asked Gary Geraghty, the monk turned guru, to write a column,' announced Claudia. 'About spirituality, finding one's path, being human, that kind of thing. I think the Irish man is ready for it.'

'But is *Irish Man*?' asked Mark, sceptically. 'The only thing Irish men regard as spiritual is the first pint of the evening.'

'Speak for yourself, Mark,' said Simon. 'Personally, I like a few rituals. Candles, that kind of thing. I have a rhubarb one. Smells very nice. And Daisy appreciates it. And I'm not averse to a self-help book or two.'

Charlie nodded. 'Finding one's path is always useful... unless that path is a rocky one, on a Greek island, accompanied by goats.'

'It's definitely worth a try,' agreed Oscar. 'Anything that gets us and our readers out of our comfort zones.'

'I have the opposite problem,' said Mark. 'I'm *out* of my comfort zone being here. I desperately want to be *in* my comfort zone of the National Library.'

Claudia smiled at him, finally understanding him. Mark was just disengaged, a square peg in a round hole, pitched up in the wrong life. He probably would never be happy, even if he did ever make it to the National Library. She hoped he found his way there. She took another bite of her Simon Special, chewing ruminatively.

'Hillwalking,' said Simon, 'is my kind of spiritual jam. I just... well... I wouldn't mind finding someone to do it with me.'

'Giving up on dating apps, again?' said Charlie, sympathetically.

Simon nodded, sighing gloomily. 'Now, *they* are the opposite of spiritual. More soul-diminishing than enhancing.'

'You'll find someone,' soothed Charlie. 'I know you will.'

'Why don't you write about the perils of online dating?' suggested Claudia to Simon. 'A dos and don'ts, the new rules and all that?'

He looked quite pleased. 'I might do. Will draft something tonight.'

'Right,' went on Claudia, 'I want our freelancers to modernise as well. Our food column has to be about places our readers will actually want to go to. And wine they might actually be able to afford. And beer. The joys of your local pub? Ask famous men to talk about pub memories. This next issue won't be quite the evolution I want, but the one after that, and we'll keep building. And Oscar...?'

'I know,' he groaned, 'you want GAA fashion. Two concepts which don't belong together, but as you have tasked me with this dubious delight, so I shall prevail.'

'We need to talk about our cover star...' Claudia said. 'I need someone big. Can everyone come up with some names and... now, this is the big announcement. We're all going out for a drink next week.'

She braced herself for the excuses or the horrified expressions. But only Oscar looked appalled.

'Not...' – he shuddered – '...a team *bonding* exercise?'

'Yes. That's exactly what it is. I thought drinks in Doheny and Nesbitt's, dinner in Luigi's, and then a game of pool. Simon's a very good player.'

'Pool?' For some reason, they all became slightly animated, bristling with the novel suggestion.

'I haven't played since college,' said Charlie.

'My father was actually a very good player,' said Oscar. 'Only my mother put the kibosh on it. Said it was common. He used to bring me to a very down-at-heel place for secret pool trysts.'

'I've never played,' said Mark. 'My arms won't reach.'

Simon laughed. 'Look, it's only a bit of fun. We're not going to play for money... but if we were, I'd take you all to the cleaners.'

'Oh, the gauntlet has been tossed,' said Oscar.

'Right, next Monday evening the great pool challenge begins.'

* * *

In the afternoon, Simon returned to the office with an *actual tin* of biscuits. 'I know it's not Christmas,' he said, with over-exaggerated munificence. 'But I was just feeling a little *flaithulach*...'

'Simon Moneybags...' Charlie reached for a chocolate wafer.

'Lord Snooty more like,' said Oscar, taking his time to choose three different biscuits. 'A *tin*, Simon? What is this? The last days of the Roman Empire?' He popped a chocolate one in his mouth. 'This is how billionaires live. Like kings.'

'No one is allowed to go into the second layer until the first layer is completely finished,' Charlie announced with an uncharacteristic vehemence obviously only reserved for biscuit etiquette.

Claudia hovered over the tin, tea in hand, suddenly craving a hit of sugar. 'I hope there are custard creams. There's literally no better biscuit.'

'I disagree,' said Charlie. 'Bourbons are in a class of their own.'

'Garibaldis for me,' said Simon. 'What a biscuit.'

'You're all heathens.' Oscar was reaching in for another biscuit. 'What about the maligned but magnificent Jammy Dodger?'

Mark had a pile beside his mug on his desk, like a little biscuit tower of Pisa. 'You've forgotten the chocolate digestive,' he said, his mouth full and spraying crumbs over his keyboard.

Claudia turned to Charlie. 'Will you write a piece about Irish biscuits for the next issue. Five hundred words...'

Charlie was looking pleased. 'Of course I could...'

'Actually it could be something you could all continue when I'm gone...' suggested Claudia, but for a moment the words felt strange. She'd be gone in a matter of weeks, back to her old life. Which was of course what she wanted...

'When you're *gone*?' Oscar eyed her. 'You're not staying?'

Claudia shrugged. 'It was only meant to be for three months...'

'And we don't know where any of us will be when the takeover happens,' said Mark, gloomily. 'I think there will be a whole new regime or we won't have a job.'

'Speak no evil.' Oscar shut his eyes. 'I can't bear it. It's the waiting. I'm not a good waiter. For anything. Buses, text messages or to hear if my job still exists or not.' Eyes open, he turned to Claudia, and gave her a smile. 'I hope you stay forever,' he said. 'I don't think we could bear it without you.'

30

It seemed that Fiona was absolutely determined to marry John-Paul and forget Cameron and Claudia knew there was little she could do except support her sister. All talk of Cameron was verboten, any suggestion that she shouldn't marry John-Paul strictly forbidden.

On Friday evening, Claudia made her way to Sandycove, where she and Fiona had gathered at Patsy's kitchen table with mugs of tea and some shop-bought fondant fancies to talk through everything that needed to be done for the wedding. Fiona had seen a dress which she had decided 'would do'.

'At the end of the day,' she explained, nibbling off the pink icing, 'a dress is a dress. And it's just too stressful to try to find *the* dress because *the* dress doesn't exist.'

They did, however, have to come up with a location for the wedding. Patsy was making notes as Claudia was searching the internet.

'Mum, concentrate,' ordered Fiona. 'How many people does Castle Leslie hold if we take the ballroom? And cross-reference it with Ballybrack House and then check Kilmeaden Hotel.'

'This one has a petting zoo,' said Claudia, staring at the screen of Fiona's laptop. 'Guinea pigs and rabbits...'

Fiona looked appalled. 'Why? Just why?'

'It's relaxing,' said Claudia, reading from the screen. '*Your wedding day is the biggest day of your life and therefore we know it can be the most stressful. We at Kilmeaden provide small fluffy animals to cuddle, which are proved to reduce stress.*'

'That's all I need,' said Fiona. 'Someone thrusting a guinea pig at me when I am trying to be calm. Cross that place off, it sounds awful. The only thing I will want to *cuddle* is a nice glass of white wine.'

'I quite like the sound of it,' said Patsy. 'It sounds nicely eccentric.'

'I don't want nicely eccentric!' yelled Fiona. 'I

want seriously stylish and memorable! It has to be *incredible!*'

'This one says you can get married in their orchard and they have chickens walking around,' said Claudia, reading from her screen.

'I don't want chickens on my wedding day,' growled Fiona through gritted teeth. 'And John-Paul's parents want to invite everyone they've ever met. And because it's only the three of us on my side, they are taking full advantage.'

'Couldn't we invent more family?' suggested Claudia. 'We could hire a crowd and call them Auntie this or Uncle that or Weird Cousin Thingy. We surely could rustle up a long-lost family member.'

'Which reminds me,' said Fiona, ignoring her, 'Mum, are you bringing Dr Alan? Because I have to work out how many will be on the top table. Claudia, I am presuming you will be on your own...'

'Well...' began Claudia, who agreed she probably would be on her own but was simultaneously insulted that Fiona assumed she would be. She suddenly thought of Johnny. Could he be her plus-one? He was just so easy to be around. And she loved how chatty he was. It was an underrated male attribute but when you found a man who liked talking as much as you did, then he had to be made a friend. But would it be weird to invite him? He was so handsome and attractive... and successful. Would it be weird to go from nice, platonic neighbour to something more? Over the last week, she'd spent many idle few minutes searching for him online and reading his reviews and interviews. How had she missed all of them? In each photograph, he looked just like Johnny but an otherworldly version. Perhaps he was out of her league?

'If Claudia is single, then we will be with each other,' said Patsy. 'Okay with you, Claudia?'

Claudia nodded. 'Or if you want to invite Dr Alan... perhaps I can find someone...'

Perhaps it wouldn't seem strange to invite Johnny because he was a close family friend, it was like inviting a cousin or something. Except one didn't usually want to *hold hands* with a cousin. Not after the age of eight or so, anyway. And not only did she want to hold Johnny's hand, she wanted to wander around town, drink pints, be hauled over railings by him. And go *home* with him. But she was being ridiculous. What about her empowering, independent pledge? She had to stop thinking about him before she made a fool of herself again. She changed the subject.

'How are things with you and Dr Alan?'

Patsy smiled. 'It's very nice and he's a very kind and interesting person. And we've been to the Francisca's wine bar in the village for more of the charcuterie platters and went to the cinema to see a showing of *Rear Window*.'

Fiona and Claudia looked at each other briefly and smiled.

'He sounds lovely,' said Claudia. 'Going to see *Rear Window*, eating cheese and drinking wine is what I want to be doing when I'm grown up.'

'And we're going to walk up the Sugar Loaf on Sunday. He's bringing his coffee and walnut cake and I'm bringing a flask of tea.'

Fiona sighed, as though exhausted. 'It sounds so simple and so perfect. Why is my life so complicated?'

It was now so obvious that Fiona shouldn't marry John-Paul, except Fiona was the kind of person you just couldn't tell what to do. Grace was right, people don't want advice, they want to be supported whatever the outcome is likely to be. But what did Claudia know? She wasn't exactly an expert in matters of love.

'The wedding doesn't have to be complicated,'

said Patsy. 'You can choose to simplify. You don't have to have a big do, with the dress...'

'Which you will wear only once,' added Claudia.

'And the two hundred guests...' said Patsy.

'And the awful parents-in-law...'

Patsy and Claudia nodded and went back to work.

'Will you two just concentrate, please!' Fiona glared at them. 'Maybe we should go to Connemara? Mum, will you check Renvyle Hotel? It's apparently incredible.'

'Will you be having a hen night?' asked Claudia. 'I can organise it, if you like?'

'And John-Paul will have a stag,' said Patsy. 'The best man normally organises that. Who is his best man? Cameron, I presume?'

Fiona *didn't* look at Claudia. 'Probably...'

'He's a nice fellow, isn't he?' said Patsy. 'I thought he was very charming at the engagement party. I had a quick chat with him about a business trip he'd been on to Rome. I said that you'd just come back from Rome on a business trip. Coincidence, wasn't it...?'

Fiona was looking increasingly agonised and Claudia felt she had to try to save her. 'Fiona and

Cameron work in the same company. He's on a separate floor though...'

'And we *had* an affair.' Fiona had the look of someone who had just pulled out a pin from a grenade and lobbed it over a fence. 'And don't say anything, Mum, because believe you me, I wish I was a better person and worthy of John-Paul. But I'm not.'

Patsy was staring at her, her mouth making strange shapes as though she was trying to talk but the volume wasn't on.

'I've made such a mess of everything,' ploughed on Fiona. 'I hate my job, my life... everything. I need to hand in my notice. I'm going mad. I've begged John-Paul's forgiveness, which he has very kindly given me, but his parents quite rightly despise me. Even more than they did before. Now I will have to spend the rest of my days tiptoeing around and trying to get everyone to like me again. And they never will. Worse, his parents have bought us a joint membership to their golf club as a wedding present and it's non-refundable. So it's full steam ahead.'

'All aboard the love train,' said Claudia.

'That's *exactly* it,' said Fiona meaningfully at her. 'Get on *board*.'

'So...' Patsy looked bewildered. 'You're still *engaged* but you've had an affair...'

'Yes, I'm a terrible person.'

Patsy paused, taking all of this in. 'No,' she said, firmly. 'Not a terrible person. A wonderful person. Just someone trying to make the best of life. None of this matters, it's okay. We all make mistakes or decisions. It's life. But...'

'But what?'

Patsy looked at her. 'You shouldn't marry John-Paul.'

Claudia was amazed that here was her mother giving Fiona advice. She didn't care if Fiona wanted to hear it or not, she wasn't bothered if it was going to be received well or anything like that. She felt something to be true, and she was going to tell her. That was bravery, thought Claudia. Braver than she had been with regards to Grace. But mothers didn't decide to be brave when it came to their children, they just were. And that's why their love and their protection powered you through.

Fiona looked at Patsy, her eyes wide. 'I shouldn't marry John-Paul? Because he's the nicest man in the world and deserves better?'

'No, because *you* deserve better. You don't want to marry him, not deep down, do you?'

Fiona's eyes were filled with tears. She shook her head. 'But I have to make it right, and if he wants to and then I say I don't, that makes it worse... doesn't it?'

'The first thing you need to do is forgive yourself. Don't wait for other people to forgive you. People make mistakes, but you haven't *murdered* anyone. This is your way – and obviously not the *best* way – of trying to sabotage the wedding, wouldn't you say?'

Meekly, Fiona nodded again.

'But ending a very long-term relationship isn't easy... and you obviously fell for Cameron...'

'It was a stupid thing to do. He's appalled as well. We haven't spoken for weeks now.' Her eyes refilled with tears. 'And never will. We've promised John-Paul.'

'Well, do you know something, Fiona?' went on Patsy. 'I am so proud of you.'

'*You are*?' Fiona looked flabbergasted.

'Yes, you're a wonderful person. You have a beautiful heart. You have been a wonderful daughter to me...'

'And a wonderful sister to me,' added Claudia.

Fiona was crying now, unable to speak. 'But I feel awful. I've hurt everyone.'

'I think it was the threat of the joint golf club

membership that pushed you into Cameron's arms,' said Claudia.

Fiona tried to smile. 'It might have been. But I have to marry John-Paul. He's promised to forgive me and I can't throw that back in his face.' She swallowed. 'I'm going to marry him. And everything will be back on track and all will be well.'

Patsy nodded. 'Whatever you want to do, I am behind you.'

'So am I,' said Claudia.

'So if I marry John-Paul, you won't hate me?'

'I won't hate you.' Patsy smiled at her. 'I was saying to Alan last night that having two daughters is the most wonderful gift. To watch two girls grow up and be so equally lovely? It's been a privilege to be your mother. Alan was asking who was like my side of the family and who was like your father's. There's an old photograph of your father in his treasure box... and, my Lord, Claudia, you look like the spitting image of him when you were the same age...'

'Wait,' said Claudia, 'his *treasure* box?'

'Well,' said Patsy, 'it's not a *treasure* box as such. It doesn't contain anything valuable, but it's how I think of it. It was just an old shoebox that he kept a few things in. It's up in the attic, I found it again the other day when I was up there looking for my old rucksack. Anyway, it's just papers and things like that. And a few photographs. And some bits and pieces. His watch, that kind of thing. Silly really. I'll dig it out for you next time you're here. It's up in the attic somewhere.' She smiled at Claudia. 'Nothing *actually* important.'

But it was *all* important. 'I'd love to see it,' she said. But first she needed to hug her older sister and tell her that she loved her and so she did exactly that.

31

Claudia spent Monday in a whirl of decision-making, meetings and editing. She had discovered that not only had she grasped what her role was, she was actually leading the team. They all looked to her for her opinion, which she learned had to be given quickly and decisively. She was enjoying herself. The major outstanding issue was who to put on the cover. Their deadline was this Thursday.

She hadn't bumped into Johnny, even though she hoped she would. She had cycled past the Spanish embassy and wondered how his *jamón* evening had gone with the beautiful Alejandra. Her finger had hovered over his name in her phone a couple of times, but thankfully she hadn't sent him a message.

Best to leave it. They were just old friends and Claudia's head had been turned by his handsome face and charming personality and the kindness he'd shown her. Perhaps, seeing Johnny again, and liking him as much as she had, then it was a sign that a manless future wasn't for her? Perhaps she would meet someone she liked as much as him?

Just after 6 p.m. that evening, a frisson of wild excitement gripped the *Irish Man* gang as they left for their night out. Even Mark had put on a jazzy shirt and had cracked a smile or two. Charlie was wearing a low-backed top that showed off a Celtic tattoo. 'A teenage folly,' she said, when they gathered around to look at it.

'Are you sure it's meant to be a Celtic knot?' asked Oscar, squinting at it. 'I think it looks like a bagel.'

Charlie rolled her eyes. 'Mam told me I'd regret it. And guess what, she was right.'

The team had been working hard on finishing that month's issue and they were ready to let off some steam.

'Well, this is either going to be the worst night of our lives or the best...' Oscar flung his scarf over his shoulder, brushing Mark across the face. 'Now, we need ground rules. I only imbibe with people I can trust.' He glared beadily at everyone. 'Whatever happens due to alcohol is a secret never to be divulged. *Omertà*? Am I right?'

'*Omertà*,' echoed Simon obediently.

'Just need you to sign here...' Oscar put a blank piece of paper in front of Claudia, handing her his special Japanese pen. 'It's an NDA. I'll fill in the details later.'

Claudia laughed. 'You expect me to write in *black* ink?'

Simon threw over his blue pen. 'Try this, but don't sign his NDA, Claud, it's a trap.'

'I'd ask your solicitor to look over that,' said Charlie.

Even Mark was smiling as Claudia scrunched up the paper and threw it at Oscar. 'And take your black pen back...' She chucked it at him, which he caught with one hand.

Jackson was standing at the doorway of the office looking at them. 'Going out, are we, Claudy-pops?'

'Just a few drinks,' said Claudia.

'And pool,' said Simon.

'We're bonding,' asserted Oscar. 'It's what teams do, apparently. Bond through the medium of convivial drinking. Did you not learn that in corporate classes? Or were you all too busy being taught how to wear a gilet?'

Jackson gave him a look which was the temperature of an ice bath. 'No, we were busy being taught how to make a proper living, not flouncing around with ridiculous scarves that were last seen in the bargain bin at a charity shop.'

He left the office, leaving the team to shrug and gather their belongings and head across the road to Luigi's. They were placed in a prime spot, just beside the pizza oven, and each handed a vast menu to peruse.

'If anyone orders pineapple on their pizza, I'm leaving,' Oscar said.

'I was going to have kiwi on mine,' said Claudia, laughing at Oscar's horrified face.

'I'm partial to banana and Nutella on mine,' said Charlie.

'Marshmallows and tuna,' teased Simon. 'Don't knock it until you try it, Oscar.'

'I like a meat feast,' said Mark. 'Enough to cause a blockage in my colon.'

Oscar shuddered. 'I hope you are all joking, you disgusting philistines.'

The waiter came over to them.

'I'll order for all of us and I hope you don't mind,' announced Oscar, theatrically, 'but I'm going to order in Italian? I feel it's only appropriate.'

Oscar took a deep breath and then proceeded to order in what sounded like the worst approximation of an Italian accent.

'Five piazza Merrionay,' he said. 'And a boutellay of the Montepulciano.'

'Is he speaking English?' said Mark.

'And some brrrread and *olive oil*,' went on Oscar, with a confident flourish.

'I think,' said Claudia, 'he's speaking some language that is yet to be discovered.'

'I feel transported to the backstreets of Naples,' said Simon.

'The back passages of Naples,' said Charlie.

Oscar handed his menu back to the waiter. 'Good, aren't I? Now, we're all having the most sublime and simplest pizzas... no extra cheese, or meat or whatever. Just simple tomato, some mozzarella and the finest slices of truffle salami... and I've ordered the wine.'

It turned out that the wine choice was perfect and so were the pizzas, so they sipped and ate, feeling that warm glow of decent wine and the joy of delicious food matching their warm feelings to each other.

Charlie smiled at Claudia. 'Since you've joined the magazine, work is so much better.'

Oscar, Mark and Simon all nodded energetically.

'Immeasurably so,' said Oscar.

'Much better,' said Mark. 'I mean, work is still awful, but it's less awful.'

'It's been really good.' Simon smiled at her.

Claudia felt touched.

They talked of magazines and journalism, of how they had fallen into this world, and experiences they had on other magazines. Claudia told them about Amanda.

'She looks unhinged,' said Oscar. 'I've shared the lift with her on occasion and she won't make eye contact. I said good morning and she mumbled something which I couldn't make out, so I said, "What did you say?" And she turned to me and shouted in my face, "GOOD MORNING, WHICH IT MOST CERTAINLY ISN'T!"' He laughed. 'It was the most aggressive interaction I've ever had with anyone ever.'

Mark told them about why he loved medieval poetry, and by this time, they were on their fourth bottle of wine, so he had no compunction in reciting some of it, and the team managed to sit in reverential silence until he had finished.

Simon told them about his journey into town on the train that morning. 'This woman came on, holding this enormous package, and her raincoat draped over it. She sat down, red in the face, slightly sweating and panting. I was sitting across from her. "How do I get to the zoo?" she said. "I'm returning a penguin…"'

Everyone around the table laughed. 'A penguin!' said Charlie. 'I don't believe it!'

'No, it's true,' insisted Simon, 'it really happened. "You've a penguin in there?" I said. "Under your anorak?" "He was all on his own on the beach in Greystones," she said, and she caught him and tied his beak… "I'm taking the poor lost soul back to the zoo, where he belongs." "He belongs in bleeding Antarctica," said this other man. And just then the guard came down the middle of the train, checking the tickets and all that, and the woman turned to him. "How do I get to the zoo? I've a penguin I'm returning." The guard, right, didn't even look surprised but lifted up the edge of the anorak and looked in. "Madam," he said, "it's not a penguin you've picked up but a guillemot. The zoo'll not take him. Best to turn around and go back to Greystones and let the little fella find its mother."'

They laughed so much that they lost all decorum. Claudia was crying. Oscar had slipped down his chair so just the top of his head was visible.

Charlie had to lay her head down and was banging the table with her fist. Even Mark was helpless with laughter, while Simon looked proud that he'd scored so highly with his story.

'More vino!' shouted Oscar. 'Wine for the guillemot!'

Finally, it was time to head up to the pool hall. It couldn't have been less salubrious, with eight large tables in the room, bright overhead lighting which made Oscar screech as though in pain, and hard benches for them to sit on. But they soon started playing, and the talents of the team ranged from dreadful (Oscar) to pretty good (Simon), and there were times when they were in bits, laughing at pretend trick shots or when Mark tried to make a shot and landed face first.

Claudia was in the middle of parading around with the cue, imitating Freddie Mercury at Live Aid, when she heard someone call her name. It was Johnny Hogan.

'What are you doing in a dive like this?'

She froze, filled with mortification. How could she have let this happen *again*? Why was she always acting the maggot in front of him? Why couldn't she be one of those ethereal women who carried themselves perfectly? Somehow, she managed to smile, as though everything was normal.

'It's team bonding,' she said, turning to introduce him to the gang. 'We're just on a staff night out.'

Oscar launched himself forward, flinging the ends of his scarf over his shoulders, holding his hand out. 'Oscar de la Bournville. Major fan. We met at the opening in Sandycove the other week. Magnificent.'

Even Simon introduced himself. 'I saw your exhibition in New York last year. It was amazing. I went around three times.'

Mark shook his hand. 'Love your work. I think you perfectly encapsulate what it means to be human. I have one of your prints on my wall.'

Charlie said nothing, just gave a wave, eyes agog.

Johnny smiled back at them. 'You're so kind. But it's just nice to be back in Dublin. Especially Sandycove... And that's where I met this wonderful woman here.' He winked at Claudia, and for some reason she felt her stomach fold in on itself. She hadn't let herself think about him for the last couple of days – she'd been too busy with work for one thing, but the other was that she liked him more than she wanted to. It was impossible and silly to like him. They were old neighbours, just good friends. But why, then, did she feel suddenly energised by his presence, as though there was a fizzing force which felt electrifying, every hair on her body stood to attention? She wouldn't have been surprised if her hair was standing on end.

Johnny nodded towards a group of men who were standing around the far pool table. 'I'm out with my old art school pals from foundation year in Thomas Street. Micko and the lads...'

Oscar turned to Claudia, and in a stage whisper said, 'So *this* is the Johnny who's your old neighbour! I just thought you meant any old Johnny, but you went out with Johnny *Hogan*!'

'But he *is* my old neighbour.'

'*Hot* neighbour,' corrected Oscar.

'Does anyone want another drink?' offered Johnny. 'I'm on my way to buy a round.'

'I'm buying *you* a drink,' insisted Simon. 'It's the least I can do.'

'I'm buying,' said Oscar, quickly. 'What will you have? *I'm* going!'

For a moment, it looked like there might be a scuffle, but Johnny laughed.

'No, no, I'm buying. It's my turn.'

'And I'll buy for the team,' said Claudia. 'I'll come with you.'

Where was this confidence coming from? Was

she really walking with him to the bar? But Johnny seemed perfectly happy and relaxed. He grinned at her. 'I haven't stopped thinking about the other night...' He laughed. 'It was... *fun.*'

'Really?'

'Yes, really!' He suddenly looked concerned. 'Did you not think so?'

'No, it was. All of it... well, not all of it. Well, yes, all of it. Did you think all of it was fun?'

He nodded, very sure. 'Yes, all of it. And... well... I didn't know if I should call you for a chat... you know...'

'You texted though...'

'Yes...' He pushed his hand through his hair. 'I did...' He smiled at her. 'I am, however, slightly embarrassed about making us climb over the railings. I've been kicking myself for being so crazy. What was I doing, pulling you over the railings? I think... I think I was just overexcited.'

'Me too!'

They bought drinks for the team and for Johnny's friends and then stood, just the two of them, talking. Johnny told her about his new studio. 'You should come down and see it. It's overlooking the Grand Canal Basin, just across from Boland's Mill.'

'It's lovely there.'

He nodded. 'The light is amazing. It bounces off the water and back into the studio. It's magical. I need to buy a kettle so I can have tea and biscuits...' He smiled at her. 'The life of an artist involves much tea and many biscuits. It's the only way of getting through. When I left Ireland for art college all those years ago, I never dreamed I'd come back, you know? I thought Ireland and me were finished and that I could only have a career away from home. But home gnaws away at you. It's a very powerful thing. I was thinking this today, looking out at the Grand Canal, thinking that this was one of the most beautiful views in the city and here I am. Home. All the time I was away, I kept thinking this one thought...'

'What if you love it?'

He laughed. 'Exactly! I don't know why I stayed away so much. I was afraid, I think. Keeping home and Ireland intact and in my memory. The people, the way everyone talks to each other, the humour. I used to walk around Dublin in my head, when I couldn't get to sleep, across Wexford Street, into Wicklow. Stop for a pint in Hogan's. Along Suffolk Street and then to College Green. I used to do the walk on Google Maps, you know? A bit sad, I know. But then I asked myself why I was staying away when my heart was here. I thought, but what if I loved it? And if I didn't, I could always move again. But so far... I'm loving it.'

'You were *meant* to come home.'

'Yeah...' He smiled at her. 'I really was.'

'How did your reception at the embassy go?' She wondered how it had gone with Alejandra. 'Did you eat any *jamón*?'

'Of course. The Spanish know their pork.'

'So no Ferrero Rocher?'

'Sadly not.' He laughed. 'Spanish food and wine. Nice classical guitar.'

'And Alejandra. Has she gone back home?'

He looked at her curiously. 'She flew back this morning, to her husband and badly behaved twins.'

She couldn't help but smile at him, and he smiled back, and for a moment, she felt more than an inner glow. She felt as though she was on fire. Oh God. This wasn't what she had planned.

They stood looking at each other. She was aware that the top of her head had just been blown off. Or, at least, that was what it felt like. And it could only have been a second or two, but it was long enough for her to suddenly see a whole lifetime with him, to see themselves together. So silly. Her imagination was far too vivid. And yet... how nice it would be.

'I'd better get back and continue my team bonding.'

He nodded. 'Maybe... I'll text you? We could go to Fitzwilliam Square again?'

'I think we might be banned. I saw our faces on Wanted posters. Dead or Alive. Have you seen these trespassers?'

He laughed. 'Well then, we'll have to find something else to do... if... you're amenable?'

'Yes...' she croaked. 'That would be nice.' And then, somehow, she managed to turn and go back to the *Irish Man* team, who were stood around gawping.

'Johnny bloody Hogan,' said Oscar. 'Jaysus. Why didn't you tell us? He's a fecking rock star of the art world. Jeepers. You're a dark horse.'

Claudia smiled loftily. 'Ah well, I have to have some secrets. I'll introduce you to my other best friends next, Harry and Meghan!'

Oscar and Simon laughed, but Charlie looked wide-eyed. 'You're serious? Oh my God.'

'I think,' said Oscar, 'that our Charlie needs a lesson in how not to be gullible. There's a night class in it at the further education college.'

'Really?' said Charlie. 'I might enrol. I need something to keep me busy now Scooby's away.' And then her face changed, as she realised the joke and they all laughed even harder.

32

The following morning, Simon entered the office carefully carrying a cardboard box. 'Doughnuts,' he explained. 'There's a shop selling them on my way from the station and I've been passing it every morning for the last three years and never bought one. Well, today I bought five.'

'Oh, thank Christ, the cavalry has arrived,' said Oscar, standing up immediately, removing the box from Simon's clutches. 'Let me unburden you. There are rumours my arse is losing its ampleness and it's time to remedy that dreadful rumour.' He took a doughnut out of the box and clamped his teeth into it. 'Divine,' he said, his mouth full. 'Thank you, Simon. Very collegiate of you.'

Simon handed the box around and they all sat for a moment eating and licking their fingers. Offices were strange places, thought Claudia. You were forced to spend inordinate time with these people and somehow, if you were lucky, you became a tribe of some sorts.

'I still can't believe you didn't tell us you knew Johnny Hogan,' said Charlie.

'I hadn't seen him for years...'

Oscar sighed. 'He's just so talented. Annoyingly so. And handsome. If I wasn't such a good person, I might be eaten up by jealousy.'

Claudia allowed her thoughts to linger on Johnny, as they had last night when she had lain awake thinking about every look or smile, dissecting every word. She didn't want to feel like this, she wanted to be free of all this, but it was just so lovely to think of him, and she told herself, it didn't matter if he didn't feel the same way, because just thinking about him wasn't harming anyone. And this too would pass. She'd be back into her manless existence again soon enough and one day, when she was old and grey, she would remember the moment in a grotty pool hall when Johnny Hogan had smiled at her.

'He's just divine,' said Oscar. 'Those cheekbones.

The jawline. Swoon! Those eyebrows. And that leather jacket. It looks like Balenciaga, but I'd guess a charity shop, bought sometime in the 1990s. Even dear old Cristóbal couldn't make such a perfect jacket that fits like a glove over that remarkably fit physique.'

'He was always cool,' said Claudia. 'He used to mow our lawn...'

'Adorable.' Oscar hesitated, his face deep in thought as though he'd had a brainwave. But Claudia was already thinking of her own one. What about Johnny as their next cover?

'What about...?' Oscar began, just as Claudia said, 'What do you think...?'

'Johnny as our next cover?' they both finished.

Simon was already nodding. 'Great idea!'

'Genius,' said Charlie.

But was it actually a good idea, or was she using a whole photo shoot as an excuse to see him again?

'Totes yes,' agreed Oscar enthusiastically. 'Sometimes the best ideas are the ones staring at you from across a brightly lit pool hall. It was far too bright, obviously, but I'd had enough wine to soften the effect. But, my good Lord, he is very, *very* attractive.'

Charlie was nodding agreement.

'He's one of those men,' said Simon, 'that you

really want to hate but you can't. He seems sound, as well as being so talented.'

'Call him,' ordered Oscar.

Claudia nodded, picking up the phone, and hearing it ring, her body flooded with adrenaline. He answered straight away.

'Claudia! How's the form?' He sounded pleased to see her.

'Not too bad. I've taken two ibrupofens and just had a chocolate doughnut. How's yours?'

'Grand. Just eating some toast, I wasn't too bad... Look...' he began, just as she started speaking. 'You go first...'

'Well, I wondered if you might be available to be on the next cover of *Irish Man*?'

'*Irish Man*? Really? The *cover*. That sounds... *prominent*.'

'Well, you're a very prominent artist. Oscar and Charlie, who you met last night, would art direct it and you'd be on the cover for our next issue. What do you think?'

'I'd love to. I'd be honoured.'

Claudia did a thumbs up to Oscar, who did a double one back and then high-fived Charlie.

'What about...?' Claudia looked over at Oscar. 'Would...'

'Tomorrow,' mouthed Oscar. 'I'll call Lorraine the photographer. We can get it all done in the morning.'

'Would tomorrow... Wednesday... suit?'

'Yes... I'm free...'

Again she looked at Oscar.

'Morning,' he mouthed. 'Eleven o'clock? Tell him to bring his leather jacket.'

'Eleven okay for you, Johnny?'

'Grand. See you then... and... Claudia...?'

But in her excitement she ended the call without hearing what he wanted to say.

'This is fabulous news,' said Oscar. 'I was worried that we were going to have to put Arnold Kennedy on the cover. I mean, he's not a bad-looking speci-men, but he's no Johnny Hogan...'

'Morning, everyone.' Foxy had entered the office.

'Morning, Foxy,' they all said.

'I've bought you a plant,' said Foxy, producing a large maidenhair fern from behind his back. 'It's purifying, good for offices, needs minimal water and prefers to be sprayed from an atomiser, so I've bought you one of those as well. I watched a You-Tube video called *Caring for your Maidenhair Fern*. Very informative. I've found watching these little three-minute plant-care videos is better than medi-tation. Which I've tried, on Alison's advice, and failed. So I think that plant care is the new therapy.'

'It has been for the last ten years,' said Charlie. 'You're late to the plant party.'

'Story of my life. I always find things out far too late.' Foxy placed the fern on the corner of Claudia's desk. 'You can all benefit from its air-purifying qualities. You too, Mark.'

Claudia was suddenly infused with joy at this incredibly sweet gesture and she lightly brushed her fingers over the verdant leaves, which bounced on their stem. 'I'll watch that video as well,' she promised. 'Thank you, Foxy.'

'Doughnut?' said Simon, handing him the box. 'Highly recommended.'

'Thank you...' Foxy picked one up. 'How does one eat these things?'

'Get your teeth and clamp on to the doughnut,' said Oscar. 'Like a Jack Russell on an ankle.'

Foxy laughed and took a small bite, trying to keep it away from his shirt. 'Oh my God,' he said. 'This is delicious. I haven't had anything like this for years. I'd forgotten what fat and sugar tasted like... I've been trying to be healthy since Alison left, sort myself out, lose a few pounds...'

'You deserve a treat now and then,' said Charlie.

'I do,' agreed Foxy. 'We all do. A doughnut is a very soothing thing. Now, young Charlie, any news about your Scooby? Still away?'

'Unfortunately yes. He reckons he was a goatherd in a previous life. He called the other day and told me he hadn't worn shoes in ten days and was eating feta cheese three times a day.'

'Living the dream,' said Simon.

'Isn't he just,' said Foxy, who turned back to Charlie. 'But he's going to realise that man cannot live on feta cheese alone. Or indeed doughnuts. He'll wake up to the fact that he has a beautiful partner waiting for him in Dublin and he'll return. I've met young Scooby and he's no fool. He just needed a bit of time out.'

'Feta cheese was used to create gouache on ancient manuscripts from the Byzantine Empire,' said Mark. 'It had important qualities of lactic acid, which was perfect to fix the colours.'

They all blinked at him for a moment.

'Very good, Mark,' said Foxy. 'Very interesting. Now, Claudia, I just wanted to check in on my editor. How is everything going?'

'Great,' she said. 'We've just booked Johnny Hogan for the new cover.'

Foxy smiled. 'Wonderful idea. Exactly what we need.'

'Mark and I are finishing the editorial... Simon is trying out a few new designs...'

'I'm not using feta cheese for any of it,' said Simon.

'Why would you?' said Mark, uncomprehendingly. 'You're using a computer.'

Foxy nodded. 'I'd better get back to work. I'm meeting William, my lawyer, now. Wish me luck.'

'How's it going up there?' asked Simon.

'Oh, you know, fighting for our lives... but... that's not your problem, it's mine. But I promise you all, whatever happens, I'm not going down easily.' He looked around to make sure no one was listening. 'It's business. Live by the sword. Die by the fecking sword. See you all soon.'

It was later, when Claudia was cycling home, that she thought about Foxy's words. He was living and dying by the sword and she was too cowardly to even tell her best friend that her partner was having an affair. There was one person who Claudia had to confront, one spectre that had to be vanquished, and that was the one and only Brian O'Brien. She had to talk to him for her own sake, for Fiona's and Patsy's. And her father's. She had to find out what had happened and why her father had landed them in such a precarious financial position. It had made their grief so much more complicated, to have left his wife and daughters with that burden was incomprehensible. Their safe, dependable and sensible father. What had happened?

She talked herself into it and then out of it. Maybe she should just leave it? After all, what was the point? What would be gained? But she steeled herself. She was going to find him tomorrow and talk to him.

33

Claudia was up to her eyes and there was no way she could take the time to go and find Brian O'Brien. Except she knew she had to. Like that pesky inner voice which made her take the job, it was now pestering her and nagging her to talk to him. She couldn't and wouldn't rest until she had. He was only a few minutes' walk away. All these years she'd worked in Hackett House and he'd been so close.

On Wednesday morning, she tried to concentrate on work, editing articles which had been emailed by freelancers. She had a quick meeting with the sales director, and she wanted to drop in on the cover shoot which was happening on the top floor. Then, she promised herself, she'd go to St Stephen's Green and find Brian O'Brien's office. It would be fine, she told herself. He perhaps could tell her something about her dad that she didn't know, perhaps explain what had happened and make it all seem much more explicable.

The photography studio was a large, bright room, beyond the offices and boardroom, on the top floor. From the large glass windows, there was a perfect view of St Stephen's Green, and beyond to Harcourt Street and along Baggot Street towards the canal. Today, the blinds were down and the lighting was low. Oscar and Charlie were already there, along with Lorraine the photographer.

She could hear Oscar's voice. 'Johnny, we just need to tousle the old *gruaig*, if you don't mind... There... that looks better. God, you have good hair...'

Claudia stepped closer, not wanting to disturb them. She wished she could tell Johnny where she was going to next, he said he'd come with her, didn't he? But she couldn't ask him, and he was busy with the shoot. And there he was, sitting on a stool in the middle of the studio attempting to smile.

'Suck in your cheeks, Johnny,' ordered Oscar. 'The way the light catches those cheekbones...'

'I couldn't live with myself if I did that,' said Johnny. 'Can't I just smile normally?'

'I think moody is better,' went on Oscar. 'What do you think, Lorraine?'

Claudia moved to the side so she didn't disturb them all.

'We're going for a simple shot,' Lorraine was saying. 'It's all about the eyes. Johnny's cheekbones are chiselled, but I think a few nice, natural smiles would work well... Johnny? Can you give us a smile?'

Johnny valiantly tried.

'More natural, Johnny,' ordered Oscar. 'The camera doesn't lie. Think of something funny...'

'I can't...' said Johnny, agonised.

Claudia lurked in the gloom, behind the camera.

Oscar gave her a thumbs up. 'He's a natural,' he said. 'Johnny, I think we might go for a topless shot next...'

Johnny laughed. 'Now, I know you're joking, Oscar...'

'I just thought I'd chance my arm,' said Oscar with a coy shrug.

Johnny spotted Claudia. 'What are they trying to do to me? I'll never be able to show my face again!' He smiled at her.

'That's it! Keep it like that!' Lorraine was clicking away. 'Beautiful. So handsome... more!'

'Let's change it up,' shouted Oscar. 'Moody,

moody! Think of death. Your dog dying! A nuclear apocalypse! Putin! Kittens being left all alone...'

'That's not moody,' said Johnny. 'That's catastrophic, you're going to have me crying...'

Claudia looked through Lorraine's viewfinder to see Johnny framed, the light catching the blue in his eyes. What a handsome man, she thought, and what a gorgeous smile.

'It's going to be a great cover... thank you so much, Johnny... I'll leave you to it.' Johnny was one of those people to whom everyone flocked and fawned over. He handled it well and didn't take the fuss and attention too seriously, but she really didn't want to be in his fan club. If she'd learned one thing over the last year since Dom, it was not to be too grateful for attention and to mind herself first and foremost.

Claudia began tiptoeing away.

'Lunch, if you have time?' called Johnny to her. 'All this smiling and looking ridiculous is making me starving...'

'Of course she has time,' Oscar said, as though he was in charge of her social diary. 'Why don't you buy some of those Simon Specials and eat them in the Green?'

'Sounds good to me,' said Johnny, smiling over at Claudia.

She turned. 'I can't. I need to do something...'

'Like what?' Oscar was indignant. 'What do you need to do that's better than going for lunch with Ireland's sexiest man and latest cover star?'

Johnny laughed. 'Oscar, please...'

'I need to go and see someone.'

Johnny was looking at her thoughtfully. He nodded, as though he understood.

If I don't go now, she thought, *I will never go.* 'Thanks again, Johnny. See you all again...'

Claudia pressed on, down in the lift, and out into the street and made her way along Baggot Street towards the Green and the Shelbourne Hotel. She crossed the road to walk along the east side of the square, looking up at the numbers on the brightly painted doors. Some houses were thicketed with russet Virginia creeper, others slick and modern offices. There was 37 and 38 and then 39. It was slightly shabbier than the others, not like the drinking club covered in ivy at number 38 or the slick financial consultants at number 40.

She walked up the granite steps towards the black door and peered at the line of about fifteen plastic doorbells, most labelled with names, including a hypnotherapist, a 'colour therapist', a tailor and even a palm and tarot reader. But no Brian O'Brien. Claudia turned towards the steps, back onto the pavement and down the steps of the basement. She tried the doorbells and if they were answered at all, she was given the same response. 'Never heard of him. Wrong place.'

Then, just as she was about to give up, a woman in a navy skirt-suit and drawn-on eyebrows was about to rush past when she spotted Claudia. 'Lost? Or looking for someone?'

'Looking for someone. Brian O'Brien. The accountant?'

The woman's eyebrows nearly disappeared into her hairline. 'Is that what he calls himself?'

Claudia nodded. 'You know him? He's meant to be in this building, but I've tried every bell and no one has heard of him.'

'He's not in *here*. He's around the back. But I'm curious why you want him.' She narrowed her eyes. 'What's he done?'

'He's an old friend of my father's...'

The woman's eyebrows were now invisible. 'Friend?'

'School, years ago... And... I need to ask him something.'

'Ask him what?'

This woman was seriously nosy, but Claudia found herself answering. 'I need to know why my father lent him money.'

The woman gave a laugh. 'Money, you say? Right. Well, good luck with that. Never lend and never borrow, especially to men like Brian O'Brien. He's slippery as a fish in the Grand Canal. And just as polluted. Go round to the mewses at the back of the houses. They're all photography studios and architects and fashion designers now. He's there.'

'Thank you...' Claudia was already moving, darting along the pavement to the gap at the end of the terrace which led to the lane behind. Her breathing was fast, that same sense of rising panic she felt that first day at *Irish Man*. But on she went, trying to steady herself, thinking what she might say.

The lane was grass- and dandelion-strewn, with purple valerian flowers sprouting from the top of the crumbling stone walls and beyond them was a row of mews houses, once the old carriage buildings for the grand palazzos facing the green, now all converted into offices and flats. Electric bikes and scooters leaned against bike racks and workers in trendy heavy-framed glasses appeared from the doors. She looked for Brian O'Brien's office. There was one which wasn't smart or cool, it was a crumbling, creaky building, the walls more dirty than cream, the window dusty. And a sign:

Brian O'Brien, accountancy and money management services and financial guidance

The thought of knocking on the door made her break out into a cold sweat and there was no way she was going to be able to conduct a rational conversation. The last thing she wanted was to give away any of her power. Not to *him*.

She took out her phone and called Johnny. She wasn't sure why, but out of everyone she knew, she guessed he would understand.

'Claudia? The shoot's finished. Ready for lunch, for this mysterious Simon Special...'

'No... I'm standing outside Brian O'Brien's office...'

'Ah. I thought that's where you were going...'

'But I can't go in...' She heard her voice wobble.

'You don't have to. You don't need to do anything you don't feel able to.'

'I know. Except I want to...'

'Wait for me. I can come straight away. I've just left Hackett House. Where are you?'

'Behind St Stephen's Green. In a mews. 39b.' She paused. 'I wish I could go in.'

'He's nothing, Claudia. You shouldn't be intimidated by him.'

'I know I shouldn't...'

'What exactly do you want to say to him?'

'I want to ask him about my father and why he gave him the money...' Claudia felt her throat seize, and her chest tighten. She wouldn't cry, not here and definitely not on the phone to Johnny. 'I just need to find out why Dad trusted him... but I can't go in... I'm scared.'

'Of *him*? He's the one who took your father's money,' said Johnny, passionately. 'He's the one who should be scared.'

Finally, she caught a hold of herself. 'Look, sorry for bothering you. I'm just going to go back to work.' But first, she had to explain why she'd called him out of everyone else in the world. He was just so solid, so sure. He had been the day of the funeral when he just took it upon himself to move the furniture around or when he mowed their lawn every week all those years ago. And he was still that person now. Someone to rely on. Someone kind. 'I just thought I'd tell you because you know what's going on.'

'Claudia, no need to explain. I'm glad you called me. Will you wait for me?'

Claudia felt suddenly better about everything. She didn't need to talk to Brian O'Brien. It would just be something she would learn to live with. But at that moment, the door opened, and there – a great swathe of pinstripe and stomach – was Brian O'Brien. He was standing in front of her, his beady eyes were ice-cold, his nose long and thin like an icicle.

'Looking for someone?' His high voice came from somewhere at the back of his nose.

Claudia ended the call to Johnny without saying goodbye, a sudden rush of adrenaline making her body fizz to attention. 'You, actually.'

'Me?' Brian O'Brien looked surprised, lifting his head back slightly so she could see up his nostrils. 'I'm busy...'

'It won't take long...' She had no idea who was doing the speaking but it did sound like her voice.

'I have five minutes.'

Nor did she know how she managed to put one foot in front of the other, as he unlocked the door, walking ahead of her. Their footsteps echoed in the tiled hallway, before he turned into another doorway and into his office. Teetering piles of files and paper were everywhere, wastepaper baskets overflowed, surfaces submerged, like falling into a paper silo at the recycling centre.

He took a seat behind his desk and Claudia perched on a pile of papers balanced on what she assumed was a chair.

Brian O'Brien's mouth twitched as he withdrew a packet of slim cigars and there was a pop sound, the hit of kerosene, as he lit the end of one and puffed on it so the tip glowed. 'What can I do for you?'

'I'm Claudia, the daughter of Philip Kelly.'

His eyes didn't move. He stared at her. The cigar smouldered.

'And...' Her throat was dry. 'And I want to know... or rather I need to ask... about my father and the money he gave you?'

34

Brian O'Brien stared at her, unmoving. Claudia wondered if he was quite all right because he was so still.

'It just seems like a strange thing to do,' she went on. 'To invest money... and I would like to know what happened.'

At last he moved his head, twisting it slightly. 'And why on earth do you think I would remember anything from so long ago?'

'I thought it could have been a significant moment. Him investing. And then dying. And owing you money...' She let the words hang in the air, wondering what he might refute. All she needed was an explanation.

He removed his cigar. 'Your father was the biggest fool I ever met.' His voice was clipped, unemotional. 'They saw him coming, all those charlatans... if I hadn't been around, then you'd have been in a far worse situation. Philip Kelly was an utter fool...'

Taken aback, Claudia tried to find the words. 'He wasn't a fool.'

'He was.' He puffed again. 'And I'd known him since we were boys.'

'Which is why I thought it was unusual that he would owe you so much money...'

'I saved him from himself many a time...' The cigar clamped between his two teeth, he pushed back his cuff to check the time on his gaudy gold watch. 'I must go.' His eyes settled back on Claudia as he stood up. 'Just know this... your father was one of those men who shouldn't ever make important decisions. He was the kind of man who people walked over because he let them.' He strode to the door of the office. 'Now, if you'll excuse me.'

Shaking, Claudia followed him out, through the tiled hallway, and to the street outside.

'Off you go,' he said, briskly, and shut the door behind her.

There was nothing she could do except walk away. Blinking back the tears, Claudia blamed herself for even going to see Brian O'Brien and for allowing him to hurt her like that. But, worse, to hurt her father's memory. She wished there was something she could do to change what had just happened, to turn back time and to have never gone to see Brian O'Brien. He was the type of man who longed for the chance to hurt someone and she had handed herself up to him on a plate. How had she been so stupid to have allowed herself to be so vulnerable. All she knew was that he was lying and he defamed her father because he couldn't defend himself. Brian O'Brien was even more despicable than she had ever imagined.

Oh Dad, she thought, *I'm so sorry. I'm the fool. I let him hurt us both. But why were you friends with him? You deserved better than him. What was going on?*

At the end of the lane, just as she was about to turn onto the Green, she crashed into Johnny. 'I finally found you!' His hands were holding her arms. 'I came as quickly as I could...' Johnny was looking at her. 'Claudia?'

'I saw him.' She stopped. 'And well... it didn't go very well...'

'In what way?'

'Can we keep walking? I need to get away from him...'

They turned towards the Green and headed back to Hackett House, and Claudia told Johnny what had happened.

'He just wasn't very nice about Dad...' She kept her voice steady. 'And it really wasn't very nice, he dismissed him...'

'This Brian dismissed your dad?'

Claudia nodded. 'He said he was a fool...'

Fool. Such a small, silly word and yet it had the power to destroy. But one thing she did not want was sympathy or pity from Johnny. If he showed an ounce of it, she'd cry, but perhaps sensing this, Johnny kept his face totally straight. 'But your father wasn't a fool,' he said, gently. 'Nowhere like a fool. He was an amazing man.' He smiled kindly at her. 'Don't take the word of someone who doesn't deserve that respect. We know the truth. Don't let someone like him change how you feel about anything. Don't let people dictate the weather of your day.'

She sighed, knowing he was right. She knew the truth about her father and why would Brian O'Brien take anything away from that? He didn't actually have the power to do that.

Outside Hackett House, Johnny turned to her. 'Promise you're all right?'

She still felt shaky. But an image came into her

mind suddenly. It was the thought of a small box in their attic at home. For some reason now, she knew she had to have it. 'My dad's treasure box...'

'Treasure?' He smiled. 'Gold coins? A chalice or two?'

'Sadly not. Just papers and things. But something tells me there might be answers in there. I'm going to go and get it tonight.'

'Do you want me to come with you?'

She was tempted. She liked being with him, Johnny made everything better and easier. But she'd taken up enough of his time, dragging him into her dramas.

'I'll be fine...'

'You're sure?'

'Surer than sure.'

'Look, have you spoken to Grace? No? Well, it might be something or nothing but I rang earlier to speak to Celia and usually Grace answers, but today Celia did. Grace doesn't work there any more...'

'What?'

'I know... and so of course I couldn't ask or say anything, but Celia, who is normally so buoyant, sounded very much subdued. I just sensed something had happened.'

35

As soon as she could leave work, Claudia headed straight to Sandycove. She had acted as normally as possible that afternoon, working hard and laughing along with some of the office banter, but she was really in a state of shock as she tried to process her feelings about her meeting with Brian O'Brien. All she knew was that she hated him, but hating him meant she wasn't free of him.

She cycled to Patsy's house on Railway Road. But instead of her mother, Dr Alan opened the door.

'Ah!' He beamed at her, squinting slightly from behind his horn-rims. He was wearing a red apron over his clothes. 'Claudia! You're looking for your mother, no doubt, well, come in, come in...' he said in his sweet, squirrely way. 'I've just made a cake for our hillwalking adventure, would you like some?'

Patsy came out of the kitchen, wiping her hands on a tea towel. 'You're not coming in?'

'I've got to see Grace... I just wondered if you had the treasure box?'

'Yes! It's in the living room.' Patsy disappeared and returned with an old shoebox, wrapped with a piece of twine. 'It's just papers and things. No gold coins.'

'Not even chocolate ones,' said Dr Alan, making Patsy laugh. He had come outside with a parchment-wrapped parcel. 'Date and walnut,' he said, slipping it into the basket along with the shoebox. 'Safe cycling,' called Dr Alan, his arm around Patsy, and the two of them smiled in the autumn evening sun as Claudia pedalled straight to Grace's house and rang the bell.

When Grace answered the door, wearing her dressing gown and old tracksuit bottoms, her face mascara-streaked, the bounce from her curly hair flattened, she crumpled when she saw it was Claudia, arms reaching for her like a zombie, falling into her arms, crying loudly. 'Tom's been having an affair...' she sobbed. 'With CELIA!' Claudia held her steady, as Grace cried her heart out. Eventually, she pulled back a little. 'I can't... I can't believe it.'

The two of them moved into the kitchen, where Grace sat on the old sofa, the very same one she and Claudia had spent hours sitting on when they lived together in their flat in town, when life seemed so much less complicated. Claudia put the kettle on, taking down two mugs from the cupboard, listening to Grace tell her story.

'So, it was the day before yesterday when Michael came into the gallery to tell me that Tom and Celia had been... you know... massive inverted commas *carrying on*. For some time, it seems. I can't get the truth out of Tom. He tried to blame me at one point, said I didn't show him enough attention and that people aren't essentially monogamous and that Celia was so flirtatious that it was impossible to resist her.' Grace shook her head. 'It would be easier if he just explained what happened, and then said sorry, and that would be that. We'd be over, obviously, so much less drama. He thrives on it, I think.'

'I saw them at the dinner party.'

Grace was looking at her, eyes wide, tears crystallising on her eyelashes. 'Saw who?'

'Tom and Celia. She was doing something under the table. With her foot.'

'Doing what?'

'I dropped my fork. And I saw...'

'Saw what?'

'Her foot...'

'Her foot?' Grace looked disgusted. 'Her foot?'

'I don't know... *manipulating*... manipulating *him* with her foot.'

Grace's eyes were even wider. 'Manipulating?' She shook her head slowly from side to side. 'She was manipulating all of us. She is the arch manipulator!' She stopped. 'But... why didn't you tell me?'

Claudia felt her skin crawl. She'd been a coward not to tell Grace. She should have told her the truth and saved her from this dreadful shock. She'd been a coward with Brian O'Brien and now she'd probably lost her best friend from lacking basic courage.

'Because I... well, I hoped it was just a moment... I should have told you...'

'Yes, you should have.' There was silence between them. 'But you didn't...'

'No... I'm sorry.'

Silence.

'It's okay,' said Grace after a moment. 'I understand.'

'You do?' Claudia felt a rush of relief and love for Grace. To be forgiven was *divine*. 'Really?'

'Of course I do. I probably would do the same. It was an impossible decision for you.'

'But I *should* have told you.'

'You're not the villain here. *He* is. And *she* is. And poor Michael. He loved Celia far more than I loved Tom, so it's so much worse for him. I mean, I *loved* Tom, but Michael worshipped Celia.' She stopped. 'God, but we all worshipped at the altar of the Celia, didn't we? No wonder Tom, Mr Psychologically Unencumbered, couldn't resist her. You know, I've been thinking that perhaps he wasn't as unencumbered as he made out to be... do you think that is possible? Do you think he was fooling us all?'

'You mean, that he's the most screwed up of all of us?'

'Yes... he went on about everyone else's faults and not his own. It was a smokescreen. He was irascible and grumpy, and lazy... Wouldn't even do the bins and would conveniently forget every week, so in the end it was easier for me to do it. His ego was so fragile. Was jealous of every man, would pick apart their looks, their clothes, their acting or whatever they were doing.' She stopped, the tears beginning to flow again. 'I'm just so glad we didn't bring a little one into the world...'

'A baby?'

'No! A dog! I was about to adopt one! That dream is gone now. And my job... my lovely job... I was so good at all the organising and I loved meeting new people. It made me one hundred per cent more interesting as a person. And now I am just boring Grace Maguire, single, puppy-less and jobless.'

'You have somewhere to live and you'll find a new job. Honestly. When Dom and I ended, it took me a while to recalibrate, but I couldn't be happier.' As she talked, Claudia realised how true it was. She couldn't be happier. And the last month had been incredible. She had been challenged and scared and she had met people that she loved and cared about. She had started the month in her comfort zone, and she was ending it feeling invincible. Why had she allowed herself to be intimidated by Brian O'Brien?

'Where's Tom now?'

'At his sister's. She called earlier to beg me to take him back, said that he was doing her head in and that she's on my side. I'm so scared about the future. Being out there again... life is easier when you're in a relationship, isn't it?'

'Sometimes. Depends on the relationship. But being on your own is incredible. What if you love it?'

36

It was 8 p.m. by the time Claudia was back in the city centre, cycling across the river and along the Quays to Fiona's house.

John-Paul looked a little surprised to see her as she stood on their doorstep, proffering the shoebox, as though she was auditioning to be one of the three wise men in a nativity play.

'Claudia... everything okay? What have you got in there? A dead hamster?' He gave a laugh.

'Dad, actually.' She tried to laugh as well, but his face had fallen.

'Your *dad*?'

'It's just a few things of Dad's. I thought Fiona would want to look through it with me.'

'She's working on the guest list for the wedding. It's already getting out of hand.'

Fiona had obviously decided to ignore Patsy's advice and push ahead with the wedding. Fiona and John-Paul were doing their best to resume their normality.

Fiona appeared in a pair of tracksuit bottoms, which Claudia knew were only ever worn when she was in need of great comfort. 'Claud? Is Mum okay?'

'She's grand. I just left her and Dr Alan looking loved up.'

Fiona visibly relaxed. 'And what are you holding? The Ark of the Covenant?'

'I thought it was a dead hamster,' said John-Paul, brightly.

'A what?' Fiona blinked at him, trying to make sense of why he was bringing dead rodents into the conversation. It was as though they were both pretending that everything was normal, but there was tension in the air, not love.

'It's Dad's treasure box. I thought you would be annoyed with me if I opened it without you...'

Fiona nodded. 'You're right. I would have been.'

'It's a bit dusty,' said John-Paul. 'Can you give it a wipe before you put it on the table?'

Fiona took the box from Claudia.

'Please, Fiona,' he said. 'It's too dirty. Here, I'll go and get you a duster...'

'It's fine, John-Paul,' she said, smiling at him. 'We'll give it a good clean. Aren't you going for your run?'

He had already slipped on his trainers. 'I won't be long.'

The two sisters sat at the kitchen table, the box in front of them.

'How's it going with John-Paul?'

'We're doing... better,' said Fiona. 'I'm still eating humble pie. John-Paul is trying to remember not to keep bringing up things. He's still hurt and I feel terrible and ashamed. I've promised to hand in my notice at work, just so I don't run into Cameron again.' She paused. 'Anyway. It is what it is. Right. Let's look at this box, then.' She blew the dust off the top of it and began untying the string. 'We can bin it, if there's nothing to see...' The string unravelled onto the table in front of them.

Claudia lifted off the lid and peered inside. It was just official-looking papers. The first was their father's birth certificate. 'Dad, the little baby...' She passed it to Fiona.

'It's funny to think of him like that, before Mum, before us. His whole life stretching ahead of him.'

His passport was in there, and his medical appointments and an appointment diary which was blank. The two of them held each other's gaze, trying to work out where all the pieces of the puzzle fitted.

'Do you remember what he used to say to us? How he was surer than sure that he loved us?'

Claudia nodded. *'I'm surer than sure that I love my two girls.'*

They smiled at each other.

'Surer than sure...' repeated Fiona. 'He was a very sweet man, wasn't he?'

'The sweetest. The nicest. We were lucky.' Claudia felt a stab of fury again at the thought of Brian O'Brien and how horrible he'd been.

'I'm surer than sure that he knew we loved him,' said Fiona.

'Me too.' Claudia placed her hands on the box. 'Let's see what else is in here.'

Under some medical receipts and what looked like share certificates, she took out a watch. It was a simple white-faced Timex, the strap broken, the hands stopped mid-tick. She had forgotten all about this watch which she now remembered he always wore.

Fiona took it from her. 'I was there that day when the strap broke. He'd been mowing the lawn and the watch fell onto the grass. He threw it over to me, telling me to look after it until he finished. He never did get round to fixing it.'

'May I have it?' Claudia turned the watch over and over in her hands, staring at it. She'd seen this exact watch before, just recently. Except the one she'd seen had a newer strap and was around an entirely different wrist. Foxy's. 'I've seen it...' she managed. 'I've seen this before...'

'Of course you have, it's Dad's...'

Claudia's brain was working in slow motion. What exactly did Foxy say? His brother had bought him *his* watch, and he had bought one for his brother, a week later. Her brain was about to explode. 'What was Dad's brother called?'

'Frank, I think. They had that falling out and they never sorted it out before Dad died.'

'Frank. You're definite? Not Foxy? Was Foxy his nickname?'

Fiona looked amused. 'I don't know... Who is Foxy?'

'I'm calling Mum.'

Claudia picked up her phone and dialled Patsy.

'Mum... what was Dad's brother called?'

'Who?'

'Dad's brother. What was he called?'

'Frank, why?'

'Not Foxy?'

'Foxy?' There was a pause from Patsy. 'He might have been. He did have bright red hair, you see. Clever man, very charming... we were at his wedding... and then it all went wrong. Fractured families never quite manage to repair themselves. There's too much work for people to do. There's too much to fix. He was at the funeral, obviously, but didn't come back to the house. He was very upset, if I remember.'

'What did they fall out about?'

'Money, I think. Isn't that always the way. As far as I recall, Frank was left money in their father's will, because he was the eldest son... silly old-fashioned rule. And Philip was so hurt by this. But instead of sharing the money, Frank used his inheritance and started up whatever business he was in and only gave Philip some shares years later when it was up and running. I think I remember Philip not wanting them, but Frank insisted, trying to make amends. And they never managed to reconnect or apologise properly. They probably thought they had time... but you know... they didn't.' She paused. 'I felt terribly sorry for Frank at the funeral. He could barely speak, the poor man. And not that I was much more coherent, but he was beside himself. I remember seeing him outside the crematorium sitting in his car, tears streaming down his face. Why? You're going through the box... what have you found?'

'I was just wondering, that's all... I'll call you back...'

Claudia put down her phone and turned to Fiona. 'Foxy is our uncle... it's too much of a coincidence.'

'Who the hell is Foxy?'

'I've told you about him. The magazines I work for are published by Foxy Publishing...'

'I thought you worked for Amanda...'

'Amanda?' Claudia genuinely had to think who that was. Amanda was several lifetimes ago. 'No... he *owns* the company, all the magazines. And...' She steadied herself. 'I think he's Dad's brother... he had the same watch...'

'It's a Timex. Who didn't have one?'

But Claudia was still thinking of Foxy. Was he really their uncle? Did Foxy know who she was? If he did, it explained everything.

37

If Claudia claimed she was his long-lost niece and he their long-lost uncle and it turned out he wasn't, she'd make a right eejit of herself. But if he was, it would explain everything – the job, the umbrella, the puncture, the pen... the kindness, the attention. She slept badly, her mind full of Brian, of Foxy and of Johnny. And in the morning, she was up early, the watch safe in her bag and the papers from the treasure box in a folder in her bag.

It was Thursday and therefore the magazine's final day of production before printing and distribution. Once it was done, perhaps she might get a chance to talk to Foxy?

After a quick slice of toast and cup of tea, Leesha

appeared, tear-streaked and forlorn. 'Something ter-rible has happened. Something truly awful...'

'Oh my God, what?'

Leesha began to sob. 'It's too hideous, like, simply the worst thing ever!'

Claudia's heart went out to her. 'Leesh, what is it?'

'I've been locked out of my social media account. Apparently I'm a bot and however much I try to tell them I'm not, they don't believe me. Like, I have to wait until they have verified my humanness. It could take ten days... maybe longer! And it's terrible, I've been offline for three days. My life as an influencer is over. I thought I'd found my life's meaning... you know? My purpose... I am going to have to start earning some money, Dad says. Get a real job.' She looked aghast. 'I don't want to go back into law. All I did was file and run about and wear flat shoes. It was hideous. My mother has a friend who has a cheese shop and she needs someone for the next few weeks and Dad says I have to do it, but the problem is, I will just smell of *cheese*...'

'But cheese is nice... and working in a shop would be a chance to take the pressure off, no more having to come up with content...'

'You mean, you don't think being an Insta-grammer is my purpose either?'

'Look, try the cheese shop... and see how it goes.' Claudia paused. 'What if you love it?'

Leesha suddenly smiled, her tears dry. 'Yes! What if I love it? I'm going to post that... where's my phone... except...' She began to cry again. 'It's all gone... my online identity, my whole *life*... all taken away, as though I no longer exist.'

Claudia put her arm around her. 'It's going to be okay.'

'Thank you, you're right...' Leesha wiped her eyes again. 'The stress has been something awful. It's been literally traumatic. I think I have PTSD.'

'You know what's amazing for helping with PTSD?'

'No, what?' Leesha looked at her with big eyes, desperate for the cure.

'Cleaning. Washing up. Hoovering. Dusting. Sorting everything out. Decluttering. It's a scientifi-cally proven cure for PTSD after being locked out of social media.'

Claudia left the house to the glorious sounds of the vacuum cleaner.

* * *

After locking her bike outside Hackett House, Claudia crossed the road to the coffee shop and ordered a double espresso. Hopefully, there would be some of Simon's biscuits left in the office, but to be on the safe side, she also ordered five pains au chocolat for the team. While she waited, she idly watched the street outside, thinking about everything that had had happened over the last few weeks... Foxy... her father... Brian O'Brien... Johnny.

And then, on the far side of the road, at the corner of Merrion Street and Baggot Street, three figures were walking in a row. One of them, wearing a green bomber jacket and yellow jeans, was the unmistakeable figure of the tousled-haired Jackson. Beside him in a navy gilet, pristine white shirt and beige chinos and his usual perfect pencilled-in stubble was Blake Moriarty. And then, on the other side, was the large expanse of Brian O'Brien.

Claudia froze, hovering inside the open doorway.

The three were talking intently, Blake's hands gesticulating forcefully, Jackson gazing at him in rapt attention, Brian O'Brien nodding and speaking. And then, just as they came closer, Jackson dropped back, lingering in the doorway of SuperValu while Blake Moriarty stood on the side of the road, as though waiting for a break in the traffic to pass, while Brian

O'Brien carried on walking towards Hackett House. And then, after a few moments, Blake Moriarty strode along confidently towards Hackett House, and then two minutes later, so did Jackson.

'Double espresso for Claudia!'

When she knew the coast would be clear, she made her way across the road and into Hackett House, where, from behind the front desk, Bernadette was looking grave. 'Morning,' she said, dolefully, her usual ebullience dampened.

'Bernadette? Everything okay?'

Bernadette's face darkened, and she pulled her floral scarf tighter around her neck. Her voice a husky whisper, she said, '*A cold wind was blowing out of the north, and it's made the trees rustle like living things.*'

Claudia was confused. 'Is that Yeats?'

'*Game of Thrones.* I know all the lines. And I thought twas apt *today of all days...*' The huskiness returned briefly. 'You see all is not well. *Winter is coming...*'

'Metaphorically?'

'And literally.' Bernadette jabbed her biro in the air towards the ceiling. 'They're up there now. The whole lot of them. Like Joffrey and Ramsay, they are. And Littlefinger...'

Claudia looked puzzled. '*Game of Thrones*?'

Bernadette nodded. 'You can learn a great deal about human nature from that programme. Whenever I am feeling a bit down, which I was last night, I put it on, and I come away feeling wiser, but this time not any less despondent. Not with those...' – she jabbed the air again – '...*eejits* up in the boardroom.'

Claudia felt a chill, as if indeed winter was coming, or, as Oscar had it, winter was already here. 'How's Foxy doing?'

'Not great. He was looking quite pale this morning. Has his lawyer with him as per. But putting a brave face on, you know him. As they went up, he said, let the games begin! All I could say before the lift doors closed was, "Fire doesn't kill dragons!" but I don't think he heard me or, if he did, I don't think he understood. Not a *Game of Thrones* fan, is our Foxy.'

In the office, Mark was already at his desk, looking even gloomier. 'Have you heard the news? The magazine's going to be sold. Foxy's meeting isn't going well. It's already lasted for three days, apparently. And more today.'

'How do you know?' Claudia put her bag and coffee on the desk, slipping off her jacket.

'Foxy's PA, Cian, told Simon who told me that Foxy looks nervous. He told Cian last night that selling the magazines might be his only option. Cian was very emotional, apparently. Loves Foxy. Would do anything for him.'

Claudia felt jittery inside, thinking of Foxy upstairs with those spoofers made her nervous. The fact that she now believed he was her uncle made the tension even worse. She'd been growing ever more fond of Foxy, but now she wished she could do something, talk to him, support him, let him know she was on his side. Poor Foxy!

'You know, despite everything, I'm going to miss this job. I hadn't realised how much I liked it.' Mark shrugged.

'It hasn't gone yet and let's just focus on finishing the magazine...' Claudia felt determination rise up within her. It wasn't just a job any longer, so much was on the line: pride, principle and perhaps even family honour. 'It might be our last...'

All morning, the team were busy editing and meticulously proofing when Jackson came to see them.

'Knock knock, people,' he said, wafting in as though he hadn't a care in the world. 'Just FYI, it's hotting up in the boardroom, I can tell you. It's all very... very... *very* exciting.' He'd long jettisoned all pretence of being Claudia's BFF. Now the board were winning, she was surplus to requirements.

'I don't know why you look so happy,' said Oscar. 'You're just a dogsbody for Blake Moriarty.'

'Dogsbody?'

'Plaything, then,' said Oscar. 'You think you're up with the big boys, when you're most certainly not. Blake's using you...'

'He's not, don't be ridiculous.' Jackson flipped his head contemptuously. 'Anyway, as soon as the consortium chuck Foxy off the board, Blake and I will cash in big time. We're going to live in Monaco... or Tangiers... or I quite fancy Las Palmas... the weather is fabulous. As are we.' He turned to Claudia. 'And to think I thought of you as my Claudy-pops. I thought you might be one of us. How wrong I was.' And with that he stalked out of the office.

Now, even Mark looked annoyed. 'He's a little flea-ridden woodcock, he really is.'

'He's a little shit,' said Oscar, 'that's what he is.' He paused. 'Marky-pops.'

'Thank you, Oscar-plops,' said Mark.

'Plops?' said Oscar. 'Pops is fine.'

'Human nature is a funny old thing,' said Simon. 'You think everyone is the same as you, that they all have the same moral compasses, the same consciences... but some people just don't. It's hard to get your head around it.'

At lunchtime, Charlie ran out to buy them all Simon Specials, which they ate at their desk, powering through the day. And then, just after 3 p.m., they declared the magazine was done and Simon began the process of saving the document and sending it over to the printers.

'I'll put the kettle on,' said Oscar. 'I'll make us all a tea. Charlie, open the biscuit tin. There's only one custard cream left and it's got Claudia's name on it.' He grinned at her. And she smiled back, knowing whatever happened, she'd made a few new friends for life.

38

'What do you think is happening up there?' asked Charlie, as they sat around drinking tea.

'No idea...' said Claudia, wishing she could talk to Foxy and perhaps help in some way. 'I could go and see if Cian can tell us anything...'

'Cian will be up to his eyes,' said Charlie. 'He's fielding all the calls from the media, bringing in teas and coffees and trying to keep all of Foxy's other work going.'

Simon looked up from his computer where the document was still sending. 'What difference will it make?'

'Feck all.' Mark shrugged. 'We're still going to be

out of a job. If they are making cuts, the least profitable will be the first to go.'

'I've loved it here,' said Charlie, smiling at Claudia. 'Especially the last month.'

'Yes, it's been fun,' said Oscar. 'The constant consumption of biscuits is a new thing for us, but an innovation that will continue. If we do indeed still have gainful employment.'

'Glad my influence has been so profound,' said Claudia.

'And you've changed the magazine,' said Mark. 'Even *I'd* read this month's.'

Claudia was touched, but she felt sad, as though it was all over. 'I've loved working with you all too. Perhaps we should have a gathering in Doheny and Nesbitt's when the issue is out? We'll invite all our contributors.'

Charlie was nodding. 'Johnny Hogan has to be the guest of honour...'

'Naturally...' Oscar looked straight at Claudia. 'He's *divine*...'

Claudia didn't answer. It was easier not to think about Johnny, every time she did, she began imagining a future together as though she was sixteen years old. It was ridiculous. And yet... how kind he'd been to her yesterday.

She took another biscuit from the tin. 'I could go up to the boardroom and loiter...'

'We could go in disguise,' said Oscar. 'Dressed as builders or plumbers... I actually was a plumber for last Halloween. Went around in a boiler suit clutching a breakfast roll. I looked fabulous, I have to say, and was so convincing that I nearly forgot who I was and started talking knowledgeably about taps and... and... I don't know... washing machines.' He took a biscuit. 'This has to be my last.' He popped it into his mouth in its entirety.

'Or we could go and pretend we need to examine the photography studio?' Claudia was now desperate to go and see how things were.

'Yes!' Oscar stood up. 'Let's go!'

Simon was in the middle of liaising with the lads at the printers and Mark wasn't interested, so just Claudia, Oscar and Charlie ventured forth.

'We went on strike last year because of the way we were being treated,' explained Oscar, as they walked to the lift. 'The board was bringing in all sorts of changes that Foxy was powerless to help. Our pay was cut, we had to do more advertorials, you know, paid-for editorials. It was all about making money, rather than producing an amazing magazine.

We were being turned into a corporate puff piece, with no personality.'

'When you joined, we were at a low ebb,' said Charlie. They had reached the lift and she slammed her hand on the button. 'We'd had this awful editor who just shouted all the time. Honestly, I was really worried that he was going to have a heart attack. I had a permanent headache from all the shouting.'

'I used to shout back,' said Oscar, 'which was exhausting, as you can imagine. My mother used to say I was a lover not a fighter and she was right. I'm back to being a lover now.'

'But he was under pressure from Blake it turned out,' went on Charlie. 'They wanted to get rid of *Irish Man* and said it was superfluous to requirements.'

'Imagine! Us? Superfluous!' scoffed Oscar.

'The board said that across all the magazines in Foxy Publishing, *Irish Man* was the least economically productive. *Irish Knitting* is ridiculously successful. So is *Irish Gardener*...'

'But Foxy loves *Irish Man* the best,' said Oscar, 'because it was his first...'

As the lift ascended, they looked at each other nervously.

'Why does it feel like we are committing a crime?' asked Charlie.

'Because we are?' Oscar leaned against the wall. 'Trespassing?'

'It's hardly trespassing.' Claudia's hands felt dry, her heart beating loudly in her ear, feeling a mixture of nausea and excitement. 'We're just going to listen at the door.'

The lift juddered to a halt on the fourth floor. The corridor was empty.

'The trick is to look nonchalant,' agreed Oscar. 'Channel the Artful Dodger. Or indeed a plumber.'

'Just say we're going to check out the studio,' said Charlie.

'Which is,' agreed Claudia, 'a perfectly normal thing for us to do.'

'Remember, nonchalance!' roused Oscar, as the three of them set off.

For some reason, Oscar was on tiptoes and walking with exaggerated carefulness, as though he was in a cartoon.

'Should we go back?' whispered Charlie.

Claudia was just about to answer when the door of the boardroom was flung open, and they heard a voice. 'I'll just get that for you, Cian.'

Cian manoeuvred himself out of the door, back-wards, holding a giant tray piled high with the remnants of sandwiches, biscuits and a stack of cups. The door was closed behind him and Cian turned, rebalanced the tray, and set off again, almost dropping it when he saw Claudia, Oscar and Charlie.

'We're just wondering how everything is going,' whispered Claudia.

'Poor Foxy,' said Cian, coming closer. 'They've rounded on him. There's a vote of no confidence and a motion to oust him from the board.'

The three of them looked at each other.

Claudia turned to Cian. 'Who's in there? Who's voting against him?'

'Oh, there's Dr Evil Blake Moriarty, a couple of other shareholders and that awful Dr Frankenstein Brian O'Brien. It's all boiling down to control of the business and who has the most shares. Dr Frankenstein has got something like twenty per cent, so he is the largest holder. Foxy's friends... Ernesto has five per cent and Foxy has sixteen per cent... and then Arnold Kennedy and Toby Rabbitte both have five per cent so that's still only thirty-one per cent.'

'Doesn't look good,' said Claudia.

Oscar looked downcast. 'It's the end of an era. The final curtain... the last throw of the dice... the roulette wheel of life has spun for the last time...'

Charlie elbowed Oscar in the ribs. 'Shut up!'

'I'm just trying to evoke a little pathos,' Oscar explained.

'Why doesn't he have the majority?' asked Charlie.

Cian shrugged. 'I'm not sure. Something happened a while back and he divested them... but it is what it is. I tell you something, I am not working for anyone but Foxy. Where he goes, I go. I wouldn't work for that shower of power-mad philistines.'

'Nor will I,' said Claudia.

'Nor I.' Oscar swiped one of the half-eaten sandwiches from the tray and popped it into his mouth.

'Nor me,' said Charlie. 'I'll join Scooby and his goats.'

'I've got to go and get rid of this,' said Cian. 'I'll let you know when it's all over what's going on.'

'We'd better go back then.'

Claudia turned around, Oscar and Charlie close behind. But the boardroom door squeaked open and there was Blake Moriarty. 'Ah, eavesdroppers!'

Claudia managed to smile back at him. 'We're just on our way to the photography studio...'

'Really? *All* three of you?'

'We're very much joined at the hip. All for one and one for...' Oscar petered out.

'Well, go along then, go and... do whatever it is you are claiming to do.' Blake paused. 'I'm surprised at you, Claudia. Here you are sneaking around...'

'We're not. We told you—'

'Well, I don't believe you,' said Blake.

There was another voice. 'Blake, we need to hold the vote...' And there, behind him, backlit like Elvis in Las Vegas, was Brian O'Brien. This was the man, the former friend of her father's, who had claimed there were failed investments, who took their father's shares, and made her mother pay back the losses over the last ten years. 'Blake, everything all right?'

'Yes, yes... just some interlopers from downstairs, trying to listen in...'

'We weren't,' Claudia insisted again.

'Why don't you all come in and tell us about yourselves,' said Brian, again that horrible smile, the smile she had first seen that day he'd turned up on their doorstep, looking for money. He turned his gaze on Claudia. 'What are *you* doing here?' He narrowed his eyes, trying to work out the connection with the woman who had come to his office yesterday and why she was now here in Hackett House.

'Nothing...' Confidence leached from her body.

'Ah, we're grand.' Oscar grabbed her hand and started to back away.

'We're just looking for something,' said Charlie.

'Thanks anyway,' said Oscar.

Brian and Blake stood there for a moment before turning to close the door. 'Just some employees,' they heard Blake say. 'Those awful ones from *Irish Man*. They truly are revolting.'

39

The blood was pumping through Claudia's body as she spun around, Oscar and Charlie at her heels, as she marched back to the boardroom and knocked with sweaty hands on the door.

'Come in,' said a voice.

She pushed open the door, somehow remembering to smile as she focused on the faces in the room. There was Foxy sitting to one side, with a man she presumed was his lawyer. There was Blake Moriarty, Brian O'Brien and four more faceless, besuited identikit men, in the same suits, with the same hairstyles, the same dead look in their eyes. Oscar, she realised, had come in with her, and she glanced at him and he was smiling too. Charlie was close behind.

'Good morning, gentlemen,' Oscar said. 'We apologise for this little break in transmission and I would like to present to you Ms Claudia Kelly, editor of one of the publications in Foxy Publishing, in fact the oldest one in the stable... and I think I am right in saying that *Irish Man* is Foxy's favourite magazine...' He looked over at Foxy.

'I like them all,' he said, diplomatically.

'Thank you, Foxy,' said Oscar, 'and now I leave you in the capable hands of Claudia Kelly. Take it away, Claud!' And he stepped to one side, his arm twirling in a flourish, as though introducing a music hall act.

She cleared her throat. 'Hello, everyone. I am here to give Foxy my full support.'

'I don't know who these two lunatics are,' Brian said, 'but she's obviously barking mad and have you seen the shoes that fella is wearing?'

'Excuse me,' said Oscar, 'but I am a fashion editor and these furry platform loafers are the *apogee* of style. Over your head, obviously.' He glared at Brian O'Brien, but Brian was still looking at Claudia, as though trying to place her.

She ignored him and reached into her bag and

found the Timex watch in the zipped side pocket. Turning to Foxy, she held it out. 'This,' she said gently, 'is my father's watch... do you recognise it?'

Suddenly there were tears in Foxy's eyes. He nodded, staring back at her. 'I do, yes... of course I do.'

'I found it in my father's treasure box,' Claudia continued.

'So you know?' Foxy was looking straight at her, his blue eyes now swimming with tears.

'I know...' Claudia smiled at him.

'I bought it for him, the week after he bought me this...' Foxy stood up, pushing up his sleeve. 'The same Timex watch, bought in Weir's on Grafton Street forty years ago this month.' He wiped his eyes with his sleeve. 'My brother, Philip, bought me this for my twenty-first, and I bought him the same one for his twentieth birthday a week later.' He smiled, holding his hand around his wrist. 'I think they were only twenty pounds or so. Enough money for us in those days. But...' He lifted off his fingers to show the watch's face. 'It's survived.' He walked to the front of the room and stood beside Claudia. He smiled at her, his eyes glistening with tears. 'I should have told you. I didn't want to scare you, but yes, you're my niece...'

'Well, I never!' There was a roar from Oscar, who punched the air.

Claudia felt Foxy's hand slip through her arm. She could feel him shaking and she realised that this meant far more to him than anything else. She let him hold on while she spoke. People were beginning to talk in loud whispers.

'My father was loyal to you,' said Claudia to Brian O'Brien. 'He stuck up for you in school, he took the blame, he even invested in your failing get-rich-quick schemes. You made him liable for losses...'

Brian had gathered himself and resumed his dead-man's gaze. 'It's all very basic accountancy.' He sounded almost bored.

'You aren't even a proper accountant,' said Claudia, taking a punt. 'You were expelled from school and therefore didn't go to university. How could you possibly be an accountant? You've been lying to everyone about your qualifications all your life?'

It was Brian's turn to go white and begin to splutter. 'I *am* fully qualified. I have all my certificates to prove everything...' He turned to Foxy. 'You're the real charlatan here. You didn't even see your brother before he died. *I* saw him, *I* spoke to him. We had lunch together the week before he died.'

Again Claudia took another leap. 'That was just

to put pressure on him about money,' she said. 'You didn't care about him. He always felt sorry for you...'

'He didn't.' But Brian didn't sound convinced.

Foxy let go of Claudia's arm. 'I'm so sorry, Claudia. It's true. We rowed, my precious brother and I, and we never made up in time. The guilt was awful. *Awful.* No excuses. I came to the funeral and told your mother how sorry I was, but I was so full of sadness and shame, I buried myself in work. I did put money in a trust for you and Fiona... but I couldn't change what had happened. I've been racked with guilt about it all ever since.'

'It's okay,' she said, gently. She handed him her father's watch, which Foxy turned over in his hand, as a tear splashed on its face. 'I'd do anything to bring him back. Nothing mattered but him. I lost so much. One row. About money. And we were both too proud, too stubborn to apologise and then too late.' He looked back at Claudia. 'And the years went on. I worked my bollocks off in here. All hours, the usual. Marriage gone as a result.' He shrugged. 'All my fault. All of it. And the only thing I had was this.' He gestured to the room. 'This amazing building. These amazing magazines. The wonderfully creative and intelligent and brilliant people who worked on them. The best people in this city – Bernadette on the front desk, Paulie and Marko in the post room, the teams in each magazine, our cleaners Betty and Baghwan have been with me for twenty years... *this* is my happy place. And these people here in this room dare to try to take it from me, just because they want to make money.' His voice was hard and they all saw a flash of perhaps the old Foxy, the dynamic businessperson, the man who had given everything to build an empire. 'I didn't do this for money. I did this because telling stories and creating a community of readers was a beautiful thing to do.' He looked around the room, eyeballing Brian and Blake and the other men. 'You are soulless fools who wouldn't know genuine beauty if it hit you in the face.'

He clutched his brother's watch.

'My little brother Philip bought me this. We had terrible, unloving, difficult parents who had no interest in us, and we bought each other matching watches as a symbol that we were a team. We thought we were invincible, that nothing and no one could come between us. But events, as they so often do, drove us apart and we were too young to know how to fix it. We thought we had all the time in the world. We thought we had *time* to make everything okay. But we just didn't have the skills to make it right, to make it better.' He turned back to Claudia.

'When I discovered that you were working on *Irish Woman*, it felt as though I had been given a second chance. For ages, I didn't know what to do. Should I introduce myself? Should I tell you who I was? Perhaps you already knew. And then when we needed a new editor for *Irish Man*, I took the chance to bring you in, to try to get to know you a bit better. I wasn't quite sure how... and I kept asking myself if I was wrong, if what I was doing under false pretences was ethical?'

Claudia's throat was tight. But she was not going to cry, not in front of Brian O'Brien. 'I'm glad you did. I've loved it.'

Oscar and Charlie were both wiping away tears and Oscar handed Charlie a large white handkerchief. 'She's been brilliant.' Oscar's voice was hoarse.

'If it is the end,' said Foxy, 'I feel as though we've given it our best shot. Gentlemen. Do what you will. Have your vote. Take my business. Buy me out. But I am taking Claudia, Oscar and Charlie out for lunch.' His arm was again linked through Claudia's. He was still shaking, but his voice was steady. 'Any preferences? Somewhere nice and expensive?'

'Ernie's,' said Claudia. 'I want to try that linguine.'

40

They had left Brian O'Brien and Blake Moriarty and the other board members and lawyers furiously talking together.

'I'm starving,' said Foxy. 'I can't remember the last time I've eaten.'

'It's the adrenaline, Foxy,' said Oscar. 'This is what it must feel like to be an Olympic athlete. Or a fireman. Or... I don't know... a Brown Thomas sales assistant in the January sales.'

Bernadette was waiting for them in reception, arms folded. 'Cian's just called and told me you were on your way down. What's going on? Is it over? Have you won?'

Foxy shrugged. 'Not yet, Bernie. It's in the hands of the lawyers.'

'The lawyers! Isn't everything? Foxy, I've worked for you for far too long and I need to know if I am expected to work for someone else because I'm not going to.'

Foxy smiled at her. 'If I have to go and work from my spare room...'

'...I'm coming with you,' she finished. 'I joined you when I straight out of a three-month secretarial course. The agency said they'd found me a job for some man called Foxy, and I thought, sounds like a lunatic. I bet he won't last two minutes in business...'

Foxy and Bernadette looked at each other for a moment, as though remembering all the years they'd had together. 'Maybe this is the end, finally,' he said, softly. 'It's been quite the ride.'

'What did you always used to say, Foxy?' said Bernadette. 'It was a Daniel O'Connell quote... your hero...'

'*I will go on firmly and with a certainty of success...*' Foxy smiled sadly.

'That's the one,' said Bernadette. 'Now perhaps winter isn't coming after all?'

Foxy looked at her. 'I'll let you know as soon as I

hear for certain.' He took her hand and held it in his. 'Thank you, as always.' As Bernadette discreetly wiped away a tear, Foxy turned back to Claudia, Charlie and Oscar. 'Come on, Ernie always sells out of his linguine... we'd better be quick. Will you join us, Bernadette?'

'I wouldn't leave my post, Foxy. You know me.'

Just as they turned to leave, Johnny Hogan walked through the main door, making Claudia's insides swoop like a seagull on a current. She couldn't help but smile.

'Ah, Johnny!' said Foxy. 'You're just in time for a plate of pasta. Would you like to come?'

'I don't want to crash on any meeting or whatever,' said Johnny. 'You all look as though you mean business.' Johnny met Claudia's eye.

Foxy sighed. 'No, we want to talk about anything but business... we want to eat, drink and talk inconsequentially about life, love and everything in between. Come on! Onward!'

They marched along, Johnny fell into line with Claudia. 'How are you? It sounds like it's been a very busy time?'

'I'm grand,' she said.

'You're incredible,' said Johnny. 'I don't know how you've done all this...'

She looked at him in surprise, but they had arrived at Ernie's and were making their way inside. One of the younger waiters showed them to a round table and five bowls of *linguine alla vongole* were ordered, along with two bottles of wine.

Oscar was looking around approvingly. 'Very authentic,' he was saying. 'I was in a place like this in the backstreets of Palermo.'

'I was there for my honeymoon... my wife Alison... My *ex*-wife actually,' Foxy said.

'Happy or sad divorce?' said Charlie. 'I love a happy divorce where they go off and live their best lives, get all empowered and burn bras and have passionate affairs with people half their age...'

'Mine is sad, unfortunately,' Foxy said. 'Most definitely. Alison got fed up of me, I never got fed up of her.' He turned to Johnny. 'Are you in a relationship?'

'No... single...'

'Happily or miserably?' asked Oscar.

'I'm happily single,' said Johnny. 'But it's not a state I would like to be in *forever*. I would like to be happily *not* single. It all depends on happenstance. I mean, if I was to meet someone I really liked, someone I admired and was beautiful and intelligent and also hilariously funny, then I would be happy to give up my happy bachelor ways and pursue her relentlessly.'

'Ah, the Holy Trinity...' said Oscar. 'Looks, intelligence and humour. I add in a sense of style, so I value the holy quaternity...'

They were interrupted by Ernie arriving behind them and placing the bottles on the table. 'Foxy,' he said, *'mi amico*... how is it going?'

Foxy stood up and he and Ernie hugged each other. When eventually they released, Ernie wiped away a tear.

'We'll get there,' Foxy said to him. 'Wherever *there* is. We had a meeting and Claudia here was incredible...'

Ernie beamed at her. 'Runs in the family, no? You and your Uncle Foxy...'

Claudia smiled back at him, puzzled. 'You know?'

Foxy answered her unspoken question. 'He's known all along. Ernie was there from the beginning.'

'Families are complicated,' said Ernie, pouring out the wine. 'These two brothers fell out over something silly...'

'What was it?' said Claudia. 'Dad wasn't the falling-out kind of person.'

Foxy nodded. 'He wasn't, you're right.' Foxy hesitated. 'I knew Brian O'Brien would want any money Philip got. He was always sniffing around, looking for handouts and money to put on at Punchestown races or some scheme some dodgy pal of his was running...'

'He was like something from a storybook my mother used to read me,' said Ernie. 'The kind of man that lives in a forest, all by himself and wishes illness to everyone else...'

'The pinstripe suits are dreadful,' joined in Oscar. 'So badly cut. I presume they are off the peg, because no tailor *surely* could be responsible. Except Edward Scissorhands.'

'I think he was a hairdresser,' said Claudia.

Johnny was nodding. 'And hedge cutter...' He grinned at Claudia. 'Sorry, Foxy. Do go on.'

'Well, that's what happened,' went on Foxy. 'Wracked with guilt, after investing the money into the business, I started seeing some returns. Philip and I never quite managed to reconcile. But I always thought that we would and that we had all the time in the world. Your father was a generous and kind man. Much nicer than me. I was hard, determined. Knew how to evade the masters at school. Knew how to fight and stand up for myself. It's just that I seem to have lost all those skills lately. Sometimes, I can't understand how I did it. How was I so determined? How did I succeed? Luck, I suppose. And a stubborn refusal to give in. But that shield is gone. There's nothing protecting me from the people snapping at my heels.'

'And Brian O'Brien is one of those who is snapping at your heels?'

He nodded. 'When you start a business, and things go well, the vultures start circling. They don't care about the world or the culture you created. They just want it for profit. To buy something and not love it, is so wrong.' Foxy smiled at Claudia. 'I can't tell you how sorry I am. And how much I wish it was different. As soon as I had made some profit, I gave Philip half of my inheritance and twenty per cent shares. I went round to your house. And there he was and your mother, and you had been born. Just a tiny baby. And Fiona was running around bossing everyone around...'

'She's still like that,' said Claudia.

Foxy continued, 'But your father was such a good-hearted person, which is why I think he was so hurt by the initial inheritance and my decision to keep it and invest it. And he felt sorry for Brian O'Brien. He'd been badly bullied in school, and your father had witnessed it all. It was a shared trauma, really. Boarding school ties you to each other, it really does. And when Brian came to him with an investment plan, which of course couldn't fail...'

'Automatic umbrellas,' said Ernie. 'Umbrellas that go up over your washing when it rains...'

Foxy nodded. 'The contract was signed, with a clause saying that if this business fails, the investors are liable for losses. If your father hadn't died, perhaps he could have extricated himself...'

'Why didn't you want to get to know me and Fiona?' Claudia looked back at him.

'I did,' Foxy insisted. 'I tried. I should have tried harder, I know. Your mother was grieving, you were two little girls and I was incapable of being the uncle you deserved. But I thought of you all often and I set up a small trust for you girls, but we'll talk about that again.'

Oscar patted Foxy's arm. 'If Claudia decides she doesn't want you as an uncle, then I am available for nephew duties.'

'And me,' said Charlie. 'I wouldn't mind a new uncle. The one I have is useless. Just gets drunk and shouts at everyone.'

Foxy reached into his inside pocket and withdrew the framed picture of him on his wedding day that Claudia recognised from his desk. A young Foxy, his beautiful bride Alison, the confetti being thrown.

'That's your father there,' he said, pointing to the hand just visible at the edge of the photograph. 'He was there that day that Alison and I were married at the registry office. It was a lovely day, we were all so happy... and then... well, it all went wrong.'

Claudia took the photograph and looked at her father's arm, and there on his wrist was the strap of his Timex watch.

'I can see him now, laughing, throwing the confetti.' Foxy was lost in the fragments of time.

'Which is why we need to celebrate life,' said Oscar. 'And first up is the launch party. Doheny and Nesbitt's tomorrow evening, 8 p.m. Johnny, you're our guest of honour.'

Johnny glanced at Claudia. 'Can't I just be a guest?'

'I suppose,' said Oscar, with an exaggerated sigh, 'I will just have to be the guest of honour.'

'We raise a glass,' said Ernie. 'We raise a glass to families and to making up and to lost years. And to uncles and nieces and everything else.'

They all raised their glasses of white wine. 'To uncles and nieces and everything else,' they all echoed.

Goodbyes were rushed because Oscar had to go and meet some designer in their Barrow Street loft.

Foxy was returning to consult with his lawyer. 'I will phone as soon as I hear anything,' he told Claudia, holding both her hands, and looking seriously at her. 'Maybe I could come and see your mother this evening? I would like to explain to her and listen to her side and say how sorry I am.'

Claudia nodded. 'Of course... I'll go over and you can come when it suits you.' She paused. 'The umbrella, the pen, the plant...'

'Too much?' asked Foxy.

'Fixing my puncture...'

'I just wanted to do what Philip would do for you, if he had the chance. Just mind you a bit. I don't know... it must have seemed a little over the top.'

She shook her head. 'No, it was lovely...' She smiled at him. 'Thank you.'

And then they all had to disperse hastily, Johnny rushing to a meeting, Foxy to talk to William, his lawyer, and Claudia back to work. But she was so full of thoughts, her head almost felt heavy as she made her way back to Hackett House, thinking of Foxy and everything that had happened. And him and her dad and how it was both wonderful and bittersweet that she, Fiona and Patsy had refound Foxy. That was the problem with reconciliations, sometimes they came too late. But then again, better late than never.

This last month had been quite the rollercoaster. She'd gained brand-new friends in her colleagues, had been tested professionally – and she hoped, had passed. She had even challenged Brian O'Brien and had discovered that facing your fears was the very best way of facing them down. Best of all, she'd even found an uncle. And, whatever happened with Johnny, she had allowed herself to imagine a life of love and romance, to allow her fancy to run free, to let a little bit of magic back in. It had been a wonderful time.

41

The flat was unrecognisable. Claudia hovered in the doorway, wondering if she had entered the wrong place. The surfaces gleamed, there was a smell of Pledge in the air and the sofa was actually discernible. The large rug in the living room even had little vacuum lines like Wimbledon's Centre Court. Claudia wandered around, marvelling at its transformation, and discovered Leesha in the dining area, sitting on a chair, her feet propped up on another, her hair tied up in a scarf.

'I'm exhausted,' she croaked. 'I've been cleaning all day... well, not just me... Mum sent over Precious. Precious by name, precious by nature, Mum says.

Anyway, Precious and I got stuck in and filled eight bags of rubbish.'

'It's incredible...' Claudia breathed in the fresh air. 'I can't believe it...'

Leesha sat up, placing her feet on the ground. 'However... bit of bad news. Soz and all that. But Dad is selling the flat, says it's about time I stood on my own two feet and not leeched off him, which is so unfair. So I've decided to move in with Roger, which is not what Dad had in mind, but I don't care, anything is better than going back to that solicitor's office. And anyway, Roger's not the worst prospect. *And* his family own a hotel in the Turks and Caicos...'

'That might seal the deal...'

'I know, right? So, it's happening in a month or so and soz it's such short notice, but I'll give you a reference, if you need one. You're quiet. Tidy. And not remotely annoying.'

Claudia smiled. 'Thanks. I appreciate it.'

So it was back to house-hunting and viewing the non-des res of Dublin.

As she knew Foxy was on his way over to Sandycove to see Patsy, Claudia wanted to be there to greet him so she made her way to the station, the papers from the treasure box still in her bag. When she called Fiona from the train, Fiona sounded slightly muffled, as though she was in a cupboard. 'I'm in the car! And I've got every single thing of mine with me because I'm moving back in with Mum. I've left John-Paul. He was as relieved as me. I can't see out of any of the windows, but if I crash, it's fine, because I am surrounded by all my bedding.'

'Are you okay?'

'I'm grand. I feel bad for John-Paul, obviously. But he'll be fine. He now can go and meet someone who loves him properly. He cried and then I cried, but we hugged it out...'

'You *hugged* it out? *Crying*? What's happened to you?'

'I've grown a heart, I think. That, or guilt has got the better of me. And another thing, I've decided to hand in my notice. Not only do I hate my job, but it means I never have to see Cameron again. I need a fresh start. Oh God. I completely forgot. What about Foxy? Did you talk to him?'

'That's why I'm calling. He *is* our uncle!'

'Oh my fecking God!'

'Yes! And he's coming over to Mum's this evening and I'm on my way.'

'Jaysus!'

'I know!'

'How's the business and everything?'

'Not great...'

'Poor Foxy...'

It was amazing how quickly family feeling kicked in.

When Claudia arrived at Patsy's, Fiona was standing by her open boot staring at the boxes inside. 'I feel overwhelmed,' she said. 'I don't think I can face the unpacking.'

'Come on, we'll do it together.'

They made dozens of trips from the car to their old bedroom, placing boxes and rugs and lamps and framed pictures in a huge pile on Claudia's old bed. Finally, Fiona collapsed on her bed. 'It's like I never left.'

Claudia perched on the very edge of her old bed. 'My flat's being sold, so I might have to move back in as well.'

'Oh God. You can't! We'd kill each other.'

'We used to kill each other then, as well...'

'Do you still read late at night with the light on?'

'Do you still snore?'

'I never did!' Fiona threw Claudia's old teddy, Edward, at her. Claudia grabbed him.

'Poor Edward! Leave him alone!'

'Maybe we'll never meet anyone,' said Fiona. 'Maybe we've had our chances and things haven't worked out... and we're destined to live with Mum for the rest of our lives...?'

It did seem increasingly likely, thought Claudia, just as Patsy knocked on the bedroom door.

'Ready for dinner? It's just cheese on toast...'

Over dinner, Fiona began to cry. 'I love cheese on toast. It's my favourite...' Fiona's emotional side had been brought back to life, as though it had been dinosaur DNA in amber. 'What if John-Paul never marries *anyone* and I have *that* on my conscience forever? What if I've ruined his life? I thought I knew what my future looked like. I thought we'd have children and a driveway and we'd wear matching fleeces.'

Claudia laughed. 'That's what you *wanted*?'

'No! Of course not! That's what I assumed would happen! I was on a life trajectory and it was nice. I knew where I was. And I've ruined everything and now you'll never be a grandmother.'

Patsy didn't seem too worried. 'We'll buy a kitten. That will be enough.' She smiled at Fiona. 'Do you know something? We're just going to get on with our lives. That's all. And I think we're going to be okay. You can't ever plan your future. I learned that when I lost your father. Life is happening now, not tomorrow or five years, or ten.'

'Thanks, Mum.' Fiona wiped her eyes, as the doorbell rang.

Claudia had forgotten all about Foxy and she hadn't prepared Patsy for any of this. 'It's Foxy...'

'Who?' Patsy looked confused, as the doorbell rang again.

'Our *uncle*... Come on, let's go and meet him...'

The three of them went to answer the door together. But it wasn't Foxy. It was Dom.

He looked a little taken aback by seeing Patsy, Fiona and Claudia together. 'Do you always answer the door as a trio?'

'Always,' said Fiona. 'You never know who might knock.'

'I came to find you,' he said, looking at Claudia. 'I didn't think it would be so easy.'

'I'll explain to Mum about our new uncle Foxy,' said Fiona, melting way with Patsy, leaving Dom and Claudia alone.

Dom smiled his winning, full-frontal toothy smile. 'How've you been?'

'Grand.'

There were so many other conversations she wanted to have and Dom was definitely the last person on her list.

'Well, *I've* been terrible,' he carried on. 'Lonely,

unhappy, miserable. You see, a year ago, I lost my best friend...'

Claudia was confused. Who on earth did he mean?

'You. *You're* my best friend. You were always my best friend, being good to me and caring about me. No one else has ever made me laugh as much.'

'Really?' Claudia couldn't recall Dom laughing very much.

He nodded. 'At first, I liked being alone. The quiet. No radio on. Being able to leave the toilet seat up or my running kit in the hall.' As far as Claudia knew, he had never run for anything more than last orders. 'But the flat was really empty without you... and...' He paused. 'Well, it was this that made me think of you. You know your plants...?'

'Yes...'

'They're all dead.'

'*All* of them? My orchids?'

He nodded.

'My ficus? My lemon tree?'

'All.' He smiled again, as though it didn't matter. 'Dead. Anyway, I thought that if the plants were dead, maybe I should try to revive *us*. I realised I didn't want us to die. In fact...' There was that off-putting toothy smile again. 'Look, we can buy more plants; you can have as many as you want. Within reason. No more than four. But I've been thinking... a lot. And well, I'm thirty-three now and I would like to get married...'

'To who?'

He laughed. 'See, you're so funny. To *you*, of course!'

'Me?' He was obviously mad.

'I am very fond of you, fonder than I've been of anyone... ever. And I suppose I love you.'

'You *suppose* you *love* me?'

He nodded. 'I suppose I do.'

Claudia realised he was under the misapprehension that this was a romantic moment, worthy of a Richard Curtis film, something they would tell their future grandchildren about.

'No, thank you.'

'What do you mean? *Yes* thank you or *no* thank you?'

'I mean, no thank you very much.' She looked at him. 'Dom, I can't believe you would think I would be happy to marry someone who killed all my houseplants...'

'I didn't *kill* them,' he insisted. 'It was an accident. Manslaughter... plantslaughter *not* murder.'

'Whatever.'

Now it was his turn to look incredulous. 'But lots of women would do anything to swap with you. I'm quite good-looking, I'm intelligent, solvent... good company...'

'Can't keep a plant alive, though, can you?'

'Will you stop going on about the plants!' His voice went squeaky.

He really wasn't getting it. Claudia liked her life as it was *now* – her precarious, uncertain life. She had nowhere to live, she wasn't even sure she had a job and she had no idea about what Johnny felt about her. All she knew for sure was that she was pressing on without Dom. And she was excited. She had woken up every day for the last month with some kind of butterflies in her stomach, the scared kind, the excited ones, the happy ones. The butterflies she now felt were the brave, adventurous sort, the kind that make you feel invincible and invulnerable, the kind that would have you running around Fitzwilliam Square late at night, not caring how you looked or what you said, because all you knew was that it was good to be alive.

'You said that you didn't have strong enough feelings for me...'

He laughed. 'That was then. I've changed. I do have strong feelings for you. *Good* ones...'

'But I don't have any feelings for you. I mean, I hope you're well and happy, I hope you have a good life, I hope you learn how to take care of plants and I hope you find your Ms Right. But she's not me.'

He hesitated. 'I'm crushed. I'm not too proud to admit it.'

'You'll be fine.' Claudia smiled at him. 'Have a nice life.'

And a nice life was exactly what she was determined to have for herself.

42

Claudia had just closed the door on Dom when the sound of a taxi pulling up outside was heard. She quickly called for Patsy and Fiona and the three of them stood at the door, to welcome Foxy, as if this was the only way they ever answered the door now.

Foxy looked straight at Patsy, holding out his hands. 'I'm so sorry. I wish I could change everything...'

Patsy took his hands in hers. 'I understand. Your parents... it was difficult...'

'Not a day has gone by without me missing him or wishing I could pick up the phone and talk to him...'

His voice broke a little, as they embraced, Patsy murmuring, 'Me too, Frank... me too.'

'I wish I'd been better...'

'He knew you loved him. I promise.'

'Really?'

'Really.'

Foxy then turned to Fiona, holding out his hand. 'Fiona?'

And Fiona, who wasn't usually a hugger but had her new dinosaur DNA, opened her arms, throwing them around him. 'I'm so glad you're finally here.'

Foxy's eyes were glistening with tears.

They brought him inside to the living room, where they sat facing each other, Foxy on the edge of the sofa, seemingly with a lot to say. He had Patsy's hand in one of his.

'It was the most wonderful, serendipitous moment,' he explained, turning to Claudia. 'I saw you one day and I stopped in my tracks. I saw Philip's face... I remember it so clearly. And so, Bernie, my faithful Bernadette, well, I had her do some detective work. Her father was a detective sergeant of the Gardaí at Kevin Street, so I knew she'd be like a bloodhound and then we were surer than sure. But I was stunned, however, when I found out. A patch of sunlight in a very dark time and it gave me hope and something of a spring in my step. Philip was looking down on me and perhaps he had forgiven me.'

Patsy smiled at Foxy. 'Oh, he wasn't a grudge-bearer, was he?'

'No, not at all. Instead, I had to learn to forgive myself... If only—'

'We can torment ourselves with the if onlys,' said Patsy. 'I decided a long time ago that I had to just focus on where we were right now. Philip loved me and the girls and he loved you, Frank... *Foxy*...' They smiled at each other. 'And here we are *right now*... Philip would be so happy if he knew.'

'Oh, he does know. I know he knows. I can feel it. And being here, in his home... well...' Foxy teared up again, gazing over at the photograph of Philip on the mantelpiece for a moment. 'It almost feels like he's right here.'

'In many ways, he never left.' Patsy patted his arm. 'Now, some tea or something stronger?'

'Something stronger, if that wouldn't be too imposing...?' Foxy picked up the bag he'd put down beside him. 'I have a bottle of chilled champagne. Forget about losing the business... and just celebrate me finding you all again.'

Fiona went to the kitchen to find the glasses and Foxy stood at the mantelpiece, peering at some more of the photographs. He stared intently at a photograph of Philip. 'He definitely got the lion's share of the handsome genes.'

When Fiona came in with a tray of glasses and the champagne, he and Fiona set up a little production line of filling and handing out the glasses, before he stood to make a toast.

'Philip was the brave one out of the two of us. He was one of life's good guys. He allowed himself to feel things, to be caring and compassionate. He was in touch with his own humanity...'

'His vulnerability,' suggested Claudia, thinking of how horrible Brian O'Brien had been and what he'd said about her lovely dad.

'Exactly.' Foxy smiled at her. 'He wasn't afraid to be himself. I was. So, to Philip. My beloved brother, your beloved husband and father. You are missed... we love you...'

It was a small ceremony of love and remembrance.

'What's wrong with me lately?' Fiona said, wiping away a tear. 'I've become an emotional wreck.'

'Me too, Fiona,' said Foxy, handing her his clean handkerchief. 'I missed out on so much, that business took up every ounce of energy I had. Now I know that the only thing that matters is... *this*. I mean, I lost my marriage because of my inability to prioritise Alison... she went to Alicante...'

Foxy looked a little defeated, as he sat sipping his champagne.

'She *left* you?' Patsy looked surprised. 'I remember the wedding. It was such a lovely day. You were mad about each other.'

'We were... and I'm still crazy about her. But she needed a change, freedom... not sat waiting for me every day.'

'So what are you going to do, Foxy?' asked Claudia.

Foxy looked over at her. 'I'm tired. I've had enough of all this. Even magazines. I have to say it's been wonderful working with you. Your ideas and enthusiasm reminded me of me, in the early days. Back then, I thought of nothing but the magazines... it was as though I was on some endless wave, surfing on sheer adrenaline and exhilaration. And now... Not so much.'

Fiona nodded. 'I think you're right, Foxy. In business, my mantra is never stay fighting if the fight is gone. You need to want to be in the ring, you need to be able for the punches, relish them, be ready to dodge them and fight back. But if you're not feeling it, if your heart's not in it, then get out.'

He nodded. 'You're exactly right, Fiona.'

'There is nothing I like more than rolling up my sleeves and getting in the ring,' said Fiona. 'But not if my heart's not in it and I don't want to see blood on the floor, readying myself for my victory lap. I just walk away. Let them have it. I'll find a fight I want to win.'

Claudia and Patsy exchanged impressed looks. They weren't used to seeing Fiona in corporate mode.

Foxy seemed impressed too. 'I used to have that fight in me. I used to love the downs as much as I loved the ups. My lawyer, William, doesn't rate my chances considering the vote of no confidence is going to go through. And so... I'm going to go to Alicante. See if I still have a chance with Alison.'

* * *

Later, when they'd all waved Foxy off in a taxi, Claudia was washing the glasses in the kitchen and Patsy was drying. 'After all these years. Frank... I mean *Foxy* is so like your father. Louder, obviously.

But the same face, the way he crinkles his forehead, his voice is exactly the same.'

Claudia nodded. She could see it too.

Patsy hesitated. 'I just want to say that I am not replacing your father with Alan. But it's nice to have someone to go for a walk with, a coffee... a chat. And he's a very interesting man. He's not your father, certainly. But... if I just think of him as entirely different, completely separate. Not a *replacement*... or a consolation prize. But a new phase...'

'A *nice* phase...'

'Yes, a nice phase.' Patsy seemed satisfied, as though she'd been wrestling with this and finally had resolved it in her mind. She smiled at Claudia. 'Sometimes you need permission in life to enjoy things, don't you? You need people to tell you to go for things or to reassure you that you're doing the right thing? It's so hard doing everything on your own. You just need a few cheerleaders along the way.'

* * *

Later, in their two single beds, Claudia and Fiona lay in the dark, their old bedroom as cluttered as Leesha's flat before the great tidy-up. From downstairs, they could hear Patsy talking on the telephone.

'Who's she calling at midnight?'

'Probably Dr Alan.' Fiona rolled onto her side, to face Claudia. 'So are we both going to live here? *Together*? Although I won't be staying long. I'll find a flat... a little one-bed, just for me. I'm dying to live on my own.' She paused. 'You know how John-Paul was perfect...'

'And nice...'

'Well... he was a bit too perfect... he didn't like me leaving my clothes on the chair in the bedroom.'

'The chair-robe?'

'That's right. And he was paranoid about crumbs. Hated them. I used to try to remove them from the butter in a kind of panic that he would find one... and I had to squeegee the shower screen every time I used it and if he found the slightest evidence that a human had been in it, he would lecture me.'

'Good grief...'

Fiona sighed. 'They aren't the worst crimes, though.' She paused. 'He also had to sleep with the window slightly ajar, even in winter, and so I would wrap myself up with hot-water bottles, pyjamas and socks and he would say just looking at me made him overheat. And he hated the heating on; we were constantly in a battle over the thermostat. Which he *always* won. And he used to go quiet on me. He didn't like conflict. Probably something to do with his parents. So he just wouldn't speak, for days on end. He once didn't speak to me for six days. I would be begging and begging and then he'd kind of snap out of it.'

'So not that nice, then?'

'I think that I needed to blow up our relationship, that it was driving me a bit mad.'

'I'm glad you did blow it up. He doesn't sound remotely perfect...'

'We all have our foibles... I'm making him out to be a monster. He's still the nicest person I've ever met. I just saw him as this saintly figure who was so much better than me and so of course I was going to sabotage it...'

'Or maybe you just weren't that into him?'

'Maybe...'

'Johnny said...'

'Who's Johnny?'

'Johnny from next door...'

'Johnny *Hogan*? He's *back*?'

'We've been... hanging out a little...'

'Have you now?'

'Nothing like that. Just we had dinner...'

'DINNER?'

'And he is on the cover of *Irish Man*... and *he's* really nice.'

'Always was. Is he as handsome as ever?'

'More.'

'*More*?'

Claudia nodded. 'Very much so.' She felt embarrassed talking about it, but it had been building up inside her for the past week and now she had to tell someone. 'He's just so gorgeous. He's fun, but so wise and intelligent...'

'He sounds perfect... but not too perfect, I hope.'

She could almost hear Fiona smiling in the dark. 'But,' said Claudia, 'I suspect he's out of my league...'

'That's ridiculous,' said Fiona. 'He most certainly isn't. I thought John-Paul was out of my league, I thought he was better and nicer and everything more than me, but that makes you just pathetically grateful and I don't want to be *grateful* that someone likes me. I want passion and excitement and someone not being able to take their hands off me and talking incessantly and happiness and joy.' Fiona's eyes were shining in the darkness. 'That's what I want. I can't tell you the relief I feel now it's over between me and John-Paul.' Fiona was beginning to fall asleep, her voice heavy. 'Love you, Claud.'

'Love you, Fi.'

43

Claudia slipped out of Sandycove before her mother or Fiona were awake, stopping for a takeaway tea and some buttered soda bread in Murphy's lovely deli on her way to the station. Holding her bike as the train rattled along the coast from Sandycove to the city, she thought of Foxy and she thought of her dad. This was the train he used to bring her and Fiona on when he'd taken them to the museum to spy the hoards of ancient gold and the bog bodies and the treasures of Irish life, before heading to Bewley's for a hot chocolate and a cherry bun. From the window, there was the ever-changing vista of sea and shore, choppy and grey, the white foam rolling endlessly towards the large expanse of sand, the birds in the shallows and shafts of sunlight. Time moved on and, then again, it didn't. You were forever that small girl holding her father's hand, on your way for a trip into town.

Just as she was locking her bike outside Hackett House, her phone rang. It was her mother.

'Sorry I didn't say goodbye this morning...' Claudia began but seemingly Patsy didn't have time for pleasantries.

'Do you have the treasure box with you?'

'The box? No, it's at home... why?'

'I need the papers... I can't believe I didn't think of it before. But talking to Foxy...' She trailed off. 'So you have them somewhere safe?'

'Yes, they're in my bag. I took out them out of the box. It was too big to carry around...'

But Patsy was obviously busy. 'Thank you, darling, I'll see you soon.' And she was gone, like a woman on a mission. Except, what exactly was the mission?

'Claudia!' She turned to see Johnny crossing the road towards her, smiling at her. 'I've been worried about all of you. I was going to call. And then I thought I might catch you before work.' He smiled. 'I don't know what's wrong with me but all I can think about is what's happening in there...' He jerked his head towards the glass doors of Hackett House, laughing, almost embarrassed and as though he was trying to make up an excuse for being there at this early hour.

Right, she had to focus. 'Foxy came...' she began, but Johnny was speaking.

'I've been thinking...' He stopped, to wait for her.

'You go first,' she insisted.

'No, you. Please.'

Her words came out in a rush. 'Foxy came to see us last night. Me, Mum and Fiona... he's our uncle...' She laughed suddenly at the absurdity of it all. 'I haven't told you. Fiona and I only worked it out from Dad's old watch. It's why he wanted me to edit the magazine...'

'Your Dad's *brother*?'

'Yes, *Uncle* Foxy... it's unbelievable, isn't it? But... he's decided not to try and defeat the board. If they are going to vote him out, he's going to let them. Before he was trying to find some kind of legal route into protecting himself. But poor Foxy says he's done. Doesn't want it any more... which means, Brian O'Brien has won. Again.'

Johnny was shaking his head. 'Wait, you've

skipped over too much. How and when... and, Jaysis, this is... *incredible*...'

'I know. I'll fill you in later...'

'I feel involved now.' He smiled at her. 'Or maybe I've made myself involved. Forced myself upon you...'

Her eye was caught by the sight of Bernadette, inside reception and behind the desk, through the glass, waving her in urgently. Johnny followed her in.

Bernadette looked desperate. 'Will someone for the love of the Holy God and Blessed Virgin Mary and all the saints including Joseph and that awful one, tell me what is going on? Foxy arrived even before me, according to Sam on security. His lawyer was next, and then now all those other besuited goons have arrived and it's not even 10 a.m. That big one with the yellow teeth, your man with the ears, the little pixie fella with the red face and then that pinstriped horror with the boot-polish hair. And of course, Mr Slime himself Blake Moriarty... so tell me what's going on. You know, I know you do.' Bernadette fixed Claudia with a look. 'I am burning up with not knowing. I couldn't sleep a wink for thinking about it all...'

Claudia didn't want to say that Foxy had said he was giving up, but she suddenly felt so sad about him and everything he had put into his business, and she thought about her father Philip and wished that he was here to have helped his brother. Claudia opened her mouth and then realised that Amanda had walked into reception behind her. She was smiling.

'Ah, Claudia... I hear that things are not going well for poor old Foxy... poor lamb. It sounds like a nightmare for him. Blake was telling me it's a mess...' She gave a laugh. 'Oh, I did warn you, didn't I? But did you listen? It could have all been done with so much less heartache for poor old Foxy.'

Claudia was about to open her mouth but instead Johnny started speaking. 'Sorry? Who are you?'

Amanda was looking at him, blinking for a moment. '*Johnny Hogan*? Oh my God. It *is* you.' Amanda gave another laugh. 'Johnny Hogan the... well, the very talented...' Claudia had never seen her so animated. '...the *renowned* Johnny Hogan. So, what are you doing here?' She looked from Johnny to Claudia, a little puzzled.

'I'm Claudia's friend,' said Johnny, shuffling closer to Claudia.

'Friend?'

Johnny nodded. 'We go back a long way.'

At that moment, the lift doors opened and Marko

from the post room exited backwards, manoeuvring a trolley stacked with magazines. Johnny's face was on the top one.

'Ah, *Irish Man!*' said Bernadette. 'Leave one for me, Marko, thank you.'

'We'd better go,' said Claudia.

Bernadette's phone rang again. 'Yes, she's here, actually. Okay... straight away.' She looked at Claudia. 'You're wanted. In the boardroom.' She thrust a pile of magazines into Claudia's hands as she went by. 'Good luck.'

'What is going on?' said Amanda. 'I mean, what the hell is happening here? Does Blake know? I'm calling him.' She took her phone out. 'I'm dialling... it's ringing... still ringing...'

Bundling the magazines to her chest, Claudia tried to think clearly, as she and Johnny stepped into the lift. Why did Foxy want her? Moral support? *Familial* support? A friendly face?

The lift doors began to close.

'It's still ringing...' Amanda was saying. 'He doesn't seem to be answering. Perhaps it's on silent... or...'

The lift began to ascend. This job, the one she had just done for the last month, was a kind of one-in-a-million role. She had loved leading a team, shaping the stories, exploring life and love and everything in between. And as for Foxy, she realised that she wanted to help him, the same way he'd helped her father with the money all those years ago. And if he was giving up, then she certainly wasn't. But most of all, it was as though she had found what she'd been looking for. She'd found an actual, real-life *uncle*.

The lift doors opened to reveal Cian. 'Claudia...' He gaped a little when he saw Johnny behind her. 'It's you,' he said. 'J-Johnny H-Hogan...' Cian's usual calm was ruffled briefly.

'Is it okay if I go with Claudia?' asked Johnny, sweetly.

'Of course. Go right ahead.' Cian smiled, smoothness restored. 'Go right ahead.' His phone rang. 'Who? Claudia's *mother* and *sister*?' He held the phone away. 'Two women claiming to be your mother and sister are downstairs. Patsy and Fiona? Can you verify their identity?'

Claudia nodded. 'They are definitely my mother and my sister.'

'Send them up,' said Cian into his phone, as Claudia and Johnny pressed on. Outside the board-room, Claudia paused.

Johnny smiled at her. 'What if you love it?'

This was it, nerves gave way to adrenaline which powered her into the boardroom, closely followed by Johnny Hogan, the renowned and exceptionally handsome artist.

'I think I do,' she said. 'I really think I do.'

44

Foxy was sitting at the large table, next to his lawyer. And on the other side were all the 'goons', as Bernadette called them: the pixie-faced one, the one with the huge yellow teeth, Blake and his gilet and, of course, Brian O'Brien.

He stared at her with unconcealed revulsion. 'Not you again. Why do *you* keep turning up?'

'I work here. What's *your* reason?'

'So why aren't you working?'

Foxy interrupted. 'Brian, would you mind not speaking to Claudia like that? Claudia is here at my behest. She is the employee I trust most in this organisation...'

Brian looked at him, knowing the reason for this implicit trust.

'I am happy to answer Brian O'Brien's question,' said Claudia. 'The reason why I am here is to make sure the board doesn't vote Foxy off. But why are you here? Why do you want to control this company? You have no interest in magazines... your specialty is novelties such as automatic umbrellas or crisp bag holders...'

One of the suits, a beaky-nosed man, pulled a face. 'A *crisp bag* holder...?'

Brian O'Brien turned to him. 'She is referring to my many investments over the years. Some have been more successful than others. The crisp bag holder was just *one* idea...' He glared at Claudia. 'Look, we are about to vote on the future of Foxy Publishing and you're holding us up.'

'Let's get going.' Blake sighed. 'There's been too much disruption. Can we crack on?'

There was a knock on the door and Patsy and Fiona were shown inside by Cian.

'Patsy, Fiona...' Foxy stood up. 'Everything all right?'

'Perfectly,' said Patsy, smoothly. 'Claudia, the papers, please...'

Claudia handed them over as Patsy began shuffling through them. 'Birth cert, driving licence, motorcycle licence... right... here we go...' Patsy held up a piece of paper. 'I suppose I should start at the beginning... if you would indulge me.' She smiled at them all. 'I have in my hand what is known as a share certificate. Frank, do you recognise this?' She handed it to Foxy, who slipped on his reading glasses and peered at it.

'I gave this to Philip, my brother...'

'That's right. Philip, my husband. Fiona and Claudia's wonderful father...'

'I gave him twenty per cent of shares in *Irish Man*,' Foxy went on, squinting at the certificate.

Brian was on his feet and was rushing forward, towards Patsy. 'You told me fifteen per cent!'

Patsy smiled at him. 'I must have got my sums wrong... bearing in mind, Brian, that I have paid you what amounts to thousands of euro over the years. Thousands. Do you remember? All that debt I was apparently liable for?'

'Go on, Mum,' urged Fiona, with another dig in the ribs.

'Well, Brian O'Brien was pretty keen to get his hands on Philip's shares and for some reason... maybe I was too grief-stricken to think clearly or maybe I was just confused... who knows?' She smiled sweetly at Brian who was now tomato with rage. 'I told him that Philip only had fifteen per cent of shares in Frank's, I mean Foxy's business. When in fact he had twenty per cent. I kept five per cent of them.' She smiled at Foxy. 'I hope you don't mind...'

Foxy shrugged, shaking his head, taking it all in. 'Of course not...'

Blake had turned to Brian. 'What the actual...?'

But Brian was staring daggers at Patsy. 'I knew it! I just knew something was going on when you sent your silly daughter around to me. I KNEW you two were cooking something up... You lied!' Brian was increasingly hysterical. 'Which is perjury at best, downright criminal at worst!'

Claudia stepped in. 'My mother didn't lie, she was just...'

'...economical with the truth,' said Fiona, pushing her way forward, forcing Brian O'Brien to take a step backwards.

'She said she gave me all your father's shares...' Brian stuttered. 'She gave me them in lieu of money... that your father owed. That investment...'

'Ha! That pointless, pathetic investment?' laughed Claudia. 'An umbrella that opens when it rains?'

'We live in the rainiest country in the world,'

Brian insisted. 'It was a no-brainer. We were going to make a fortune on them... it wasn't my fault that the agreement meant you were obliged to pay all debts if it failed. And your mother, as his beneficiary, was liable... and she lied! She told me that she would give me *all* the shares... I reduced the money as a result...'

Now Foxy turned on him. 'You told me Patsy had given you *all* of them.'

'I thought I did have them. I was misled...' Brian threw a deadly look at Patsy. 'By this criminal here.'

'Sorry about that,' said Patsy, coolly.

'Did you not look at them?' asked Blake to Brian. 'Did you not read the bleeding small print?'

'Of course I did. It said fifteen per cent and I thought it was enough to get me on the board... Blake, you *have to* believe me.' He put up his hand to try and grab on to Blake but only managed in clinging on to the top of his gilet. Blake shook him off.

'So...' Blake was thinking out loud, doing his sums in his head. 'That's... how many...'

'What the hell is going on?' roared Brian O'Brien.

The two lawyers were whispering together. Claudia was also trying to add up in her head how many shares the board had and how many Foxy and his side had. Would that loss of five per cent push it to their favour?

Foxy turned to Claudia, his eyes suddenly shining, and began to laugh. He turned to the lawyer. 'Tell me, what do you think?'

'Well, we need to check with the share registry service, but these should have been handed over if a new owner was to claim. I don't think any transference of shares was legal. But until we're able to check, I can't say for sure. But if the shares were not transferred legally and the fifteen per cent that Mr O'Brien claims to own are not his, then they are all in your brother's estate's possession and Mr O'Brien does not own a single share.'

Claudia looked at Foxy. 'Dad's shares, plus yours... Arnie's, Ernie's, Toby's... is that enough?'

The lawyer called from the back of the room, 'It gets us over the fifty-one per cent.'

'Does it now?' Foxy was still smiling, his arm now around Patsy and Fiona. 'How interesting... that kind of shifts the power.'

The lawyer nearly smiled. 'I think, Foxy, that we can take it from here.'

Blake thrust his face into Brian's, his nostrils quivering, spit spraying. '*You* lied! *You* told me you had more than you have. You promised me. Do you think I would do a deal with *you*? Do you honestly think I would have *you* as a business partner? It's over! It's fecking over!'

He went to grab at Brian O'Brien's neck but as Brian tried to protect his face his arm swept around and glanced off a cup of coffee on the table which flicked up and circled in the air, its contents spraying all over Blake.

'My GILET!'

One of the goons handed over a raft of paper napkins which Blake ineffectively mopped his gilet with, fixing Brian with a murderous look. 'Jesus... it's destroyed. It's over...'

'It's a *gilet*, Blake,' said Brian. 'It's replaceable.'

'No, it's destroyed. I can't go round with coffee stains. Have you *tried* removing coffee from clothes? But I tell you what else is finito and that's our bid. We don't have the power to vote for anything. So... I'm out. I resign from the board and as editor-in-chief and as the CFO.'

Foxy looked at him silently while Patsy slipped her arm around Claudia. 'Okay?'

Claudia nodded.

'The rest of the board...' Blake turned to the other men in the room. 'Resign or stay? All those in favour of resigning, put up your hands?'

The five members of the board raised their right hands.

'Brian?' said Foxy. 'Although technically you had no business to be on the board.'

'I resign too,' said Brian, sulkily.

Johnny, Fiona and Patsy had their arms around each other, jumping up and down, as though Ireland had just scored a goal.

Foxy cleared his throat. 'Well, gentlemen, I'm glad that's cleared up. And those who will be selling their shares, please talk to my lawyer today and we can have this deal done as soon as possible. Okay with you, William?'

His lawyer nodded, handing out his card to the board members.

'And gentlemen,' continued Foxy, 'if you wouldn't mind vacating the building, please? We've got some cleaning up to do. Security will show you all out. Cian?' Cian's head immediately popped around the door. 'Ask Sam to organise security to escort these gentlemen from the building and Blake can clear his desk.'

Cian nodded, already on his phone.

Once the goons had filed out, Claudia and Foxy grinned at each other.

'So you're not giving up?' said Claudia. 'You're *not* going to Alicante?'

'Oh, I'm *still* going to Alicante. I want my Alison back. If she'll have me, of course. But I have to try. But...' He paused. 'I know who I want to appoint as the new CEO. My *other* wonderful niece, Fiona Kelly. Fiona, you told me last night that you needed a new challenge. I wonder if you would like to accept a role as CEO here at Foxy Publishing?'

Fiona smiled. 'Why don't we give it a go?'

'And Claudia, hopefully, will remain as editor and also editor-in-chief? I want to keep it in the family. Just like I should have done with Philip, all those years ago.' His eyes shone again with tears. 'I can direct operations from Alicante. Working part-time. Joining Alison's yoga glasses. A cava or two at happy hour.'

There was a knock on the door. Cian poked his head inside, still smiling. 'A visitor, Foxy.'

And then, stepping into the boardroom, was a beautiful woman in her early sixties, with ash-blonde hair, dressed in smart jeans, flat sandals and a black sleeveless top... showing toned and tanned yoga arms.

'Alison!' Foxy launched himself on her, his arms around her, his head pressed into her, making muffled sounds, while Alison clutched back at him, her face pressed into him. Finally, Foxy lifted his head, his eyes red, gazing at Alison, as though she was some miraculous vision. 'How did you? When did you?'

'Patsy called last night,' said Alison, gazing back. 'I took the first flight this morning.'

'Come on,' said Patsy. 'Let's leave them for a moment.'

45

Patsy, Fiona, Claudia and Johnny filed out and piled into the lift, talking excitedly.

'You were magnificent,' said Johnny to Claudia.

'Wasn't she just!' said Patsy.

'You all were,' said Johnny.

'And *you* called Alison and told her to come back to Dublin?' said Fiona to her mother.

'Her number was on her yoga website, and I didn't know what I was going to say, just thought she might like to know what we knew...'

'So what happens now?' asked Johnny.

'I'd better get back to *Irish Man*,' said Claudia, as the lift opened on the third floor, 'and bring them up to speed.'

'And we're returning my wedding dress,' said Fiona.

'So, you've left work...? You'll never see Cameron again...' asked Claudia.

'Who?' Johnny looked between them. 'Was he the man I met you with who wasn't your fiancé?'

Fiona nodded; tears in her eyes. 'I miss him...'

'Which one?' asked Patsy. 'John-Paul or Cameron?'

'Cameron.' Fiona wiped her eyes. 'I feel like my heart is broken...'

'Call him then,' said Johnny.

'I can't,' said Fiona, agonised. 'I said I wouldn't. I promised John-Paul I wouldn't. We both agreed. I've left work. I have to start again... except... I miss him.' A tear rolled down her face, as Patsy placed an arm around her.

'It's not easy to say goodbye to someone,' she soothed. 'I know...'

'But this isn't like he's dead,' wailed Fiona. 'He's alive and well. And will probably go off and meet some very nice woman and live happily ever after while I get all wizened and bitter and live in a house full of things I have bought in the charity shop until I can't leave the house because the front door is blocked.' She took a breath for air, glancing at Johnny. 'I'm sorry. I'm not normally like this.'

'No, she really isn't,' agreed Claudia, trying to think what to say, but Johnny got there first.

'Call him. Call this Cameron. Tell him what you told us. You miss him. See what he says. You have nothing to lose. Your heart is already broken, it can't get much worse...'

Fiona shook her head. 'No... it can't... but I promised.'

'Promised!' said Patsy. 'You were economical with the truth, that's all! I agree with Johnny. Call him.'

Fiona turned to Claudia. 'What do you think?'

'Call him!' She grinned at Fiona. 'What have you got to lose?'

'But...' Fiona's lip wobbled, her eyes big. 'I don't want a small life, I don't want to stay in my box, being good, being nice, doing the right thing. I want to live...'

'So, call him,' said Johnny. 'Live big, live large. You deserve more than a small life. Or just buying stuff from charity shops. Take risks. Get out there. Because...' He glanced at Claudia.

'...what if you love it?' she said, making Johnny laugh.

Fiona nodded. 'I will call him. After I return the wedding dress.'

'I think that's the right order of things,' agreed Patsy.

Claudia turned to Johnny. 'There's a party tonight...'

'Oscar has already told me.' He smiled at her. 'I'll see you later... if that's all right with you.' He looked straight at her and she felt something crackle in the air.

'Yes,' she said, looking straight back at him. 'It most certainly is.'

'And we'll be there,' said Patsy, slipping her arm through Fiona's.

'And Dr Alan *has* to come, Mum,' said Fiona, who had brightened up slightly. 'If he's to be our new stepfather...'

'So there will be a wedding after all!' said Claudia. 'Fi, no need to return your dress. Just give it to Mum.'

'Girls,' said Patsy, rolling her eyes. 'That's quite enough.' She turned to Johnny. 'Honestly, the two of them never stop acting the maggot again.'

Fiona was smiling again, thankfully.

'I'd better go,' said Claudia reluctantly, pressing the lift button, wishing she didn't have to leave, knowing that these three people were very much her favourite people. Even Johnny, who she'd only re-known for the last month, was the one person she wanted to see later.

The lift door closed behind her, as she stepped onto the third floor, trying to focus and breathe, she marched straight into the office.

Simon looked up. 'Finally!'

'Halle-bloody-luia!' said Oscar.

'At last!' Charlie had a half-anxious, half-hopeful expression on her face. 'So, what's the news? Do we still have jobs?'

'I think so.' Claudia sat down, clutching her dad's Timex watch. The strap had broken and she realised that she had been holding it on all this time.

'So, tell us,' said Oscar. 'What's going on?'

'Foxy won,' said Claudia, to cheers from the team. Simon grabbed Oscar in some kind of head-lock, Charlie jumped up and down and even Mark punched the air.

'Yeeesss!'

'The board members have resigned. Blake's gone... and the others...'

'The one who said my shoes were ridiculous? The one with the nostril hair who looked like a fancy-dress Dracula?'

'He's gone as well.' Claudia felt a certain feeling of satisfaction, as though one or two ghosts had been laid to rest. She was going to phone Grace to make sure she would come to the drinks tonight... and what about Johnny?

'What's that in your hand?' asked Mark.

'My dad's watch. The strap is broken. It needs a new pin or something.'

Mark took it from her, examining it.

'By the way, our Mark has news,' said Oscar. 'He's got a new job...'

Mark looked up from examining the watch, nearly smiling. 'I heard this morning. I'm being taken on at the library. Assistant keeper of the manuscripts...'

'He gets to wear white gloves every day,' explained Oscar. 'As long as he doesn't paint his face white or wear a stripy top he won't be mistaken for Marcel Marceau.'

Mark looked at them all. 'I'll actually miss you all.'

Oscar gave a snort. 'Oh, no you won't. Give it a rest. But we might miss you from time to time.'

'Are we still having this launch or what?' said Charlie. 'People are already starting to call about it, they said someone mentioned to them that everyone involved in this month's issue is invited.'

Oscar looked quite pleased. 'As long as the drink flows and there is food. *Will* there be food?'

'Crisps?' suggested Claudia.

'That'll do.'

Simon nodded. 'We could always go and play pool later...'

Claudia turned to Oscar. 'I need to look amazing. Is there anything I can borrow? Or some make-up? Make me look nice?'

Oscar studied her up and down. 'No,' he said, 'you're glowing. You're already perfect as you are.'

There was a scream from Charlie as she stared at her phone. 'Scooby's back! He's just landed! Says he just caught a flight home and never wants to eat feta cheese ever again. He wants some Dairylea Lunchables!' She looked at them all, her face shining. 'I couldn't love him any more than I do.'

'Almost as much as he loves processed cheese,' said Oscar. He turned back to Claudia. 'Now, we need to think about our Cinderella here. Right... what do you need?' He shook his head. 'Nothing. You're glowing. You're already perfect as you are.'

46

Doheny and Nesbitt's was looking its very best, full of drinkers and post-work-week revellers. In the corner, a band was playing traditional music, which floated into the air, above the noise and laughter, the talking, the pints being filled and consumed, and the sound of a usual Friday night in the middle of Dublin City.

Claudia was at the far end of the bar, in an area which opened up into the main room, sharing the long mahogany bar over which a million pints had slid. The whole of the *Irish Woman* gang were there, along with Bernadette from reception and Marko from the post room. And there were people in intricately knitted jumpers who were from *Irish Knitting* and there was a group in the corner playing fiddles and a bodhrán and a tin whistle, all from *Irish Music*. There was Ernie talking to Arnie Kennedy, Lorraine the photographer was chatting to Toby Rabbitte whom Claudia recognised from his regular media appearances. And there were the freelancers, their reviewers and their writers and Foxy Publishing's advertising and sales teams.

Fiona, Patsy and Dr Alan were standing with Foxy and Alison, talking. Or rather Fiona and Foxy were in deep conversation, while Patsy and Alison were in the midst of their own intense chat, their arms were even linked, as Dr Alan was listening and nodding along.

And then Claudia noticed a man making his way through the crowd, weaving through the bodies, his eyes fixed on Fiona, looking serious and determined. Cameron. Fiona turned, her face transformed into a huge smile as he wrapped his arms around her and they stood for a moment, suspended in time, their bodies melting into each other.

They were going to be okay, thought Claudia. There was love and then there was that other kind, the one infused with passion and excitement, the

one we should hold out for, never settling for anything less. The kind of supercharging love which
makes you feel coveted, consumed and so delight-
fully happy that you can face anything. The kind of
light which never goes out. Fiona and Cameron had
released each other and were now talking, quietly.
And then Fiona laughed loudly, Cameron beaming
back at her, his hand around hers.

Grace, wearing a pair of red dungarees, slurped
her gin and tonic through a straw. 'God, I love being
single.' Grace took another long, noisy drink. 'I think
single life is the only way forward, I really do. I was
reading your brilliant article in *Irish Woman* about
how some people are just not meant to be in relationships. They're better being on their own. That's
you and me. And now, Tom's moved out, I can have
cheese in the fridge again...'

'I didn't know he was dairy intolerant...' Claudia
looked again at the door. Still no sign of Johnny.

'Just intolerant of any cheese that wasn't extra-
mild, bland cheddar. Foul-smelling Camembert was
another Tom repeller. Should have deployed the
cheese and the boiler suit much earlier... he came
back yesterday to collect his stupid certificate from
off the wall and took the opportunity to say that

some people are too narrow in their understanding of relationships... and was just about to say something else when I told him I'd had enough of hearing his voice and encouraged him over the threshold. I closed the door and called the locksmith. And I met Michael in the village. According to him, Celia isn't interested in Tom. She was just seeking some excitement and she's a repeat offender. Tom wasn't her first dalliance and Michael says as much as he loves her, he's decided that it's time to end things once and for all. He wants to find someone who won't have affairs. It means that the gallery won't be funded so who knows what will happen.' Grace glanced over Claudia's shoulder, a big smile on her face. 'Oh, hello, Johnny... what are *you* doing here?'

And there he was. All leather jacket and that chiselled, handsome face, the light swathe of stubble, those Aegean eyes and his lovely hands which were now wrapped around Grace, hugging her, but he was looking at Claudia. Smiling. 'Hello,' he said to her, over Grace's shoulder.

'Hello.' Claudia smiled back. Her stomach flipped over.

Grace looked from Johnny to Claudia and back to Johnny again, confused.

'I've been thinking of you.' Johnny was looking straight into Claudia's eyes.

'Have you?'

Grace involved herself. 'In what way?' she said, puzzled.

'Oh, *every* way...' Johnny was looking straight at Claudia. 'I've missed you...'

'Missed her?' Grace seemed slightly perplexed. 'When did you last see her?'

'This morning...'

Claudia's whole body was melting, from the inside out and from the outside in.

'Well, this is interesting,' said Grace, thoughtfully. 'Well, go on then, what are you waiting for? Hug her!'

And Johnny's arms were around Claudia which was just as well because she wouldn't have been able to hold herself upright, as she sank into him, his body against hers, as he spoke softly. 'Maybe we could trespass in Fitzwilliam Square? But only if you promise to pretend to be a phoenix again...'

She laughed. 'I promise. But you have to promise me something too...'

'Anything?'

'That you prolong the ephemeral...' She grinned at him.

'It's a deal. So we're being phoenixes in Fitzwilliam Square and waltzing?' He still had his arms around her.

Grace was shaking her head. 'Something tells me that we won't be living together watching television in our pyjamas...'

Behind them, Oscar and Simon arrived. 'Oh, of course!' said Oscar. 'We should have known! The two of you can't take your hands off each other!'

'It was just a hug,' Claudia insisted, as Johnny released her.

'If that's just a hug, Johnny can hug me any-time...' Oscar opened his arms. 'Come here, Johnny. I want one of those as well.' Johnny obediently stepped forward to be enthusiastically squeezed by Oscar. 'Oh, you do give good hugs, Johnny Hogan. Simon, you're next...'

'You're grand,' said Simon, 'but thank you...' He smiled shyly at Grace.

'Grace, these are my colleagues at *Irish Man*. Oscar and Simon...'

'Charlie and Scooby are on their way,' Oscar was saying. 'We met them eating chips on a bench when we were cutting through St Stephen's Green...'

'Scooby wasn't wearing any shoes,' said Simon.

Oscar nodded. 'He says they hurt his feet after

being barefoot for so long.' He paused. 'I do hope he has reacquainted himself with underpants however.'

Grace quickly shook Oscar's hand, before turning her full beam on Simon.

'Good to meet you...' She was looking at his T-shirt which had a picture of Freud and the words 'Dr Fraud'.

'Are you into psychoanalysis or therapy?' Grace asked, cautiously.

Simon laughed. 'God no! I prefer to just get on with life and be as good a person as possible. Oh, and mind my dog. She cures everything. *And* have as much fun as possible.'

'I couldn't agree more,' said Grace.

'Oh, by the way...' Oscar reached into his inside pocket of his jacket. 'Mark gave me this to give to you...' He pulled out an envelope. 'Apparently it just needed a new pin which was bent out of shape and he said he is sorry he couldn't come tonight but he was going to meet his new colleagues.'

Claudia opened the envelope, and inside was her father's watch. The strap still original, the face perfect, the hands making their slow ticking journey. She slipped it on her wrist and Johnny helped her do up the catch.

Amanda marched straight up to Claudia. 'I hope

you're happy,' she fumed. 'Blake's gone and he's taken Jackson with him. And now I hear that Foxy is your uncle! Nepotism at its finest... I *knew* there was a simple explanation!'

'She's the best editor I've ever worked with,' said Simon.

'I concur. A tremendous editor...' Oscar beamed at Claudia. 'And fun... that night in the pool hall is still making me laugh...'

'Well, it's no skin off my nose because I've been offered an amazing new job,' went on Amanda. 'Heard this afternoon. Head of in-house marketing communications for Grady-O'Gara the accountancy firm. I've handed in my notice and I'm leaving in a week. You'd all *better* come to my leaving drinks.' It was quite the threat.

There was a tapping of a glass. Foxy had silenced the room, his arm around Alison. 'Ladies, gentlemen... writers, editors... friends...' He smiled. 'Thank you for coming this evening to our celebration of the latest edition of *Irish Man* but also a celebration of life. As many of you know, we have been going through a challenging time, but this evening, I am looking at a sea of friends who have sustained and supported me and the business. Thank you for your commitment, enthusiasm and talents.' He paused, bringing Alison's hand towards him, pulling her in closer. 'First, I want to speak about my beautiful wife. We first met many moons ago, I knew then, as I know now, there is *nothing* I love more than her.' He brought her hand to his lips and kissed it gently. 'I've had other cheerleaders and friends, including Cian Donaghy and Bernadette Claffey. And of course, my old pals Arnie Kennedy, Toby Rabbitte and Ernie di Lucia. Thank you all for keeping me sane and being on my side.' He raised his glass as the three men gave a cheer.

'G'wan, ya good thing!' shouted Bernadette.

Foxy smiled at her. 'But there is an absent friend to whom I want to pay tribute. My brother, Philip.' Foxy's voice cracked a little. 'We'd been estranged when he died, my life's biggest and most enduring regret. It stayed with me, the shame and the sorrow of that, gnawing away at my edges and however much I pushed it away, there it was, my brother dying without us being friends. You can work hard and enjoy success, but you can never outrun your sorrows or your shames. They'll always catch up with you. And then, a year ago, when Alison decided to spread her own wings, I was humbled and crashed to earth.'

Alison had tears in her eyes.

'I thought that was it for me,' Foxy went on. 'The jig was up. What was there to live for if I didn't have the love of this woman? If I didn't have family?' His voice broke again as Alison clutched his hand. 'But I've always been lucky. Always. When I've been on the ropes, something good always happens. The universe has been generous when sending help and assistance. One morning, not too long ago, I was walking through reception of Hackett House feeling a little despondent, down in the dumps, when a young woman passed me. She looked exactly like my brother Philip. Exactly. His eyes. His smile.' He looked over at Claudia. 'It was like I'd been struck by lightning. Was I imagining it? And so, Bernadette did a bit of research and... we discovered that the universe was giving me a second chance. Only this time, I wasn't going to waste it. It was, I am sure of it, a sign from Philip.' He was still clutching Alison's hand. 'Or perhaps just a wonderful coincidence but I can say with certainty that without Claudia's tenacity and talents, I wouldn't be here now, my business intact, my wife beside me and facing a sea of my friends. Thank you, Claudia.'

Everyone turned and looked at Claudia, giving her a surprisingly rapturous round of applause. She blushed and caught Fiona's eye, who grinned at her.

'Now...' Foxy paused, looking around. 'I have a few announcements. This afternoon, after a long lunch, we made a few decisions, and one is to relocate to Alicante. Alison's career as a yoga teacher is far too important to give up. And yes, I will still be running the business but from a little office in the spare bedroom of a flat on the Costa Blanca, overlooking the beach. But Foxy Publishing is in good hands. My niece Fiona Kelly will be the new CEO and she comes with a fantastic pedigree and experience of the corporate world. More than that, I can trust her. Welcome to the team, Fiona.'

There was another round of applause.

'So, raise your glasses to my nieces, Claudia and Fiona. And to my wonderful sister-in-law, Patsy. And let's remember my younger brother, Philip. We miss you, Phil.' He raised his glass, his Timex watch glinting in the light, matching the one on Claudia's wrist. 'And to my Alison. Thank you for sticking by me. I love you more than I love my magazines.'

Arnie from the back of the room shouted out, 'Impossible,' and Toby called out, 'We don't believe you!'

Foxy, laughing, said, 'It's true. I've worked too hard and too much, but I know that Alison and family is what is most important to me. We have decided to bi-locate to Dublin and Alicante. Over there, I will be known as Alison's husband and will be on tea-making duties...'

'Tea-making! Get out of that!' Toby again.

'Okay, sangria-making.' Foxy smiled. 'To Alison!'

'To Alison!' everyone in the room chorused.

Later, Foxy and Alison joined Claudia and Johnny. 'I've found a flat for you,' said Foxy. 'I've had Ernie on the case for the last month. One of his tenants has just moved out...'

'Really? That's amazing!' Claudia felt as though all the weight of the last year was being lifted off her shoulders.

Alison was smiling. 'You're going to love it. It's on my favourite square.'

Claudia and Johnny looked at each other. 'Which one?'

'Fitzwilliam. Number 26. And the rent is reasonable,' said Foxy. 'But it's only a one-bedroom...'

'That's all I need,' said Claudia, feeling a rush of relief. No more sharing, no more box room.

'You know, he might be persuaded to sell it one of these days,' said Foxy. 'If you like it enough...'

'I already love it,' she said. 'I can't wait.'

* * *

It was after midnight when Johnny and Claudia stopped in Fitzwilliam Square and locked her bike to the railings. The sky was black, shot through with a billion beautiful stars, the night jasmine scenting the air.

They peered up at number 26, which was way up on the top floor.

'You'll get a key to the park,' said Johnny.

Claudia felt excited. 'We can have picnics in the summer...'

'Come on...' Johnny was already pushing himself over the railings. '*This* time, it's not trespassing, because you're a resident...' Johnny held out his hand to pull her over and then she was on the other side, in the shrubbery, in the moonlight, and she and Johnny were holding hands and running towards the bandstand. Where they kissed for the first time.

She and Johnny lay on their backs, holding hands and counting the stars, one of which was perhaps her father looking down at her.

I love you, Dad. And Mum, and Fiona... and her whole life. And the future and best of all, this moment, right now, being bathed in the light of the moon, the sparkling night sky above, the city in darkness and perhaps a wonderful new chapter about to begin. Who knew what would happen? She might just love it.

* * *

MORE FROM SIÂN O'GORMAN

The next book from Siân O'Gorman, is available to order now here:
https://mybook.to/SianOGormanBackAd

ACKNOWLEDGEMENTS

Thank you to my wonderful agent Ger Nicholl who cheers me on all the way. And to the brilliant Caroline Ridding and Boldwood Books family, it's so lovely to be part of your story. And to Ross Dickinson for his meticulous editing. You are a joy to work with. To my daughter, Ruby, who makes me so happy. But this book is for my mother who taught me everything I know. I will miss you.

ABOUT THE AUTHOR

Siân O'Gorman was born in Galway and now lives just along the coast from Dublin. She works as a radio producer alongside writing contemporary women's fiction inspired by friend and family relationships.

Sign up to Siân O'Gorman's mailing list here for news, competitions and updates on future books.

Follow Siân on social media:

facebook.com/sian.ogorman.7

x.com/msogorman

instagram.com/msogorman

bookbub.com/authors/sian-o-gorman

ALSO BY SIÂN O'GORMAN

Friends Like Us

Always and Forever

Mothers and Daughters

Life After You

Life's What You Make It

The Sandycove Supper Club

The Sandycove Sunset Swimmers

The Girls from Sandycove

For Once in My Life

If We Could Turn Back Time

The Boy Next Door

Boldwood

Boldwood Books is an award-winning fiction publishing company seeking out the best stories from around the world.

Find out more at www.boldwoodbooks.com

Join our reader community for brilliant books, competitions and offers!

Follow us
@BoldwoodBooks
@TheBoldBookClub

Sign up to our weekly deals newsletter

https://bit.ly/BoldwoodBNewsletter